THE RAVEN THRONE

STARSIDE SAGA, BOOK 4

ERIC KENT EDSTROM

To J

1

———

WORDS TO DREAM

The dragon glides on leathery wings scaled with brilliant blues that turn to green when the sun strikes at just the right angle. It soars high above the island simply known as "the Colony."

In Starside, two thousand miles to the west, a raven does the same. Its feathers are blue as well, but no human eye detects this when it's in flight. It wings above the city, a black speck riding currents that lift it higher and higher above the tumble of buildings and streets that climb the slope toward the Citadel.

That's where *she* resides. But the raven is not visiting *her* today.

The bird squawks and swoops to circle above the other young woman, the one who has awakened. Kila Sigh.

The citizens who see the bird tap their ears and say three times: "Die, Raven, die." But it's all for naught, for such feeble spells have no power over the bird. Across the city, goodwives shudder and pull shawls over their shoulders, and even in the darkest passages of the Abbey of Til, Donse Masters shrug deeper into their robes.

Across the town, where Terriside borders the Blasted Quarter, the Coin of Pol removes her medallion and gives the relic a toss. It lands on edge, spins until it comes to a stop, still standing. It is the third time in three days that it has done so.

In the thinnie cavern town deep beneath the city, the survivors of Kila Sigh's mercusine attack are still mostly abed from the sickness that has swept their ranks. A young man, now their leader, tilts his head back and swallows the last of his wine. "Kila Sigh," he says. "You'll know her by the gray cat she keeps company with. And her golden hair."

The man he addresses wears all black. Even his head is shadowed deep within hood of his woolen cloak. The thinnie leader sets a bag of coin on the table as payment.

But the shadowy man doesn't take it. He merely stands, bows ever so slightly, and departs, leaving a scent of spice in his wake.

The raven circles ever lower, watchful of the girl in the bell tower window. Though it can't speak, it speaks. Words to dream.

Why? Kila Sigh. Why?

Why don't you fly?

2

THE PURPOSE OF PROPHECY

There was almost always a strong wind in the morning, especially in Gristenside. That morning it rushed from the ocean, laden with warm moisture unusual this close to Winternight. Kila stood atop the bell tower, holding an urn full of ashes.

The Voluptuary, Sens Renna, Sens Beth, Finta Sahng, Yiqa, and the boys crowded in with her. The Voluptuary spoke words. Finta spoke words. The boys spoke words.

Kila said nothing.

She removed the lid, tipped the vessel over the railing, and poured Wen into the breeze. Oly was not there.

Fallo had relayed Oly's opinion of the ceremony earlier. *Lop says Oly doesn't think Wen is in that jar. He is gone already, so there is nothing to see but ash.*

Kila felt the same way. Wen was not his body. And his body had barely been part of him, not since the sickness had come over him. She wanted to remember the lithe, fast, stealthy Wen. The Wen who loved her without sugary words, but with a gleam of pride in his eyes as he watched her master new skills.

She would remember Wen's keen insight, his uncanny ability to plan a theft. She would remember how he called her "sister" when upset with her.

And she would always remember the dream they'd shared. Of setting up as legitimate recovery agents, to get back what had been stolen from others. Father's dream had become Wen's dream had become hers.

"It's odd how you can remember the future, isn't it?" she said to nobody in particular. "Not what will happen, but what you wanted to happen." She thought remembering that future —now permanently lost—would ache in her chest far longer than memories of the painful past. You could lose gold, money —even friends—and time would numb it. But when you lose the future you have lost hope, and there is no balm for that.

The ashes poured into the wind and fluttered away along the Divide and over the northern stretches of Gristenside. Some swarmed against the Starside wall and floated to the Westbunk, the fortress of the Watch. Some swirled over the manses of the Radiancies. Some wound around the tower and wafted to settle atop shop roofs. Kila supposed some would even fall into sewer grates and rest in thinnie tunnels. Others would coat the streets and be trod upon by atlens pulling carriages.

Wen was everywhere now. And nowhere.

Nowhere. Like Kila.

Later, she found herself in the library of the novitiates'

ward, sitting in an overstuffed leather chair, books all around her. The hearth from which she and Ragin had once climbed to the roof was ablaze with a roaring winter fire.

Ragin sat across from her, gaze lost in the middle distance. He had kindly not offered soft words of sympathy. She didn't think she could bear his pity. It was bad enough that the Sensuals all gave her the worried-brow look, as if she were a lost child.

"We need to talk," came a voice from behind her.

The Voluptuary dismissed Ragin with a look. He touched Kila's shoulder, then departed. The Voluptuary arranged herself in his seat. Her stout face was haggard, her black and gray hair pulled back more severely beneath her jeweled headpiece. Bare shins showed beneath the hem of her multi-layered robes, spider-webbed with purple veins.

She leveled a hard stare at Kila. "We must talk about the Donse Master who accosted you when you last confronted the Hargothe. I have already questioned both of the boys." She was referring to Dunne Yples, a Donse Master who had witnessed her ashing of the thinnies. He'd gone mad and insisted she was the foretold destroyer of the world known as Dem-Kisk. He had tried to kill her, but Henley had saved her.

"He said I was Dem-Kisk," Kila whispered. She lifted her gaze to meet the Voluptuary's. "Am I?"

The fact that the woman didn't answer immediately told Kila enough. "Then I should be locked up. Or—"

"No! Never speak such goose-headed idiocy again. Don't let such thoughts into your mind. Renna, be a sweetie and fetch me a copy of Exine's *Notes on the Prophecies.*"

Kila hadn't noticed the placid-faced Sensual's presence. But in less than a minute the requested book was placed in the Voluptuary's hands, and the Sensual had retreated into the shadows.

Kila didn't entirely trust the Voluptuary—she didn't entirely trust anyone—but the Voluptuary had helped her and Wen. And the woman hated the Hargothe. That made them allies in at least one thing.

The woman thumbed through the tome until she found the page she wanted. She read: "Of the Prophecy of Dem-Kisk, what is truly known? Ask any goodman or goodwife and one is likely to hear the Way of Til's interpretation. 'He will come to decide the end of the world.' But in the text there is no mention of such a decision. The prophecy—if it even is such—only tells us how we will *know* Dem-Kisk. It speaks in imagery most dire, but what a muddle it is! And so we return to our initial discussion in chapter one of this disquisition: What is the purpose of prophecy? I submit, again, that it is not to forewarn us, or to prepare us to do something about the future. The purpose of prophecy is to signal to us that the fore-told time is upon us. Nothing more. The fulfillment affirms the word of the Theb. Nothing more. We need not fear Dem-Kisk. In fact, we should rejoice when he—or she—arrives. For it will affirm the truth of the Theb and the rightness of our faith in the gods."

The Voluptuary closed the book and folded her hands atop it. "Exine was a farmer. But his thinking on the purpose of prophecy is the clearest and most reasonable I have encoun-tered. It is, of course, considered heresy by the Way of Til."

In answer, Kila recited, "'You will know Dem-Kisk by the flames, by the charred bone, by the ash.' That sounds like what I did to the thinnies."

"Before you were born, the warehouses at the bottom of Terriside burned. Flame, charred bone, and ash. Did that signal Dem-Kisk?"

"But what if I *am* the one foretold?"

"A fair and reasonable question. One I have pondered for a time. At first I was convinced that you should remain here and study. Now that Goolsoy is ash upon the wind, I do not think there is anyone here qualified to instruct you. That is why I encourage you to go to the Garden."

Kila blinked. The Garden. "Dunne Marlow and Highest Binel said the same."

The Garden was an island in the Ansin Ocean, far to the south. There, the three seats of the Triumvirate existed outside the control of any nation.

The Voluptuary tapped the book with a stubby forefinger. "You would be welcomed into Ori's Home, where you could train in safety. And scholars there may have deeper insights into the question of Dem-Kisk."

"And if I say no?"

The Voluptuary's fingers stroked the book on her lap. The woman's eyes fell on Kila's queller. "I'm mostly concerned about your safety, child. Dunne Yples must be somewhere, lying in wait. I have Yiqa out searching for him, but it's interesting how swiftly he vanished from the Hargothe's crypt."

The woman's eyelids lowered as she watched Kila. "You, yourself, vanished once. Have you forgotten?"

The fire suddenly failed to keep Kila's skin warm. "You mean he dymensed, don't you? You're saying a demayne took him?"

"You do know someone who consorts with demayne."

Dunne Marlow. Kila knew where he was hiding. The great black space with the columns. The Derslin Wheel. "I can't imagine Marlow wanting to be saddled with a madman like Yples."

"Perhaps you're right. Maybe Dunne Yples is locked back in his cell. All I know is he's a danger to you. The Hargothe, too." The Voluptuary stood. "That's why I've booked passage for you on *Sparrow*, a fast ship owned by Raginalt's father. The voyage to the Garden takes only two months. The Garden is lovely. I believe you will thrive there—after a time."

"And what if I refuse to go?"

The woman's face didn't change, remaining stern and handsome and outwardly calm. But her voice hardened. "You will go." The Voluptuary left and Sens Renna went with her. Once alone, Kila stood and began to pace.

She didn't fear the Voluptuary's implicit threat. They could try to hogtie her and throw her aboard a ship, but they had better be certain to quell her if they did. Kila had a knack with the mercus when she got desperate enough. But such thoughts didn't come with much heat.

Because she didn't feel much at all.

Even the grief of sending Wen into the wind had dulled, and that only revealed a deeper misery. Nax was gone, the bond ripped away by the Hargothe.

Kila felt hollowed out. But now she knew what she had to

do, thanks to the Voluptuary. That talk of dymensing had sparked an idea.

Kila had to find Marlow. Which meant she had to get back to the Derslin Wheel.

Though she'd walked out of that strange, dark cavern, under her own power, she'd been bagged and dragged into a cart before she'd discovered where in the city she was. There was only one way to find out. She needed to find the strongman who worked for Marlow. A heavy-handed man called Grig.

3

DEALING WITH DEMAYNE

A half hour later she was in Terriside, studying the buildings bordering a stretch of the Street of Sorrows. The taverns were doing great business, the crowds eager to warm themselves against the newly-arrived winter with copious quantities of beer, wine, and trezz.

She kept her hood up and pressed silver plugs into a few palms. By midnight she had found Grig, the leader of the men who had recently bundled her into a wagon and taken her to the abbey. He was bleary-eyed and trezzed to the rafters. A flutter of eyelash, a sharp press of her knee in his groin, and a flash of silver were all the encouragement he needed to disclose where Marlow's jeweler's shop was.

She was off to the roofway, leaping alleyways and dropping copper plugs in toll pails until she came to the shop. Getting into the shop required no skill at all. The rear door was unlocked.

She descended to the cellar and approached the illusory

stone wall in the corner. She passed through, feeling a weird chill skim across her flesh, like plunging through ice water.

Into blackness she went, her queller off so she could feel her way ahead with her mercusine senses. She remembered it was a long walk, so she picked up her pace.

A light in the distance drew her forward, though it didn't appear to come closer until she was nearly upon it. It shed a reddish glow across a strangely patterned floor. She looked away from the twisty tiles as a wave of dizziness hit her.

The columns stood all around, each with a symbol etched into a flat section cut into the front. Marlow called it the Derslin Wheel, but she had no idea what its purpose was.

Marlow was asleep when she found him, lying on a pallet of blankets in the center of the ring of columns. The lone whale-oil lantern burned near him, illuminating a small oval of the floor. The faint smell of flowers hung the air, too.

Of Dunne Yples there was no sign. Kila wasn't surprised. The last thing Marlow would want was the care and feeding of a madman.

She shoved him awake with her foot.

He blinked away sleep and sat up, eager. "A sharp thinker, you are, dearie. A sharp thinker to have found me."

"The Hargothe stole my bond with Nax. I want it back."

The light of realization sparked in his eyes, as if a puzzle piece had fallen into place. "Of course you do, my dear. Of course. And I may be able to help with that."

"What do you want in return?"

"You insult me. Do you think my loyalties are for sale?"

"It wouldn't be loyalty if it was for sale. I just want your services. A demayne."

He pursed his lips and squinted at her. Finally, he nodded and grinned. "You make a fair point. But forget about payment. You can return the favor someday, I'm sure. Besides, it is in my interest to deny my brother the bond with your cat. He has always sought such, but not out of love of animals. He has some other aim, some use for the bond I have never divined." He waved his hands, as if shaking the question away from him. "But are you truly committed to this course? Dealing with demayne is not to be undertaken lightly."

"Can you return the bond to me?" When the Voluptuary had spoken of vanishing, using a demayne to get Nax back had been all Kila could think of. She didn't want to do it, but she didn't see any other choice.

"No. And no merculyn I know could do so. But the demayne Flaumishtak will know how. He knows more of the mercus than the sum of all knowledge held by the Way of Til."

Kila had a sense of just how much that particular demayne knew. She'd used what she'd learned from him—without knowing how—to heal the Hargothe. Which raised another question. "I saved your brother's life, Marlow. Did you know that?" She told of the technique she'd picked up from the demayne.

"By Kil's flaming eyes, what a feat," Marlow said. "Explain it to me. Every Sense in every proportion."

"I don't remember. I just did it. I had to, I thought, to save Nax."

Marlow was on his feet now, muttering to himself and

tapping his fingers together. "This explains his newfound strength. Whatever you did, it did more than save his life. You invigorated him."

That was not what Kila wanted to hear. But she didn't care much, either. "I just want Nax, and then I'm leaving Starside."

"Yes. You should go to the Garden. The Way of Til will welcome you, even though you are a mere girl. They'll overlook that deficiency once they hear of your power."

He must have noticed Kila's indignation, for he pumped his hands at her. "I'm not saying *I* think your womanhood is a deficiency. Pol knows, the most brilliant person I ever met was of your persuasion. Ah, but don't let my chatter worry your pretty little head. Til respects power above all things."

"You think I'm Dem-Kisk."

Marlow stammered a moment too long. Realizing she would not be convinced by any lie he offered, he simply nodded. "I fear it, but I don't truly know. How can anyone know? The prophecy is rubbish, in any case. You should read Exine on that."

"I have."

"Oh. Well, let me prepare to summon Flaumishtak."

"What does one pay a demayne?"

"All sorts of things. But Flaumishtak only wants one thing. Dragon scales."

"Might as well ask for Kil's teeth. Where am I going to get a dragon scale?"

Marlow grinned. "Scales. As in, more than one. I know where to get them. The Eerie. And you, dearie, are just the one to retrieve them."

The Eerie. A cavern perched high upon the mountain behind the Citadel. It was where the messenger wyrms in Her Enlightened's personal flight roosted. "There hasn't been a dragon there in over a ten-year," she said.

Marlow dismissed her concerns with a wave of his hand. "They shed loads of scales. The Eerie is thick with them, or so my previous source told me. I, uh, am no longer in good standing with her. But you could get some, I'm sure."

"How many will the demayne want?"

"Let's ask!" Marlow set about arranging rocks in a pattern on the floor. "I must warn you, if Flaumishtak is released before the rite is complete he will kill us both and then likely destroy the entire city. Or he'll share an ale with us and tell us stories before making us kings. He's capricious like that. But don't worry too much. I've done this several times without incident."

Kila did not feel much encouraged by Marlow's monologue, but she was committed to getting Nax back, whatever the cost.

The rite was not very interesting, and involved Marlow reading from a tome in a language that set Kila's teeth on edge. And it went on and on and on. Kila was about to drift to sleep when the green fog swirled into existence.

The great beast appeared, his fearsome features looking vaguely annoyed. His regal and bestial mane of hair swept back from his wide face, becoming tendrils of smoke where the wispy ends should be. He had his arms folded across his massive chest, hands tucked in the sleeves of his thick robes. His wide, bulbous nose hung over a slash of mouth, the corners of which were turned down in an expression of grim dissatisfaction.

Marlow bowed formally. "Great Flaumishtak, welcome again. We have need of your services."

The demayne eyed Kila. "If you won't let me have her, I don't want to do anything for you."

"It is she who seeks to bargain with you," Marlow said. "To recover her Beloved One from the Hargothe and restore the sacred bond between them."

This got the beast's attention. The eyes narrowed but the mouth softened. "What of the bond? What of the Hargothe? Speak it again." An especially foul reek wafted from him. Burnt hair and charred bread.

Kila stepped forward and cleared her throat. Despite her determination, her palms were cold and damp and her heart raced. Flaumishtak was nearly twice her height. "The Hargothe transferred Nax's bond from me to himself. And somehow he has compelled her to rejoin him in his foul crypt. I want her back."

The demayne stroked its beard, which shed wisps of smoke that curled away into the dark above him. Nodding sharply, he said, "I like a being who speaks plainly. Take note, Marlow. I shall help you, Kila Sigh. But the cost is steep."

"Then speak plainly," Kila said. "How many dragon scales do you require?"

"One thousand."

"One thousand?" Kila and Marlow said together.

Kila imagined the size of a dragon and how large a single

scale must be. Then she realized she didn't have the vaguest notion. "Can I even carry that many?"

"You could carry ten times that in a sack," Flaumishtak said. "They are light as feathers, no matter the size of the wyrm."

"I'll give you ten," Kila said. Father had taught her to bargain. If someone opened with an outrageous number, then the only strategy was to counter with an outrageous number.

Marlow squawked in indignation. Apparently, one didn't bargain like a Cheapsgater when dealing with a demayne. But Flaumishtak merely laughed, a booming, human-like guffaw, but punctuated with wheezes that sounded like chains dragging over stone. "This is not a negotiation."

Kila glared at him, but realizing she had no bargaining power, she relented. "One thousand, though I don't know how long it will take me to collect them. Now, let's go retrieve Nax."

"The bargain is struck!" the demayne said, voice booming with more weight than volume. A solid chill coalesced around Kila, as if her shirt had turned to ice. The feeling intensified, then faded.

"May I step out?" the demayne asked Marlow.

"You may."

The demayne offered a surprisingly delicate bow and stepped from the ring of stones. His hooves clopped on the tiles, though a swirl of fog shrouded them. He began a mercusine invocation, and soon Kila was swept into mercus green.

When it faded, she found herself in the Hargothe's crypt. The Hargothe lay upon his bed, Nax's slim gray body nestled next to him. A length of twine was fastened to Nax's neck and tied to a bed post.

The Hargothe rested a pale, long-fingered hand on her body. Both appeared asleep. Kila made to go to her, but the demayne stopped her. "You must allow me to do what is needed."

The demayne cupped a hand and began a swirling motion, just as he'd once done when healing Ragin. Soon a violet light streaked with gold filled his hand, the glow painting his monstrous face purple.

Kila wished she had Cayne in her hand. As soon as the demayne returned Nax's bond to her, she was going to jump on the Hargothe and kill him. Her fingers itched to clamp around his throat again. She considered removing her queller to better see what the demayne was doing, but she feared her mercus powers would alert the Hargothe.

Flaumishtak poured the violet light on Nax's head. The cat's eyes popped open and she stretched. When she noticed Kila there, she meowed mournfully. Kila waited in expectation, longing for the touch of Nax's mind upon hers.

At a slight motion of the demayne's black-clawed forefinger the twine parted and fell away from Nax's neck. He beckoned and she stood and leapt onto his arm, then climbed to perch on his shoulder.

"Have Marlow summon me again when your payment is ready," he said. With a twist of his wrist, the demayne flared into bright green light and was gone.

Kila stood there, stunned to wordlessness.

"So, you have returned to me," the Hargothe said. "But

where is my Beloved One? Where is my sweet Ishmilla?" He sat up and patted the mattress all around him. "I can't sense her!"

Kila's nostril's flared as she cursed the demayne. "That overgrown goat tricked me!" He'd stolen Nax right from under her gaze.

"Remove the queller, girl," the Hargothe commanded. He sat up easily, then stood. Where he had once been frail, thin of chest, and skeletal of limb, he was now broad-shouldered, hale, and strong. "It will not go well for you if I must call the guards. For once I drain the rest of your mercusine, I will give you to them for their sport."

Kila ran.

4

RECOMPENSE

The corridor outside the Hargothe's crypt was lit only by whale oil lanterns, and those were infrequent. The bang of a slamming door resounded behind her. The Hargothe followed, ringing a bell to summon acolytes to stop her. She put her head down and sprinted to where she knew a winding stair led up to the cathedral.

She had some familiarity with these halls, for she had once before descended here to meet and kill the Hargothe. That had not worked out. But she had escaped, with Fallo, Ragin, and Henley's help. The stair was blocked by a group of acolytes responding to the Hargothe's summons, their shadows huge on the final curve of the stairwell wall.

Kila kept going, barging through an iron-bound door and continuing past prison cells. She didn't pause to study them, but they were low doors held in place by simple wooden bars on hooks. This was where Henley and Dunne Yples had been held. The horror of being locked in such a small dank space gave her more speed.

As she ran, the wall-mounted oil sconces grew fewer, and the halls lay in deep darkness. She chanced a look back but didn't see anyone. She noticed a passage to her left. Total blackness. She dove into it, relying on her thief's training to guide her feet.

It didn't work. Her foot stepped into emptiness and she fell.

Stone steps met her shoulder, her knees, her back. Abruptly, she came to a stop. She lay flat on her back, eyes to a hazy gray ceiling. Above the thud of her heartbeat and the rasp of her laboring breath came the call of distant voices.

The speed of her retreat had given her a moment's respite. Picking herself up from the damp and grimy floor, she tested her limbs. The pain in her knees was nothing compared to that in her shoulder. That was thanks to Yiqa, who had once pulled it from its socket. Kila rubbed it and let out a breathy curse.

The voices were growing louder, but they were indistinct and hollow. She imagined the Hargothe screaming orders to befuddled acolytes.

She offered a few curses to the darkness. "If I ever get my hands on that Kil-kissin' demayne . . ."

An empty threat, of course. Flaumishtak was untouchable, no matter her supposedly grand mercus powers. For one, she didn't know how to use them. Secondly, he had Nax.

She crept further along the corridor. The short flight of stairs she had taken the hard way had ended in a section of tunnel. It couldn't be properly called a hallway, for the ceiling was so low that Kila had to crouch to keep from bumping her head. The walls were rough, hewn from bedrock. The gray light that filtered from ahead glistened on a sheen of greasy dust coating the floor. It was slippery and cold on her bare feet. It smelled of a forgotten root cellar full of rot.

The tunnel ended in a round chamber stuffed with barrels and crates, each emblazoned with the symbol of the Way of Til: the Father God's Hand, palm out, fingers splayed, three-pronged crown in silhouette above the middle finger.

There was no window. The crypts and prisoner cells were too far underground. The light came from a shaft in the ceiling. A chimney flue. Past fires had coated the walls in black soot, and the ceiling was enameled with it. The room was meant for garbage burns.

She stacked a few crates and empty hogsheads to form a climbing platform. She was up and into the shaft in seconds, back pressed to one sooty wall, her feet braced against the other. It was exactly like climbing out of the novitiate's ward chimney. Except in this case the shaft was many times taller.

Heights did not frighten Kila. Falling did.

"So let's not fall," she said, echoing something Wen used to say. She supposed he'd gotten the advice from their father. Kila's memories of Father were vague. She shook her head and kept climbing. She didn't like to think about the past. Especially the early years of her life.

The voices of pursuit were drowned by the hollow howl of wind crossing the top of the shaft. Kila had no idea where the chimney flue would come out. She just hoped it wasn't in a courtyard where Donse Masters meditated upon their holy magnificence or some such. It turned out to be atop the Abbey, the chimney protruding from the tile roof that over-looked an interior courtyard. A cloister of double columns surrounded it, providing dry passage when it rained. At the moment, nobody was out.

She studied the lay of the rooftops, looking for a path that would get her out of the Abbey.

The Divide loomed above her, its top hazed by smoke drifting from Gristenside. Closer by, but mostly hidden behind the towers and spinets of the Cathedral, was the Starside Wall. If ever there was a reminder of Her Enlightened Majesty's supreme power in the city, this vantage provided it. The hoardings of a watchtower stood atop the Starside Wall, positioned directly above the Cathedral. She wondered if some long-dead Enlightened had placed it there to demonstrate the position of the Raven Throne above the Way of Til. How it must burn Highest Binel to have that constant reminder looming over him. She could only guess at the disgust felt by the Hargothe.

Her eyes scanned away from the Divide and Starside Wall and down to the nearer towers of the Abbey. She didn't make a habit of climbing to dead ends that forced her to climb back down. She wanted a rooftop that led to another rooftop.

The air was crisp, but the wind did not cut here so cruelly as it would higher up. Kila's bare feet were getting a bit numb. She needed to get moving.

Wiping a sheen of soot onto her trousers, she went to the nearest tower. It was thicker than the others and closer to the Cathedral, which formed the center—skyward-reaching—

focus of the entire Til complex. The brickwork was well maintained, as were the downspouts. She climbed one like a ladder, reaching a ledge that circled the tower midway. It was only as wide as her foot, more of a decorative element than a practical one. Evidence that pigeons had found it a satisfactory roost crunched and squished beneath Kila's toes. She proceeded to the corner and peeped around.

With no good finger-holds available, attempting to go around would tempt Pol's ire. Kila didn't rely on luck to keep herself alive when running the roofway. She wouldn't gamble here. Fortunately, there was a window right in front of her.

She thrust her elbow into the bottom pane, hoping to shatter it. She was rewarded with a sharp shock through her forearm. The buzzing numbness flared in her fingertips. She shook it out, cursing. The pane hadn't even cracked.

Cupping her hand to the glass, she peered through the window. Nobody was in the room beyond. She hoped it stayed that way.

If she loitered here she was going to be discovered one way or another, for she was completely visible to anyone in the cloistered courtyard below. She saw now how thick the glass was, likely to bar the cold winds that would strike against it. She peered through to the left and right to see how it was latched. There was a simple brass handle with a rounded wedge that drew secure under a bracket. A common design and good against thieves. There was no lock to pick, no gap to slip a slim metal shim through.

"Goolsoy, if you're watching from Ori's great pool, send me what aid you can."

This was ridiculous. And it wasn't going to work. Except it had to, because Kila's toes couldn't feel the ledge anymore. Climbing down with numb feet would quickly turn into the fastest descent of her short life.

She removed her queller and put it in the front pocket of her trousers. The zing was upon her instantly, the copper and tin alloy of the downspout shining a reddish color, the wrought iron spikes atop Cathedral spires glowing even duller reds. Someone was cooking a ham. The scent drifting to Kila's mercus-enlivened senses from some far kitchen in Gristenside.

Stomach rumbling, body shivering, Kila turned her attention to the brass window latch.

This should be simpler than unlocking the door in the Rose Hall at the Baths of Ori. After all, this was just one latch, not a bunch of hidden lock tumblers. And this was metal, Kila's specialty. The brass glowed a dull gold, though the light did not cast rays onto the objects around it. With the glow came a bell-like tone, a resonance of the alloy.

She tested her other senses against it. No taste at all. Which suited her fine. Licking metal was not a favorite pastime unless it was to bite a gold skillet to test its quality. There was a slight odor to the brass, very faint beneath the delicious fumes of that goodwife's ham. Kila discovered she was rubbing her fingers against one thumb, the universal gesture for money. Her fingers lifted from her thumb and she *felt* the smooth latch handle. She closed her eyes and forced herself to drop the words "brass," "latch," and "handle." The mercusine was brightest when the world remained unnamed.

And now the sense of touch grew more pronounced. The

surface was warm, she noted. Her fingers continued to explore the mercusine feel of the latch. The less she thought about it and the less she sought to grasp it, the firmer the latch handle became beneath her fingers. She tapped a stubby fingernail against it, heard the click.

She imagined how turning the latch would increase the feeling of pressure against her finger. There, right in that spot on the fleshy area between knuckles. Kila lent pressure to the contact. The latch handle resisted. She increased the feeling of pressure.

Like bone grinding on bone, the brass latch wedge began to slide. The vibration trembled against Kila's fingers. The sound was the very real rasp of the latch coming loose.

All at once the mechanism released, the latch inside turned, and the window seemed to sigh as it came free. Kila pressed her hands to the glass and pushed. The window swung in.

And then she was inside. The shouts of acolytes and Donse Masters greeted her. She looked to a descending stairwell to her right. They were climbing up to get her, lured by her exposed mercusine powers.

She dug out her queller and slipped it on. The world went mute and dull.

Kila ran the other way, through a short series of halls to a double doorway blocking her path. She burst into a lush apartment, the floor covered with thick rugs, the walls adorned with tapestries and curtains. Fire burned in a grand hearth, and luxuriously upholstered divans and lounges surrounded a seating area featuring a statue of a naked woman holding up a lantern. It was lit with mercus light.

She chose a door at random. Inside she found the largest bed she had ever seen. Flimsy veils draped from its canopy, and the bottom was festooned with a velvet ruffle and gold rope. A fire burned here, too, and the windows were shrouded by thick curtains.

Kila stopped, and scanned for a way out. The voices of pursuit were louder now, and footfalls sounded in the corridors she had just recently fled.

Someone stirred in the bed. The curtain parted, and a young woman with tousled hair peeped out. She couldn't have been older than nineteen, and she wore exactly what she had worn in the first moments of life. Nothing.

Another face appeared behind hers, older but not old. Kila recognized him instantly.

She swept into a mock bow and said, "Beggin' yer pardon, Highest Binel. I seem to have upset the honey-hive, may Til grin ya good." She turned, eyeing another door. But Highest Binel called to her. "Come here, Kila Sigh. That way leads to my wardrobe. You'll be trapped."

Kila let out a black blasphemy. The naked girl laughed. But Binel just waved for Kila to approach. "You must hide here."

"The first place they'll look is under the bed," Kila said.

"Not under," Binel said. "Get in. Trust me, they will not intrude here."

Kila stared at him, not believing her ears. Only the shouts of coming captors moved her from the spot. She dove over the girl and landed in a warm, blanket-covered realm of skin, perfume, and darkness.

A rustle of bedclothes and a few soft murmurs from Highest Binel to his naked guest were all that Kila heard as a warm, heavy blanket swept over her. Something jabbed her ribs. "Lie still," Binel hissed.

Legs closed in from either side, and Kila found herself hiding between two very hot, and very unclothed people. A voice cut through the weight of the down-stuffed covering that lay upon her. "She was here, Binel. Didn't you feel her?" It was the Hargothe, though his voice was louder than Kila had heard it before. She cursed herself for healing the man. But she had done more than that. She had given him new strength.

"Who was here, Seer Hargothe? Perhaps if you allow me to dress and we can talk in my—"

"Your bed companion is no secret from me, Binel," the Hargothe said. Even coming through the sound-deadening down, his voice was acid.

The air was so stuffy that Kila found herself straining to breathe. Every inhalation seemed to draw in nothing but her own hot exhalations. She shoved the girl's thigh with her elbow. There was no need for her to press in like a frozen puppy.

"Forgive me, Seer," Binel said. "She is nothing to me."

The naked girl's legs stiffened and she let out an injured gasp. "But you said you loved me!"

By Kil's throbbing handle, what a pickle-bird that girl was. If circumstances had been different, Kila might have taken the girl aside and given her a good talking to. As it was, she wanted to pinch her behind and call her a doodle-headed ninny. Did she truly think a man sworn to celibacy would marry her?

The Hargothe was mumbling too softly for Kila to understand, but his voice droned on for an eternity. If Kila didn't get out of this bed soon, she was going to lose her mind. Strange how she'd been so cold before. Now she half-wished she were naked, too. She didn't dare move, or the Hargothe would—

Wait. She realized the man was blind. If she moved, he would hear the bed rustle, but he would assume it was the other girl shifting around. Kila inched backward, trying to stay as flat as possible. Finally, she turned and lifted the bedcover enough to allow an inflow of fresh air at the foot of the bed. A sharp toenail dug into her bottom and she had to stifle a yelp. She dropped the cover and returned to her stifling tomb.

Wait 'til Wen hears about this, she thought. He would laugh so hard he'd turn red. And then she remembered he wouldn't ever hear about it. Wen was dead.

The Hargothe said something else, a final condemnation of Binel's weakness of flesh. Then his presence left the room. Binel lifted his side of the blanket, allowing light to ooze in. The resulting display of skin did not escape Kila's notice, unfortunately. She squirmed out of the covers and sprang from the bed. "That'll give me the horrors for a fortnight," she said.

Binel was pulling on a dressing gown. The girl had slumped into a pillow and was staring sullenly at the shrouded window.

"Why didn't you hand me over to him?" Kila asked. Highest Binel had schemed with her and Dunne Marlow to have Kila kill the old man. But she'd failed and Kila had even knocked Binel out using a mercusine method she couldn't remember. If anything, the man should want her hanging by her heels in Dunne Medow Plaza.

He had a handsome face, young for a man of his position. It was not so much serious as it was haughty. "Because, as flawed as I am, I am not without compassion. Nor am I stupid. The more he drains you, the stronger he becomes. He is already too powerful. But he is convinced—for very good reason—that I will keep nothing from him. If he probed my mind the way . . . But that is none of your concern. What I want in return for my mercy is a promise."

"Which is?"

"You will leave Starside. Preferably for the Garden, but if not there you will go somewhere far from here. You may be —" He stopped and glanced at his companion. "You may be that which we discussed."

Dem-Kisk.

"You should read Exine," Kila said.

Highest Binel did not see any humor in the comment. He frowned and motioned for the girl to depart. She gathered up her clothes and slipped out, throwing dagger-glances of jealousy at Kila before closing the door. She was plump, pretty, and doe-eyed. Kila doubted she had ever heard of Exine.

"I am familiar with the apostate known as Exine," Highest Binel said. "Did you know he was a farmer?"

Kila decided she didn't care about the Highest's opinion. She had more faith in the Voluptuary. Besides, she liked

Exine's interpretation better than the Way of Til's. "Do you have any dragon scales I could buy?"

The Highest cinched the belt on his robe and moved to check his hair in the looking glass in one corner of his luxurious bed chamber. "How many do you need?"

"You're not going to ask why? But of course you aren't. You know what sort of creature desires such a thing. I suppose you are aware of what Marlow has been up to?"

"He was expelled from the order for his dabbles in demaynic summonings. I must warn you that consorting with such dire beings is utterly despised by Til. You will suffer on this plane from the beast's duplicity, and you will suffer in Til's presence when he judges you for your actions during this life."

The lecture sounded like a formality, something said without any thought about its meaning.

He went to a wardrobe and dug a wooden box from the floor in the back. He set it on the bed and removed the lid. "I got this when I visited the Eerie when I was a boy. My father took me there to see Noxianthenes. "

Braggart. Kila crept close enough to peer into the box he'd opened. The sight of the objects within took her next words— and her very breath—out of her body.

Nestled on a black velvet cushion was a wondrous disc. Roughly circular, it was the size of a small dinner plate. Slightly concave, it thinned at the edges to razor fineness. The color of the shiny surface swirled from aquamarine to emerald. The scale was polished to mirror brightness, and gave the illusion of such depth that Kila was tempted to press her finger into it and feel the cool depths within.

As it was, Binel slapped her hand when she moved it toward the box.

"I collected this from the Eerie, freshly shed from the great wyrm itself. I own nothing more prized. How many did the demayne name as its price?"

"One thousand."

Binel snorted and closed the lid on his box. "And you agreed to that ridiculous amount?"

"What choice did I have?" Kila said. She backed away from the man and his bed. She hadn't come here to be mocked. "If you will kindly point the way to an exit, I will leave you to your scales and your women."

Binel put his box away and turned to regard her. He didn't seem concerned that he was facing a girl who could bring ruin to the world. "Do you believe the demayne expects you to pay?"

"Why else would he have named the price?" A hot feeling was beginning to well in Kila's gut. She recognized it as her instinct that she'd been swindled. The beast had wanted to free Nax from the Hargothe, but not to return her to Kila. He had taken her for himself. By striking the bargain, he'd gotten himself permission to leave the circle of stones—and had named such a high price—he could rest easy knowing that Kila would never be able to pay.

"Did Marlow know?" she asked, fuming. She should have known better than to trust that fallen Donse Master. He was far too smooth of tongue to be trusted.

"What do you think? Does Dunne Marlow strike you as stupid?"

He was many things, but stupid wasn't one of them. "It wasn't a fair deal. It doesn't count." But she didn't need Binel's laughter to confirm what she'd already deduced. Marlow had known that Flaumishtak's deal was impossible. But that raised another question. Why had Marlow helped her at all?

Binel anticipated it. "None of us want the Hargothe to go on living, much less to increase in power. Removing the Beloved One—excuse me—the Despised of Til from the Hargothe was only sensible." He paused and regarded Kila. There was none of the haughty superiority in his eyes now. Instead, there was a look of curiosity. "What is it like, speaking to one of them?"

"To a cat? It's like speaking to your best friend. Insults, teasing, brutal honesty."

Just talking about her bond inflamed the gaping wound in Kila's heart. She took another step back. "Just point the way and I'll get out of your life forever. I'm done with the Way of Til and all of you hypocrites."

If Highest Binel was insulted, he didn't show it. He merely shrugged, still absorbed in the idea of talking to a cat. Was that longing in his face, or mere stupidity? Kila didn't know and didn't care.

"You would be safe from the Hargothe at the Garden," he said. "While I cannot send you there in my official capacity as Highest, I'm sure I could arrange through Marlow to get you a berth aboard a ship. Consider it recompense for the loss of your animal."

"I'll tell you what recompense I want," she said. "Return my blade."

Highest Binel looked momentarily confused, but then the dawning of a vague memory came over him. "You mean the stolen Shadline blade I caught you with? Why on earth would I relinquish an artifact of such immense value to one to whom it clearly does not belong?"

"Because I'm going to turn you to ash if you don't," she said. Kila put her finger around the queller and started to remove it. The effect on Highest Binel was instantaneous. He held up both hands, face going pale.

"There's no need for threats. And if you remove that the Hargothe will be here instantly. Not only will he destroy you, he will know I was concealing you from him." When Kila left her ring in place, he relaxed and moved toward a bureau sitting against one wall. "I don't know how you came into possession of such a weapon, but I doubt you truly understand what it is."

"It was my father's. He never said where he got it."

"And your father's profession?"

"Locksmith."

That was true. Wen had apprenticed with a locksmith, too, for a while. Those memories were vague for Kila. The fact that Father had left locksmithing in favor of lock-picking was irrelevant. As for the blade being of the mythical Shadline sort, she had many doubts. For one, she didn't believe the Shadline cult existed. Second, the stories were so fanciful—featuring duels and blades with strange powers—that they seemed designed for impressionable boys. Finally, she had never seen a Shadline blade to compare Cayne to. In the stories they were all mostly swords.

Binel had removed a bundle of blue fabric from a bottom drawer. "This belongs to the Way of Til," he said. "All mercusine relics do, by rights granted at the synod of the New Pantheon." He unwrapped the blade, the black sheath and hilt sucking in the light. "But as a Donse Master and Highest of Til, I am not permitted to bear a weapon."

Kila held out her hand. "Stop with your nonsense. You will say anything to justify stealing that thing from me."

"I am not making this up, Kila Sigh. This relic is of an age before man. It was imbued with the mercusine by the first race. That makes it an artifact of Til. To pretend otherwise would be to shirk my holy responsibilities. But let us accommodate you."

Kila smirked and waggled her fingers. "Yes, let's."

Highest Binel brought Kila the blade, holding it in both hands the way a Donse Master would carry the effigy of Til for a Tilsday congregation: With solemn respect.

Kila realized he was serious. She looked at Cayne and could see nothing about it that suggested mercusine abilities. But then, she had always assumed it was merely a very fine blade. Father probably had stolen it long ago. But now that she was looking at it more closely, she recalled how she had killed an acolyte with it. Did Binel know that? It didn't seem likely. But Kila would never forget that moment. It was the first time she had ever taken a life with a blade. The man had sought to take her to the Hargothe. She'd had no choice. Cayne had penetrated to the man's heart as easily as it could have into an over-ripe melon. And his blood had stained the hilt but not the blade.

"I am Binel, Highest of Til. In His name, I bestow this holy blade into your possession, may it serve Til through you. And when you have gone to join Him, this blade will return to the Way so that it may once again be put to use in Til's service upon this His world."

Kila took the weapon and cinched the sheath straps around her right thigh. A sense of rightness settled on her. She did not like being unarmed these days. Binel stepped back, chanting under his breath. When he was done he smiled at her. "See? No need to ash me. I can be of assistance to you. Remember that if some day you do truly become Dem-Kisk."

Kila was tempted to punch him the gut for saying that. But when it became clear he wasn't joking, she merely glared. "The exit?"

"This way," he said, extending an arm. It led to the same closet he had warned her from entering when she'd arrived in his bedchamber. Soon it was clear why. He went to the rear wall and pressed his palm to it. Something mercusine must have happened then, for the wall shoved inward and rotated on one side to open a gap. Beyond, darkness. "My preferred route from my quarters when I'm leaving to attend to unofficial business. It will lead you to the kitchens. From there it is simple to walk out into the plaza."

A door at the bottom of a winding stairwell opened into a hallway. It bustled with servants, acolytes, and scullery maids. The smell of roasting atlen and boiled cabbage filled the overheated air. Kila kept her head down and wound through the kitchens until she spotted a door. She went through it and was happy to find herself in the cold wintry air of freedom.

5

____

RITES OF SUMMONING

The Way of Til discouraged immortalizing past Donse Masters by naming things after them. The obvious exception was Dunne Medow Plaza. But there was another one, known only to the followers of the Way and the few scholarly types who came to visit the Abbey. It occupied an enormous series of halls on the east wing.

The Library of Dunne Francis LiMillar was not as large as the library at the Garden, but what it lacked in quantity—a mere 20,000 volumes—it made up for with quality. The books, scrolls, and parchments here were lovingly organized, curated, and maintained by an order within the Way known as the Readers. These men were full Donse Masters but preferred the honorific Reader over Dunne.

The Hargothe had considered a life as Reader once. That was before he truly understood the power available to him through the mercusine. But the Library of Dunne Francis LiMillar held jewels of knowledge, much of it appropriated from Radiants' estates during the great Purge of Light. Some of these texts were filled with heresies about the so-called "small gods" and the fern-eater cult. These abominable practices were outlawed by the synod of the New Pantheon, and the books were declared Wrong. Possession of one of them could result in numerous punishments, including burning at the stake.

The Hargothe now walked among the stacks, breathing in the calming scent of the books. The aged leather bindings gave off a perfume he associated with his most joyful days as a young acolyte.

The men attending him walked a few paces behind. He didn't need help to stay upright anymore, and he certainly didn't want to hear the repulsive sound of his elderly servant's breath whistling in and out of his nostrils. That old man was at the end of his usefulness entirely. Soon he would have to go. A pity. Perhaps he'd be allowed to live while he trained a young replacement.

The other man in attendance was the head of the library, Reader Oloft. He was quiet, and his nostrils did not whistle when he breathed. He smelled clean, and his voice was naturally soft. These qualities made him tolerable to the Hargothe.

"Demaynic summoning is just to your right, Seer Hargothe," the man said. His voice was deferential, but also colored with disapproval. Such materials were not for respectable people. The library kept the volumes merely for the sake of completeness, and also against the day a demayncor show up in Starside and the order needed to study the ways of their enemy.

The Hargothe held in his mirth. There had been demayn-cors in Starside since he and Marlow had arrived from their far-flung plantation. They had pilfered numerous books from this section, seeking the keys to bringing demayne to this world to do their bidding. But the Hargothe had not had the knack for it that Marlow had.

What the Hargothe—then known as Acolyte Tenn—possessed was an ability to influence the minds of those around him. The power had quickly flowered and he could not keep his abilities secret from then Highest Simyn. His path had necessarily turned away from demayncy when he became so painfully sensitive to light and sound he'd been forced to put out his eyes and seek refuge in his crypt.

He stopped and turned to the books in question. His long, thin fingers trailed over the spines, feeling the leather and the embossed gold letter-work.

"Is there a volume the Seer Hargothe specifically desires?" Reader Oloft asked. "I could pull it down for you."

"And who will read it to me?" the Hargothe said. "These words are not safe for any simple acolyte's eyes and mind."

The Reader cleared his throat. "Perhaps a Reader could be spared to read you a few passages." The man didn't sound too keen on having to give the assignment to one of his charges. "May I ask why the Seer has this sudden interest?"

"Because there was a demayne of the highest order in my crypt when I awoke. It stole something of great value to me. I would recall it, retrieve my possession, and punish the beast for its insolence."

A strangled gulp was followed by: "I see. Well, of course I

am only too happy to assist you. I suppose Fromb's *On Summoning Fell Beasts* would be the place to begin. I must admit, I have only glanced through it. The book is Wrong. You do understand, do you not?"

The Hargothe understood completely. The Reader had likely read the entire volume with great interest. It was the nature of man to do that which was forbidden to him. The Hargothe did not care. He merely wanted his Ishmilla returned to him.

"Fromb was an imbecile, repeating stories told by half-witted trezz-wives. Pull down Rigothz."

The gasp that followed his utterance was truly magnificent. The name of the Kil-turned Donse Master Rigothz was not to be spoken within the walls of the abbey. Hargothe didn't care for such rules. Was Highest Binel going to confront him and make him do penance? No.

Reader Oloft knew the Hargothe wasn't subject to the usual order of discipline. He merely bowed and called to an assistant for his gloves to be brought. Rigothz's book on demaynic summoning might be declared Wrong, but that was no excuse to defile it with one's bare hands.

The Hargothe felt the tension radiating from the head librarian. It gave him a slight headache. "If Rigothz's words offend you too much, you can seek penance from Highest Binel when we are done."

The Reader's robes rustled and his lips smacked as he pulled down the volume in question. His odor turned sour and he continuously cleared his throat.

The Hargothe's elderly servant came forward to guide him

toward a reading room the Reader had prepared. Not needing this assistance, the Hargothe shrugged free of the old man's grip and touched his mind with fear. A gasp and a forlorn cry was followed by the putrid reek of the man having soiled himself. "Attend to yourself, man. I shall call for you if I have need of your assistance."

The seer continued unaided. He did not need anyone to be his eyes for the mere purpose of walking into a room. He could feel the space around him better than most men could see it. The mercusine reported to him all that surrounded him, though he did not know how it did so. Til's grace lay upon him. That was enough.

In the reading room, the Reader opened the volume and flipped through the introductory pages. "I am unfamiliar with *Rites of Summoning*, Seer. Forgive me while I take a moment to—"

"Chapter thirteen, Oloft."

"Yes, Seer." Then followed the sound of pages being flipped and the wash of dry, musty odor of very old paper. The Hargothe even detected the earthy note of the oak galls used in the ink.

The man cleared his throat four more times before beginning to read. "The subject at hand is the summoning of high order demayne. This is not to be attempted lightly. The dangers are well known, and if one has a heart full of—"

"Skip the warnings, Oloft. Rigothz was brilliant but superstitious. Get to the summoning. I need names and stones. That is all I care about."

The Reader mumbled under his breath as he read through

the useless introductory matter. The Hargothe remembered feeling the same impatience when he'd first read the book. Why couldn't a writer get to the point at the outset? Why did they always bury their useful material beneath mounds of wordy inanity? If only there existed a person to read the manuscript and cross out such superfluities. Alas.

Finally, the Reader cleared his throat and read. "The stones needed are ten in number, their sizes are these: One like an apple of the miretree, two the size of an autumn pumpkin. Three of a man's head, and four of pig's orbs." The Reader made an odd coughing noise and his robes rustled. He continued into the Hargothe's silence: "These the demayncor must place in the shape of the Crown, and repeat the invocation ten times without error. The spell—for want of a better word—is a naming rite, calling the attention of Father—" Oloft groaned.

The Hargothe said, "Simply reading what is before you does not put the words into your heart. I will not condemn you for speaking the phrase 'Father Kil.'"

"As you say. But allow me to continue with what follows immediately after that blasphemy. '. . . calling the attention of Kil, for whom names are of utmost power. If He smiles upon your efforts, the stones shall receive these names and remain unknown to the summoned demayne. Should the beast learn but one of the stones' names, it will break free of all bonds and wreak havoc untold. Many are the dead who have witnessed this carnage, few are those have done so and survived. All of hell's worst tortures are the carnival of the Firelords. Beware!"

Such dramatic writing. While the Hargothe did not doubt

the dangers, such dire warnings did naught but ignite curiosity in the young.

Such had been the case for him and Marlow. But Kil didn't listen to the Hargothe, and so the stone names did not take. But Marlow was favored of Kil, and his summonings succeed without fail. This presented a problem for the Hargothe. There was no reason to believe his invocations would meet with more success now. He was clearly favored of Til, and so the Despised God would do nothing to aid him. He would have to pursue other means.

There was one besides Marlow who he was confident could summon the beast. Unfortunately, she despised him, and not without reason. But now that he thought about it, she would be perfect. And getting her to the stones might not be all that difficult.

The seer closed his empty eyes and felt along the mercusine web for his old servant. The man was a flickering candle among dim flames. But the Hargothe knew his servant's light as well as he knew Kila Sigh's.

The man felt the Hargothe's summons and showed up wheezing a quarter of an hour later. Reader Oloft sat in silence except for the occasional nervous throat-clearing. The Hargothe didn't dismiss him. There was another matter to address with the man.

The elderly servant bustled in, "Seer, how may I assist you?"

"I require an audience with my sister."

"Seer? An audience?"

"Do I make a habit of saying things I do not mean?"

"No. I shall send for her at once."

"No. I will go to her. She remembers me as I was. I will enjoy surprising her with my renewed vigor. Send notice that I am coming. Then arrange for a carriage. Horse-drawn. I cannot abide those foul atlens."

"Yes, Seer." The man scurried away to make arrangements.

"Reader Oloft," the Hargothe said. "What you will feel next is pain."

The man uttered a questioning grunt and then started to gasp and convulse, fingernails scratching at the table. The Hargothe didn't need to touch the man's head to enter his mind. The process of blanking a man's memories was simple if you didn't mind tearing holes in it.

With time and practice, one could put in all manner of false memories to cover what was blanked. But the Hargothe didn't have time to waste on a nothing like Reader Oloft. And he didn't much care about the consequences to the man. He would likely not serve as head Reader for long. But most importantly, he would have no memory of the Hargothe reading from a book declared Wrong. Nor would he know that the Hargothe was bound for Gristenside and the estate of his sister, Radiant Juni Peline.

6

THE LIGHT OF YOUR ATTENTION

Kila didn't want to go to the Warren. There were too many memories of Wen there. And it wasn't as if she had left anything behind. She didn't want the old fish oil lantern or the piles of rags they'd used for beds.

But there was one thing she did want.

Oly, have you found Startle yet?

Yes. The cream-colored ball of animosity had not been in sight the entire way to the Warren. He had come to a truce with Kila, but that wasn't going to make them friends. Even now the bond was like a prickle of heat on back of Kila's neck.

Well, where is he?

No answer. And there likely wouldn't be one.

Kila was tired and her feet were numb from the long run along the roofways and then the long-cut through the sewers into Cheapsgate. She was tempted to stay here for the night.

But she knew she wouldn't sleep. The Warren was haunted now by the ghosts in her heart.

First was Nax, a void that left her bereft, as if her own name had been taken from her. And second was Wen, her brother and lifelong companion. Her teacher.

The den was no place for her. But more than that, it was farther from her goal.

The objective of her visit—a black and white splotched cat named Startle—nosed through the carpet door that had served as Kila's only barrier from the outside world for the better part of a year.

She knelt and held out a bit of dried beef. The cat stalked close, posture low and wary. But he knew Kila, and after only a moment's hesitation accepted both the treat and a chin scratch.

"I'm not coming back here, Startle," she said. It felt a bit odd to be talking to this cat. She realized that she had never spoken to any of the others prior to this. But she doubted Startle could understand her spoken words the way Oly could understand her sent ones.

The cat rubbed against her leg and began to make the contented buzzing noise. The sound brought a pain to Kila's throat, and she flashed on memories of sleeping in this tiny room, Nax atop her chest and vibrating with this same sound.

Startle will not come with us. He's too stupid to understand the advantages of the atlen barn. Oly sent an irritated skin-crawl sensation. *Which is exactly what I told you would happen.*

The truce was thin indeed. She and Oly agreed on nothing

except that Nax had to be found and her bond to Kila restored. *Let him know where—*

He knows exactly where all his litter-mates are. I've told you this over and—

Tell him again. Tell him he's welcome.

The concept confused Oly. But Kila felt certain that telling Startle he was welcomed would make a difference despite Oly's assumption that a cat could go wherever it pleased, regardless of welcome.

I told him. Let's go.

Kila stroked Startle from ears to tail, then made for her secret entrance of loose planks. A short climb later and she was atop the Warren. The slums of Cheapsgate stretched upslope to her left. Beyond it stood the ring wall, the outer limit of the city of Starside.

The combined smoke and reek of rotten fish surrounding the Warren smelled like home. But it was no longer *her* home. She didn't truly have one.

She trotted along the roofline, leaping up or down when the elevation of the cobbled-together repairs and dormers required. And when she finally dropped to the roofs of the ramshackle hovels that made up Cheapsgate, Oly was there. He loped alongside her, sending irritated emotional jabs every now and then.

I didn't ask for this bond, you know, she sent to him.

A long silence followed, absent all of his rude sendings of fur being rubbed head-wise and tails being yanked. Finally he sent, *Wen asked for it. He said that I needed to look after you.*

An ache formed in her throat. She swallowed it. What she

should feel was anger. How dare Wen saddle her with his ornery cat? Did he truly think she was so hapless she required this cream-colored tangle-ball to keep an eye on her?

She couldn't raise much ire in the end. She had loved Wen, and it was clear that he had loved her. And though Oly seemed to despise her, his regard for Wen's wishes were touching. Maybe there was more to Oly than thorns.

You're too slow, Oly sent. He darted ahead and disappeared.

Instead of giving chase, Kila slowed to a stop. A figure in black had appeared in front of her, the swirling tails of his cloak settling around black trousers and slim shoes that reminded Kila of Yiqa's. His face spoke of strength, but the faint lines around his eyes did not necessarily indicate age. He could have been twenty or forty. He wore a sword at his side.

"You are Kila Sigh," he said. "You must come with me. You have oaths to speak."

"Are you trezzed or are ya just daft? I'll be followin' you to my granny's weddin' afore I'll let ya drag me off t' the old man." He had to be one of the Hargothe's creatures. A mercenary or bounty hunter.

"Let's dispense with the Cheaps-talk, please. You have never been the waif you claim to be." He stepped forward, no threat explicit in his posture, but neither was he relaxed. He was tightly wound, like a clockmaker's coil. Ready to unleash violence in an instant.

"Not a waif? That's interesting," she said. "My belly would argue against that, as empty as its been these past few years."

"The atlen eggs you steal from the boys' barn keeps your appetite sated. And I'm sure the Sensuals will feed you if you miss a meal." He stopped a pace away, hands loose at his sides but one near enough the hilt of his blade. "But you have new responsibilities to bear, and with them comes advantages of coin."

Father had warned Kila of hucksters and their promises of wealth. Strangers offering money with one hand were picking your pocket with the other.

Kila knew many in Cheapsgate whose entire living depended on swindling the passengers stepping off ships. She had laughed along with them as the wide-eyed marks walked off with a vial of seawater that was sure to cure whatever ailed them. So she would be a Radiant's daughter in a crinoline before she would fall for this fool's tricks.

She made to step around him. "Ya need to work on yer banter, my friend. You'll pilfer no sap's coin with that dung-tongued hooey."

The man didn't move to intercept her. But as she passed him a chill swept from her crown to her toes. She gave him a second look. But he was gone. She spun, searching for the ledge he must have dropped from. But the roofs here were all joined. She stomped in search of a hidden trap door, but only provoked the angry residents below into shouting theories about her low parentage.

The temptation to remove her queller was enough to make Kila grip the ring, but Oly sent a warning surge of anger at her.

"Stupid cat," she mumbled. She hated when Oly was right.

The man's appearance and his whole bucket of bilge-water was a trap. But why had he just vanished? He looked deadly, and Kila had no doubt he could've given her a tooth-scraper of a fight.

She rubbed her arms, still tingling with the chill of his disappearance. There may have been something mercusine afoot. She wondered if the man was even a man. In stories, demayne could take on any form they wanted if they were given permission to do so.

Perhaps Highest Binel had warned Marlow that she knew his schemes. If he was sending people after her, then she would put a quick stop to it. How, exactly, she didn't know. But not knowing how to do something had never factored into her decisions in the past. And she was still alive.

Oly went back to the atlen barn, which suited Kila just fine. The more distance between them, the fewer unwelcome opinions she received.

The jewelry shop stood on a stretch of lower Terriside Street of Sorrows frontage where the wealthier merchants shopped and did their business. The store was closed, the front windows papered over to obstruct curious eyes. She noticed a mark above the front door, a vague nick in the wood frame. Father had taught her to never to steal from such a place, for it was protected by the Owls. Kila had robbed numerous marks on the street, but she and Wen had never resorted to robbing homes or stores. That was the purview of the Owls, and nobody who expected to live long crossed them.

Or so the story went.

Kila had come to believe the Owls were a myth, a phony organization of villains created by the Terriside merchants themselves to keep real thieves away. Kila had once asked her friend and barkeep, Critt Sanglo, about the Owls. He had merely shaken his head and whistled. "I'm not stepping off that yardarm, dearie. It's a black and roilin' sea ye be sailin'."

Whether they were real or not, Kila and Wen had always kept an eye out for the scratch-dot-scratch of their sign. She proceeded to the rear of the shop. This time the back door was locked.

So, Marlow knew she would be coming. She pulled her canvas roll of lock-picking tools from her pocket. Father had made these long ago. Wen had held onto them. Now, Kila had them. Aside from Cayne, it was the only thing of her father's she possessed. She undid the strap and unrolled the canvas. Nestled into individual pockets were an array of slim metal probes, hooks. Some flat-headed, some pointed, and of various thicknesses. Kila had practiced with them under Wen's tutelage. The idea had been to knock over a Radiant's greathouse and make off with some gold platters or forks or jewels. Perhaps that had been a childish fantasy, but it had motivated Kila to learn the workings of locks.

They were not that difficult once one understood the way tumblers moved. Kila was tempted again to remove her queller. When you could see the metal bits, you could open a lock just as easily as you could turn a key. But the mercus vision wasn't necessary for a lock this simple.

The lock released with a satisfying click.

Fifteen minutes later she walked into the whale-oil glow of Marlow's camp in the weird chamber of nothingness. The mysterious columns stood all around, each carved with a different symbol. The demaynic stones still lay where they'd been when she'd left with Flaumishtak.

Marlow was there, too. He sat on the floor, leaning against a handcart full of supplies. He was puffing on a long-stemmed pipe, the smoke rising around his head like a ghostly gray wreath. He pursed his lips around the stem when he saw her. "I was expecting you earlier."

Kila drew Cayne and began to toss it and catch it by the hilt. "I thought we were aimed toward the same thing," she said. "We both wanted the Hargothe to lose Nax. We both wanted him dead. But Highest Binel informed me today that you knew the demayne's price for Nax would be so ridiculously high I'd never be able to pay it. Did you think I would just accept being swindled?"

"Don't be silly, Kila Sigh. I know you will never give up. But the price is the price. Perhaps you'd be better off gathering dragon scales than sneaking into Donse Masters' bed chambers."

The temptation to stab him was difficult to resist, but she had stabbed him once before and it hadn't done more than nick him. He was protected by some mercusine trick that made his flesh like stone.

She sheathed Cayne and removed her queller. The metals around her blazed with mercusine glow. The column symbols, the brass of the lantern, and the iron in Marlow's blood. The man lowered his pipe and started to stand. Kila focused on the gold ring he wore on one pinky. She sought it with all her senses, focused on its tone, its smoothness. Her fingers pinched, stroking the contours of the outer edges. She wanted to yank it from his finger, but the more she sought to grip it, the less solidity she felt beneath her fingertips. Instead, she did her old trick of adding to the glow. This was heat.

"Are you unwell?" Marlow asked. "Your face looks—"

He yelped and shook his hand. Hissing and hopping, he plucked the ring from his finger and dropped onto the tiles of the cavern. The ring bounced with a clink, then rolled to rest at Kila's feet. It lay there in front of her toes, glowing red as a fire ember. She stopped adding to its glow, and the heat faded.

She cocked an eyebrow at Marlow. "I'm showing restraint."

He tapped the dottle from the pipe. "And I appreciate it. But this demonstration was quite unnecessary, no matter how marvelous." He put his pinky in his mouthy and glowered. "That hurt."

"Did you send a man in black to find me in Cheapsgate?"

"No."

"He said I had to take oaths. He also hinted that there was money to be had."

Marlow began to add tobacco to his pipe. "I was wondering when *they'd* step into the game. That they allowed you and your brother such freedom for so long is rather unusual."

"What are you talking about?" Kila was sick of his little mysteries. Why couldn't the man just speak direct and save everyone some time? He was almost as bad as the Voluptuary on that count.

"You are a Shadline, obviously. Or—that is—you *will* be one. That dagger has the unmistakable look of a Shadline blade. And you are already so moved by the force of destiny, how could you be anything but a Shadline?" He laughed and shook his head.

She drew Cayne again and held it to the light of the lantern. "Everyone says this blade is stolen. Maybe so, but nobody ever accused my father of being in a sword cult."

"Does it need sharpening? Does it rust? Does blood remain on the blade when it cuts?"

The answer to all these was no, but still . . . Father had owned the blade since she could remember. A headache came over her, so sudden and blinding she doubled over and pressed her fists to the sides of her head.

"You are not well. Please sit. I will prepare some tea."

Kila didn't have much choice. The pain didn't relent. She leaned against the cart.

"We could save time if you would boil this water." Marlow held up a small kettle. She couldn't bear to look at the stove-flame, much less use the mercus to heat water. Even if she knew how. She shook her head and covered her eyes.

"No?" Marlow put the kettle on a small whale-oil stove.

The smell of the steeping tea eventually reminded her to put on her queller. The moment she did, the pain subsided. The oddest thing.

"Your father was an interesting man," Marlow said. There was an invitation in this statement, a question he wanted Kila to answer. The Voluptuary had tried the same thing, but Kila wasn't going to tell them a Kil-damned thing about her father. Those were her memories, and they had nothing to do with anyone else.

But Marlow wouldn't let it go. He handed her a dainty

porcelain cup and took a seat next to her. "The black-cloaks keep close tabs on every Shadline weapon." He reached to flick the black blade in her hand, making a dull ringing that was quickly swallowed up by the chamber around them. "If I had to wager, Cayne here is new to them."

"My father had it for years, and Wen after him for several more."

"I didn't say 'newly forged.'" He took a sip of tea. "I meant that it is newly discovered. The blade itself is at least two thousand years old. Else it would not be a Shadline blade. That it was in the hands of men all that time and not known to the black-cloaks is beyond Til's ken. That is, it isn't possible."

His eyes were serious, brow furrowed. "So they either allowed it to remain free in the world, or they did not catch wind of it until recently. And how would that be possible? Perhaps other forces concealed its existence." He took another sip and sighed. "That is good tea for being mere hard black. Doesn't even need honey."

Kila's head had cleared enough that she could drink her tea. The lantern light still seemed too bright. But with the queller on at least she could bear to have her eyes open. "Whether it's a Shadline or Smith Freck's castoff is no care of mine. The black-cloaks can recite all the secret oaths they want and leave me out of it. This blade is mine. It stabs and cuts and that's all I need or want from it."

Marlow reached to pour more tea from his kettle. "But that is not all it will want from you. I'm no lore-master, but like your bond with the cat, the blade has bonded to you. For what purpose I know not, but it won't long remain a secret."

He nudged her with his elbow. "If you would learn more, go with the man the next time he appears. The black-cloaks would be powerful allies . . . or powerful foes."

Kila smirked. "When I have my thousand dragon scales and can spare the time, maybe I will." She wondered if she would. The weird notion that perhaps her blade had an ancient mysterious origin made her head flare with pain again. As did the fleeting thought that her father might have known what the blade was. That made her wonder if he'd aspired to become part of the black-cloaks.

Marlow turned to look at her, seeking eye contact she did not want to give. Not wanting to appear weak, she met his gaze. He looked sympathetic. That was his way of charming her into trusting him. Well, it wouldn't work.

"Why don't you go get the scales you need, Miss Sigh?"

"What? From the Eerie? You think I should just climb up there and collect a sack full of them?"

He didn't smile, or even so much as flash an eyebrow. "Yes."

"I've never even been to the Citadel. I'm sure there are a bunch of gates and guards between me and it. And in case you weren't aware, my face is known to the Watch."

"That is of no matter. I will take you there."

"And won't the Hargothe have you killed the moment you step foot outside?"

"Not necessarily. He would use me for my talents before making me a permanent part of the wind. But his methods are unpleasant."

"I'm aware."

He made a pained laugh. "Indeed. Imagine growing up with him."

She couldn't imagine such a thing. And she didn't want to. "Why don't you skip to the part where I say no."

"Because you will say yes, my dear. I have it all planned. But for it to work, you must loan me your queller." He paused while Kila uttered a long series of Kil's-tongue curses. When she ran out of steam, he continued. "I must remain quelled to avoid being discovered. But you, Kila, do not require such protection."

"The Hargothe would agree. He would love for me to go about with a naked mind."

Marlow retrieved his pipe and began to tamp in fresh leaf. "Always making assumptions. But you, my dear, have such facility with the mercus that you may learn a skill I have only dreamed of. You can surely mask your own power. And I will teach you." He seemed quite proud of his generosity, puffing away as he put a flashtaper to the bowl of his pipe.

This offer was at least as suspicious as the cloaked man telling her she had oaths to take. "Knowing you, there's more in it for you than me. What's the trick?"

"No trick. You keep mistaking my errors of judgement for outright duplicity. Do not forget, I was hoping to get you out of Starside when we met with Binel the first time."

She remembered. They had conspired to send her to the Garden and put under the leering eyes of the Donse Masters there. Hardly a favor. "You will never return my queller to me, will you?"

He merely smiled at her. "I would beg your indulgence to

keep it for a while. At least until this misunderstanding with my brother can be resolved."

He meant until his brother was dead. Kila had every intention of making that happen soon. But without the queller it seemed more likely the Hargothe would find her, drain her mercusine power, and have her body tossed into the garbage burning room down the hall from his crypt.

If Marlow could truly teach her the skill of masking her own power, then perhaps it would work. But that didn't solve the greater issue of how she would get to the Eerie. "Even if I got to the Eerie without drawing the Hargothe's notice, it's high upon the mountainside. That is not a matter of climbing a rain gutter to a roof. It'll be cold up there. And surely Her Enlightened has her Fell Guards posted every few feet."

Marlow puffed, making the herb in his pipe crackle and glow. He blew a great gout of smoke into the air. "How many young men have asked to court you?"

"I have little time for making eyes at boys. Besides," she said, "I'm not really the type to draw that sort of attention."

"Believe me, young lady, you have everything a young man might desire save some padding on your bones. You are well formed, of expressive brow, and have a charming elfish quality in your chin and nose. You have the most remarkable eyes I have seen since losing my dear Spin Hetta. The reason young men do not approach you is twofold. First, they fear you will stab them, either with your sharp tongue, or your Shadline blade. Second, they assume the fortifications surrounding your heart are too strong. And so they do not approach. Do not make the same mistake about going for the Eerie that lads make about your affections. Each goal can be won by a determined heart."

Indignation warred with embarrassment in Kila's gut. She wanted to smack the grinning Donse Master. One did not speak of such things, especially an older man to a younger woman. Who was he to offer such counsel?

Marlow didn't waver under her glare. "Do not point the light of your attention too much on my advice about love. I meant to turn your thoughts to the Eerie. I assure you, the Fell Guard counts on assumptions to keep intruders away. My former source for scales returned there many times. You know you will attempt it, for what other choice do you have?"

It came back to Nax, of course. Kila had to satisfy the demayne's terms or she would never regain her Beloved One or the bond. "Can you teach me to ignore the mountain chill as well as how to mask my mind from the Hargothe?"

"That I cannot, though such skills were written of in tomes long since declared Wrong. In time you may gain insights for how to do just that. But I shall fetch foul-weather gear to protect you during your climb. And I shall procure a satchel, that you might easily return with the booty you steal."

He held out his hand. She looked at it. Now it came to a decision. She either trusted this man to do as he promised, or she attempted to reach the Eerie alone. "I've seen Highest Binel's dragon scales," she said. "They were each the size of a dinner plate. A thousand of them will weigh at least as much as the same number of gold skillets. Even if I gather them, the climb down from the Eerie will be impossible."

"Did Binel allow you to handle one of them?" When she

didn't answer he nodded knowingly. "I thought not. Then you did not have a chance to discover that you were looking at eight of them, all nested together. Allow me to assure you that each scale is as light as a tuft of atlen down. For the dragon to fly, it must carry as little weight as possible. Even the beasts' bones are rumored to be riddled with holes, like a sea sponge."

Kila was certain there were lies in his words, but she didn't know anything true about dragons. Until this very day she had assumed that the Shadlines were pure fancy.

"How many stabs of this blade can your body deflect?" she asked, holding up Cayne.

He swallowed, revealing what she had suspected. The limits of his invulnerability were nearly reached already. "Good. Then know this. Should you fail to do as you have promised, I will find you and we'll count the stabs together. Then we'll both know for certain." She pulled off her queller and handed it to him.

He made a little flourish with his hands, as if honoring a Radiant. "You shall never have to count stabs in my presence, Kila Sigh. This I swear."

There was no telling with this man. He always spoke with a mix of sincerity and sarcasm. Whatever his true intention, he was clearly eager to get on with it. He stood, brushed off his robes, and gathered several small items into a sailcloth bag. "I shall return anon."

"I'm going to eat all your food while you're gone."

His grin wavered, and Kila took pleasure in it, knowing he had incurred great expense bringing these supplies here. He had obviously not left the Derslin Wheel, and he had not asked any of his hired goons to bring it. No, he had summoned a demayne of some lesser class to bring it all to him. But that had surely cost him well more than the supplies would fetch in Starside.

"Be my guest," he said, reestablishing his smile. "And do remember my hospitality when you come to hold the fate of the world in your hands."

With that, he tramped into darkness. It was only long after that Kila realized he had not taken the whale oil lantern with him. Had that been out of consideration for her?

Or out of fear of her?

7

─────

TIME-REIN

enley Mast scooped the last spoonful of stew and ate it. Then, cheeks reddening with shame, he took a chunk of bread from the platter and sopped up all that remained in the bowl. No one was else in the Baths' dining hall save Raginalt Keel, a novitiate doing penance in the scullery.

Had Henley shown such terrible manners in his father's house, he would have been sent to sit on the floor with the hounds. And those rascals would have stolen the rest of his meal in half a heartbeat.

But hunger compelled him to eat every crumb and spot of the hearty stew. More than hunger. He had gone into the dungeon cell beneath the Abbey of Til as a somewhat hardened lad of the street. But part of him had still been the soft son of a rich merchant. Even his years aboard ship did not compare with the cold and desolate world of namelessness. Inside that cell, the old Henley Mast had died.

A different boy had been born, one nurtured by starvation, madness, and hopelessness. From now on Henley would take no soup as certain.

But sopping up soup made him feel like a prisoner. Furtive, animal. He ate the bread and pushed the bowl away. Raginalt came forward to collect it. He was taller than Henley and a few years older. And he was a Keel, the family who had burned down Henley's house.

"Raginalt," he said, acknowledging the lad. It was hard to do without growling. The Mast and Keel families had feuded so long that Ragin and Henley had learned mutual animosity in the crib.

And yet Raginalt had saved Henley's life. As the fire swept through the Mast house, and the rest of the Keel brothers ran through it to make sure Henley's father and armsmen were all slain, Raginalt had come to Henley's room and helped him to the window where he'd climbed to safety.

And so Henley had lived.

"Please sit, Raginalt."

The lad was blond, broad-shouldered. Henley supposed he had a pleasant enough face—to anyone not familiar with his father Hackworth Keel. The resemblance was unmistakable, though he did not possess the habitual smirk that marred his father's face. Instead, his countenance was placid, even earnest. It must have been that quality that made Kila so twitchy around him. She had never spared any of them the jabs of her wit, but Raginalt got double his share.

Raginalt sat on the long bench across the table from Henley and folded his hands. It was strange to see him in the somewhat scandalous filmy robes of a novitiate of Ori. Novitiates were rarely seen outside the Baths, and most were female. The robes surely drew a lad's notice when a novitiate girl happened to swish by in them. Kila had apparently worn them once. He could only imagine her chagrin, and he did imagine—or tried to—what she might have looked like in them. But Raginalt was clearly at home in the getup.

"I have to thank you, Raginalt. I'd be dead if you hadn't pushed me out of that window." Raginalt hadn't shoved him, so much as guided him so that he could climb down and avoid flames and blades. "And I suspect that is why you are no longer welcome at House Keel. I'm sorry for that."

"You have naught to apologize for. It was my family who destroyed yours."

"But I have more to apologize for. When you were on the way to the cathedral to sell the cat you got from those sailors—"

"You mean Oly."

"Yes. Well, Fallo and I had planned to rob you that night."

"Kila beat you to it."

Henley winced. "Actually, she simply beat us. Then she went after you. But good came of it. If we had succeeded we would have taken Oly straight to the cathedral, and none of our cats would know us."

Raginalt moved Henley's bowl aside. His brows scrunched over his nose and he said nothing for a long time. Finally, he looked up. "And I wouldn't know Kila."

"Don't fool yourself. Nobody truly knows Kila."

Raginalt snickered and gave a sad smile. "As true as that?"

"As true as that."

A presence entered the dining hall that made both boys turn to see who had come in. Henley stood and offered the Voluptuary a bow.

She was no taller than he was, but she might as well have been a giant. She radiated authority like a mercus light. "Sit. Both of you."

They sat. She joined them, taking a seat next to Ragin. She propped her elbows on the table and rubbed her hands together. "I won't make you stay, Henley. But I think you should."

Right into the conversation, as usual. "I appreciate your generosity, Voluptuary, but I don't want to become a novitiate. I don't want to do anything but leave Starside." And leave Kila Sigh, he didn't add. She frightened him as much as she charmed him.

"You have awakened to the mercus, lad. The Hargothe will not let you slip through his fingers. Where is your cat?"

"Hunting. You have a rat problem, in case you didn't know." He felt his face flush, knowing that it was turning bright red. He shouldn't have said that about the rats. But she had made him angry. As if he didn't know the dangers of the Hargothe. He knew them better than anyone save Kila.

The Voluptuary didn't seem particularly offended. "I felt the mercus ebb and flow as Kila and the Hargothe contended for her power. It wasn't nearly so bright as her ashing of the thinnies, but no one with a whisker's sensitivity to the mercus could have failed to feel it.

"But there was another presence flaring upon the mercusine during that battle. It, too, was centered in the Hargothe's crypt." She shivered at her own words. Few had ever seen the tomb-like chamber where the old man lived.

Henley had not admitted to himself that he'd used the mercus. He certainly hadn't told Kila or Fallo, and especially not the Voluptuary. If Kila knew of it, she hadn't said anything.

"You aren't denying it," Raginalt said softly. His eyes were wide, and he leaned back as if seeing in Henley a sudden danger, like finding a spider in one's wardrobe.

"Your power is strong, Henley," the Voluptuary said. "Stronger than Sens Goolsoy's was, may Ori embrace him eternal." She leaned forward, eyes intense and penetrating. "Tell me what you did. Mercus feats of any kind are difficult. Most with the skill can merely sense it. But I felt you moving it, and the feeling was watery and strange. I had a note from the Coin of Pol asking for confirmation of it. She claims to have spun three smiles when asking the medallion if another merculyn had awakened."

Henley looked at Raginalt. The blond boy had been there in the crypt shortly after. He had helped Henley and Kila escape. Raginalt was—and it took a moment to really recognize the truth—a friend now.

Far away, Huff pounced and killed a rat. He sent waves of grim satisfaction and pride to Henley. This boosted Henley's fortitude. The Voluptuary had been a friend, too. And a friend to Wen and Kila, though Kila would hardly admit it. He could risk telling her.

"I don't know what I did," he said. "It came out of desperation. Dunne Yples was going on about Dem-Kisk and trying to kill Kila. I just . . ."

Both the Voluptuary and Raginalt were watching him, eyes drinking him in. He was not accustomed to such attention from anyone. It made him uneasy, and he looked away and rubbed the back of his neck. "I don't know if I did it or not. But the world turned sort of green and everything moved slower. Much slower. Everything but me. I was able to deflect the Dunne Yples's final blow. Then I knocked him out. I thought I'd killed him. And then it all returned to normal and I was more exhausted than I'd ever been."

The Voluptuary didn't say anything. She seemed to be waiting for him to continue. But he'd told all there was to tell. He'd never had any of the experiences Kila described: the keener sight, the ability to smell what the family on the floor below the Warren den were cooking for dinner. He certainly had never seen metals glowing.

He coughed and avoided the Voluptuary's eyes. "As I said, I don't know that I even did it."

"Oh, you did it," the woman said. "I assure you. A mercus feat not accomplished in an age, and even then by only one merculyn. Her name was Duri LiMinluit."

Both boys gasp at mentioned of the first Enlightened's name. She was not well thought of. "You mean the one they named the Harridan Gate after?" Raginalt said. "She wasn't a merculyn. She was god-touched."

The Voluptuary let Raginalt's mild blasphemy slide. "Is that what the Donse Masters say?" Shaking her head, she pressed her palms to the table as if seeking its solidity to keep her on an even keel. "Her disgrace is a myth, propagated by the Way of Til to weaken the Raven Throne. The resulting revolt cost thousands of Terriside lives and turned Cheapsgate from a thriving dockside village into the horrid slum it is today. The word 'harridan' is all the evidence you need. The Nares of the Thebkine Table have always sought to reduce women to hounds. They've had a bone in their craw about us since compromising on the Triumvirate at the synod of the New Pantheon."

She heaved a great breath, again seeking to control her ire. She failed. "Those men *are* what they despise. Those be-robed . . . swirehogs!"

She held her breath a moment then released it. This time she did relax. With her composure back within her control, she smiled wanly. "Duri LiMinluit was steeped in the mercus. Our library has three separate accounts of her power, written by her contemporaries—all of whose works have been declared Wrong by the Way of Til—and these accounts agree that Duri's powers were unmatched in her time.

"There was one witness to her feat of time-rein, a man who served in her household as a do-all. He had been summoned to her quarters to repair a rattling window. As he worked upon it, Her Enlightened Majesty entered the room. Naturally, he ceased working immediately and paid the proper obeisance by bowing and lowering his gaze to his feet.

"This is where the story becomes quite weird. When the man straightened and resumed his work at her insistence, a gull flew into the window, jarring it loose from the frame and shattering it. As the pieces fell toward the workman, a flash of green filled the room. It lasted a mere moment. When it passed, there wasn't a shard of glass upon the floor. It was all contained in a priceless vase held in Her Enlightened Majesty's own hands. The gull sat upon the carpet, dazed but alive. The workman had moved three paces aside from the window in less than a click of a tongue."

Henley could envision the scene as if he'd been there. He knew what the Enlightened had seen. What she had done. "But why expend so much power for a mere do-all?"

The Voluptuary shrugged. "She was the Enlightened, seeing what others could not. But judging by events that followed, she merely sought to protect her future husband from injury. She was a seer and must have seen a grave future ahead if the accident had proceeded as fate directed. Few can confront and turn aside the force of destiny."

Henley blew out his cheeks. Part of him was relieved. "That means I probably won't be able to do it again. And maybe the gods touched me to save Kila. She is Dem-Kisk, after all."

Raginalt swore and stammered an outraged denial. The Voluptuary waved him to silence. "That is not decided, young man. A possibility, but not yet a fact."

Ragin paled, then turned slightly green, like a land man at sea for the first time. Henley sympathized. But he'd had more time to accept that the ravings of Dunne Yples were not mere fancy, but a truth inspired by direct witness of Kila's destruction of the thinnies. "Still, if I did do that time-rein thing, it doesn't mean I know *how* to do it. I didn't feel anything happening."

The Voluptuary merely stared at him, unblinking, mouth pursed in the manner of one patiently allowing someone to say silly things to get the ideas out of their minds. "Lean forward," she commanded. "My arms aren't long enough to reach you."

When Henley leaned the wrong way, she sighed. "I'm not going to hit you, you sheep-headed dolt. I'm going to show you your own power. You obviously won't take my word for it."

Hesitantly, he leaned forward. The Voluptuary motioned him closer until he was nearly folded in half, his gut pressing into the edge of the table.

She placed her dry, warm palm on his forehead.

Heat flashed up and down his spine as the world snapped into keen detail. The smell of his soup jumped out first, proving he had not gotten every bit from the bowl. The grain of the wood table, which had been polished glossy by ages of use, was now rough to his touch. He could even see the ridges of the grain, like tiny waves upon a dun ocean. He pulled away, sucking in a breath and feeling his hair stand up, a chill coursing over his scalp. His muscles contracted, forcing his hands into claws and his back to pull inward, his chin rising until he was squinting at the ceiling.

The Voluptuary nodded in satisfaction. "I don't have Goolsoy's delicate touch, I'm sorry to say. But this will pass."

Raginalt was swearing under his breath. Henley heard every syllable as clearly as if it were whispered into his ear. Abruptly, the tension released and his body slumped.

Breath racing and body tingling, Henley panted and stared dumbly at the dining hall around him. He could still see more keenly than he'd ever seen before. Every sound that reached him was crisp and clear, as if the source were right next to him. In fact, he heard the conversation of two novitiates who had come into the kitchens to help the baker prepare the next round of bread for the afternoon meal.

"You may not be able to accomplish a time-rein again. I don't know, and my preference would be that you do not. The gods are jealous of their domain, and time and the force of destiny are not to be trifled with. But you saved Kila. That speaks to your importance in this game. So I ask you again to stay here and train. The Way of Ori can protect you within the confines of the Baths. If you leave, you are on your own. In this, the Coin and I agree. I will not detain you. But you will most certainly be recaptured by the Donse Masters if you leave."

"I don't want to be a novitiate."

"Then don't."

"What?" Raginalt blurted. "That's not fair."

"As you well know, Raginalt, little in life is."

"Stay forever?" Henley said. "I don't want to be trapped here. I just want to collect enough coin to buy passage on the first ship south." His heightened senses were too much now. The swarm of smell and sound pressed in on him as surely as the walls of a prison cell. The whole world was cloying and much too close. He covered his face with his hands. "Don't make me stay."

Huff was coming, a single point of goodness in the world. He didn't speak, but merely moved. And then he was there, climbing into Henley's lap, a warm comfort.

"It is best to not think in absolutes like forever and never," the Voluptuary said. "Face what is for long as it is. That is all anyone can do. But don't discount your strength. Though untrained, you possess a deep reserve of the mercus. You need not remain defenseless for the rest of your life. But to grasp your power, you must accept it and learn it. Trust me, it is a gift. One few get."

The Voluptuary got up and smoothed her robes. "Raginalt, you have another ten-day remaining in your penance, correct? Stay with Henley for as long as he stays in the Baths."

Raginalt shot up and swept a deep bow. "My pleasure, Mother Voluptuary. He will want for nothing."

The woman left. Henley realized she had gone without an answer from him. And what answer could he give but to accept her hospitality? At least they tolerated Huff's presence. Those who lived here held no love for the Way of Til, and the promise of two gold skillets was apparently not enough to tempt them. That assumed they could catch Huff if they wanted to.

Kila is up to something, Huff sent.

Did Oly tell you something?

She was at the cathedral and then she climbed an outer tower. Whatever she did, Nax is gone.

What do you mean gone?

Huff didn't expand on his comments, but sent a wave of annoyance for being asked what 'gone' meant.

Is Nax dead? Henley doubted even Kila could bear such finality. And Oly's unwelcome bond had been nothing short of a hair shirt to her, as if her suffering hadn't been sufficient.

Huff didn't send any grief through the bond, but he was agitated by the loss of Nax. He didn't say anything more, so Henley was forced to deduce that Nax was either beneath the realm of sleep or dead. Either way, Kila would be in agony. And there was nothing Henley could do to ease it.

"What it is it?" Ragin asked. "You look like the scream-clown stole your mother."

"Kila's cat has gone missing."

"Yes. The Hargothe took her. I was there, remember?"

"No. Huff says Nax is *gone*. I need to find Fallo and discuss what we're going to do." He stood and felt the awkwardness between him and Raginalt return. Being an enemy was a habit not easily shed. "Again, thank you, Raginalt. You are a much better man than your father."

"That's not saying much. But thank you. So, let's go find Fallo."

"He isn't here at the Baths."

"I see. So you're going to risk getting caught by the Hargothe's men. You heard the Voluptuary. I dare not leave the Baths without permission again or who knows what penance she'll give me."

"I don't be long, Ragin."

"It's your neck, Hen."

"Don't call me Hen." He didn't wait for Ragin to agree. In minutes he was upon the roofway and running for Terriside.

8

UNQUESTIONABLY A MERCULYN

One good thing about the Derslin Wheel was that Oly's presence had faded to a mere itch in Kila's mind. And that made her curious about what this place was. *Where* it was.

She had been reclined against the handcart and watching the lantern flame flicker for a while, and now she was bored. She stood and stretched.

She approached the nearest column, instinctively avoiding the demayne summoning stones Marlow had left out. Symbols were carved into a flat section cut into the face of each column. The one before her was familiar to her. Three diagonal slashes, starting from upper left.

She had added to their glow once before and had ended up on the floor. Marlow called this place a Derslin Wheel. She should have asked him what it was. Maybe when they weren't planning some stupid caper with a demayne or to kill the

Hargothe or to steal a thousand dragon scales she would remember to do so.

With her queller in Marlow's hands and him off to wherever he was, the mercus was a constant presence. It took nothing to bring the mercus glow to the symbols around her. The silvery light of the unknown alloy grew and sparked into existence all around, showing even more columns out of range of the lantern light.

She cocked her head and allowed the slashes to fill her vision. The trick with the mercus was to not name anything she sensed. Not slashes, not lines, not a column, not a glow. In the realm of the mercusine, names placed a barrier between the sensing of a thing and the knowing of it.

The glow intensified the more she relaxed. It took on dimension, became a cloud of light streaked with blue and swirling with indigo. Sparks of white peppered the field of glow. Kila moved closer, bringing her eyes within an inch of the column. The sound surrounding her was no longer the usual bell tone of metal. It deepened and separated into constituent noises—at first a hush wind through trees, but then growing into the roll and crash of the surf. Salt air wafted over her face, moving her hair, and embracing her with balmy warmth.

She closed her eyes, enjoying the marvelous cleanliness of the breeze. Her bare toes wriggled, no longer feeling the cold tile beneath her feet, but now damp sand.

Surprised, she opened her eyes and cursed on a long out breath. "Kil's teeth!"

She stood on a sandy beach, an endless ocean spreading before her. Far out, a great beast of the depths broke the surface to arc and dive, its undulating body following in a slow slide until a forked tail splashed into the air before slipping from view.

Panic rose in her, making her shoulders climb to her ears. She turned and sighed with relief to see a doorway leading to the dark cavern of the Derslin Wheel. She stepped back into the relative cool of the chamber. The portal remained open.

Kila's body thrummed with the mercus. She went through again, stretching her arms to let the freshening breeze sweep over her. She laughed and turned her face to the sky.

She screamed at the sight of death swooping toward her. A dragon. She backpedaled until she fell through the portal. Her elbows rang with pain as they struck the floor.

A shadow occluded the doorway and then was gone. Kila's grip on the mercus faltered and the door hazed over with white and was gone.

"Kil be a merry maiden!"

That was what Kila was thinking, but she hadn't said it. Marlow had. He stood behind her, a heavy bag slung over one shoulder. His mouth had dropped open and his lips moved as he struggled to form more words.

He dropped the bag and went to the column. Pressing his hands to the symbol, he leaned his forehead against the fluted section above. His shoulders sagged and he slowly turned back to face Kila, shaking his head. She still sat on the floor, exhausted and a bit shaken.

She pointed at the column. "Dragon. I nearly got eaten."

"Is that what that shadow was? I couldn't tell. Thanks be to the Triumvirate that it could not pass through the portal. How did you manage to open it?"

She shrugged. "I just listened to it."

Marlow swallowed. He looked more shaken than when she'd burned his finger with his own metal ring. "What you just did . . ."

"Let me guess. It hasn't been done in an age, and even then it took two hundred Donse Masters and a fishmonger to do."

Marlow stammered and then laughed. He offered her a hand to stand. She took it.

"The fishmonger was just there in case something went wrong," he said.

Now Kila laughed. "I wasn't trying to do anything. I was just curious."

"I've been studying these columns for a ten-year and I haven't seen so much as a spark from any of them. Pity none of them lead to the Eerie."

"Where *do* they lead?" She was after dragon scales, not entire dragons. Even so, she wouldn't mind spending an hour more on that beach. It had seemed so peaceful, so clean. The kind of place she would be able to take a nap and wake up rejuvenated.

Marlow began pulling items from the bag. The first was a parka. "Seahound skin. Try it on."

While Kila stuffed her arms into the thick, fur-lined sleeves of the parka, Marlow pulled out boots, stockings, a fur hat, and a leather backpack. "Perfect for carrying a heavy load while keeping your hands free."

"To fight? I thought you said the Fell Guard relies on assumptions to guard the Eerie. And are you going to answer my question about where that portals lead?"

"I cannot answer it. I don't know. Until now, I didn't know if they opened portals or merely concentrated power to accomplish mercus feats inside the circle. Was that a beach I saw?"

Kila plopped onto the floor and eyed the stockings with skepticism. She had never worn any before. Her feet were callused, tough, and nearly black with filth. She didn't trust the boots to give her feet and toes the grip she needed to walk, much less to climb the Eerie Stair.

Marlow noted her hesitation. "You might be surprised, Kila. The stockings are wool. They will keep you warm even if soaked through. The boots are lined with wool, then atlen skin for comfort and fit. The outer is seahound to ward against water. You will thank me when you reach the Eerie." Kila drew on the stockings, grimacing as the fabric entombed her skin.

The boots felt like huge lumps of numbness. She walked around in them and found it impossible to do her thieve's-step technique. "I hope there's nobody up there. I'll sound like a trezzed-up clogger approaching in these."

"Yes, yes, never mind that. If a Fell Gaurdsman stops you, you can ash him with a thought."

Kila bit her lip. Marlow might be right. Or she might fail to so much as warm his belt buckle. But the truth she didn't want to admit to this man was that she didn't *want* to ash anybody. Except maybe his brother.

Marlow rubbed his hands together and took her in. "Now, onto the training. Masking is really quite simple in concept, though it requires a constant effort to maintain. That last bit is why I don't leave this place unquelled. My powers are great compared to most, but compared to you my powers are like a flashtaper in the wind." He removed Kila's queller ring from his finger and put it in a pocket. "Have you learned to feel the mercusine within others yet?"

"No."

He made a face. "Did the Voluptuary teach you anything?"

"I was busy."

He shook his head in disgust. "Wasted potential is a finger in Til's eye. Whatever you were doing with that column, do that to me. Simply look at me without naming. Allow my mercusine potential to reveal itself."

Kila shrugged out of the parka and tossed it to the floor. She took position in front of Marlow and looked at his forehead. She thought she'd laugh if she looked in his eyes. The whole thing felt weirdly intimate, and she didn't like it one bit.

"Relax," Marlow ordered. He closed his eyes, which removed a distraction. Letting her vision relax, she allowed her mind to fall into the subtle realm of the unnamed. Her sense again opened to all that lay around her.

She raised an eyebrow when she discovered Marlow had acquired a blade of his own while he was away. It was steel, finely wrought, and secured beneath his robes. She suspected a hole had been cut in that pocket to allow him to withdraw the blade at need.

His blood glowed dully, concentrated at his heart. But his whole body had another glow, this one fainter, less made of light as it was of haze. Kila put her attention on this.

"Yes. You feel it." Marlow opened his eyes. "That is what the Hargothe feels when he searches you out. It is this potential that you must learn to mask in yourself." Abruptly the mercus vanished from Marlow.

He grinned and made a slight bow. Tension drew his eyes tight and his smile turned to a grimace. "That's all I can manage."

The mercus haze returned to engulf him. It seemed fainter now, but Kila didn't know if that was because he'd expended so much effort at masking himself or if she had grown distracted enough to lose focus. "And you want me to do that the entire time we are out there?"

"Yes. Just remember, if you lose the mask, you will be a beacon to the Hargothe. But for him to come to the Eerie to collect you would not be a simple task. No Donse Master has dymensed in five generations. Speaking of which, if you learn *that* trick, you must show me. I've read every scrap on the topic and I have not dared to try it. If one makes the slightest error, the results are usually quite gruesome. A person arrives at their destination to find their feet embedded in the pavement, or they appear a thousand feet in the air and plunge to their death."

He was talking about what the demayne Flaumishtak could do. Disappear in mercus green. She had enough to focus on now, and as useful as dymensing might be, she would rather not kill herself. Her feet had never failed her yet.

"Masking is not about quelling," he said. "In fact, a queller pulls a constant flow of mercus from the wearer. It isn't much, but it provides power to the relic. One particularly weak in the mercus might be terribly harmed by wearing one."

"So I have to use mercus to hide it. How?"

"If you'd accepted any of the Voluptuary's training, you would know of the concept of the 'bolt.'"

He clasped his hands behind his back and began to pace. Chin tucked, he lectured. "A bolt is a combination of sensual energies. Bolts can be of a single sense, like sight. Or it can include all twelve of the senses in a single burst."

"Twelve? Do you have extra eyeballs and earholes?"

He made a face. "I see this lesson will be supremely remedial. There are the five senses of the flesh, one of intuition, and six of the demaynic realm. Those last ones are not generally accessible without first employing bolts of the first five. You need not concern yourself about them. I suspect your higher feats are tapping into those senses without your awareness. When masking, we prepare bolts of clear opposites. For example, with light we deploy shadow. With sweet we counter with bitter. Smooth, rough. The perfume of the lilac with the reek of rotting rats. And finally, for sound we bring forth the same tone twice and 'slip' it."

Marlow acknowledged her incomprehension by clicking his tongue. "I am well enough rested to demonstrate sound slip, I suppose."

He took a slow, deep breath and brought forth a high-pitched ringing. Like a little glass bell whose ring never faded. "Now the slip." Another pulse of the same tone sounded so that the air to both sides of Kila's head was shimmering with sound. Moreover, she *saw* the mercusine waves as they appeared. They moved and undulated like the great sea beast she had seen through the portal. The waves were mirrors of each other and then slid to become exact opposites. And it was at the moment they aligned in this fashion, the sound stopped. And yet they were there.

"I can still see the mercus haze around you," she said.

"That's because I masked only sound. To mask all of my mercusine potential requires that the first six senses be masked simultaneously. Hence, the concept of the bolt. These combinations are difficult at first, but with practice they come forth as freely and effortlessly as your swearing does. Attempt to try it with light first."

Kila didn't even know how to make light, and her perplexed blinking made Dunne Marlow offer a curse of his own. "Merely see the light you wish to produce," he said. "Really, for you it should be easier than spitting."

Kila supposed it was the same as when she added to the glow of metal. It wasn't something she did so much as desired. It was an intention to add something. She held up a finger and focused on adding light to it. At first a glimmer appeared and faded. It was hot. She instinctively removed the heat.

"Two tricks at once," Marlow said. "You truly are a show-off."

Kila didn't pay attention to the man. He was always saying something or other that had no relevance to her. The light appeared on her index finger, a bluish-white flare of light that cast sharp shadows behind Marlow and turned his face a pale, sickly blue.

"Now add dark to it," he commanded.

The phrase "add dark" confused her. How does one make something that is itself an absence? But the mere question provided an answer. She sought to remove light from the light she created. Both flows came as easily as sipping tea. The light went out, but she could still feel the mercus powering both.

"The order matters," she said absently.

"Kil and Marol had a cow!" Marlow swore, then gaped at her. "I was setting you up to fail and you figured out the trick before I could gloat. Go on. Add smell. The senses that carry are the first you must mask. Taste can go last."

The senses fell to Kila's efforts, one after the other. Maintaining each pair of negations didn't require any effort at all. Kila wondered what the worry was all about. "This is easy."

Marlow looked as if he'd swallowed a groanberry. But he motioned for her to continue. Now that she'd spoiled his fun, he was impatient for it to be over. When Kila had at last masked all five, he nodded in grouchy approval. "Well done, ho-hum. I see that you will be an annoying student. You have no idea how many years of study it took me to learn that skill. And I can maintain it for a few seconds. Maybe minutes if I had the right kind of heller. But you just throw bolts into existence and wonder if it's time for supper."

"Now that you mention it, I never did eat any of your food. I could use a biscuit and a slug of ale." She found the mercus flows to be much less heavy than the effort required to heat up metal. She walked in a circle, did a little spin, squatted, drew Cayne and threw it through a series of tricks. Her last toss went awry and she dropped the blade. It went skittering into the dark.

She retrieved it and returned to sit with Marlow by the lantern. He had dug out a couple of apples and set up two tea cups. He removed a flask from his person and poured a two-finger measure into each. He raised his cup. "To Kil's Daughter and her Frightful Friends."

Kila took up her cup, sniffed. Trezz. And not the cheap, watered-down swill they served in Cheapsgate taverns. Not that she was much of an expert. Father had always warned about trezz, and Kila didn't like the effects. Or the taste. She clinked cups with Marlow and threw back the liquor. It went down smooth and hot.

Once she'd recovered from a coughing fit, she leaned back and observed her own effortless mercus feat. There was something familiar about what Marlow was calling a bolt. "When I healed your brother, the senses came together like this. Some negated, I think. But others required . . . I don't know the right word. Like when certain colors are pleasing together. Or when two singers float up different notes that mesh."

"The word you seek is 'harmonize' and it is a fundamental concept in the higher mercus feats. Such sensual expressions are much more difficult than the negations required for masking."

That was interesting. She had once watched Flaumishtak heal Ragin. He'd brought forth dozens of subtle energies, leaving her befuddled and entranced. That marked the first time she'd ever been truly interested in learning the mercusine arts.

"Hey, I'm a merculyn!" she said. "Just like Phillys the Red."

Marlow snorted. "You are nothing like that old crone. But to the main point you're making, I concur. You are unquestionably a merculyn. And as such, you have great responsibility. As you grow in your abilities, fewer will be able to stand against you." He looked into his empty cup. "And the lure of ever greater power will tempt you."

"Says the man who dabbles in demayncy."

"Bah! What does a little more darkness matter in this world?" he asked.

That he had sought to excuse his actions did not make sense.

Kila shrugged. She'd not point the shaky finger of righteous outrage at him. After all, she robbed men for coin.

Marlow set his cup aside. "My point is that your course and my brother's may start from very different places, but the pull of the mercusine may draw you toward the same destination. No child is born a despot. The decay of mind and morals is as gradual as the procession of the hours. Be mindful of what you desire."

She grunted. "I only want one thing. Nax. Then I'm leaving Starside forever."

"Which brings us back to your Beloved One. Shall we go to the Citadel?"

"We shall," she said in her best Gristenside snob-tongue. She collected her seahound parka and backpack. They began the walk to the cellar, moving through a shapeless blackness of the other-realm cavern.

"If we ever return here," she said, "I'll show you how I opened that portal."

Surprisingly, Marlow said nothing. His face was set, like a man walking to his doom.

9

ABOUT A SCANDAL

The Radiants lived in such luxury that the very air of Gristenside smelled different from the rest of Starside. The greathouses stood at much higher elevation than the rest of the city, so none of the chimney smoke and foul-house reek of the lower quarter reached them. And if the wind turned easterly—as it had today—the ocean added a humid freshness to the air. The Hargothe, however, detected the grisly smells of the wharfs, for he was immersed in the mercusine.

The carriage rattled up the slopes, the ride smoother now that they had passed into the rich quarter of the city. The clop of the horses' hooves made for a nice rhythm that provoked memories of his youth.

They arrived at the estate of Radiant Peline, his sister. What a remarkable rise to power she had enjoyed. A plantation overseer's daughter should never gain admission to such a house. But like the Hargothe, Juni had been born ambitious.

She hadn't the faintest spark of the mercus, so her rise had required less subtle methods.

She would argue—*had* argued—that her techniques were more subtle, but she was a woman and didn't see her own wantonness for what it was.

The Hargothe smirked at the thought. Juni could just as easily have ended up the cup-madam of a Cheapsgate brothel. But one moment of chance—of bumping into her future husband at Tilsday service—had delivered her to the Street of the Diadem.

The carriage came to a stop and the Hargothe stepped out unaided, though his elderly servant made all manner of concerned noises to see him do so. The man was worse than a nanny.

The forewarning of the Hargothe's arrival had resulted in a greeting party. He felt the shapes and presence of the household staff assembled at the front entry. Standing at the top of the steps was his sister, her daughter, Quinn, at her side. The Hargothe ascended, allowing his empty gaze to sweep over those to his left and right. He knew how his empty eye sockets made them shiver. Soon they would be spreading the news of his good health all over Gristenside. That was good, for the Radiants needed to know that the Hargothe was real and he was vigorous.

He gained the top of the steps and stopped in front of his sister. She smelled familiar, though she had splashed on some toilet water meant to smell like flowers but which merely irritated his nose. "Dearest Juni. How long has it been?"

"Seventeen years, brother. Please do come in." She didn't

offer assistance, which irritated him more than if she had. He followed, tracking her footsteps and those of her daughter. Quinn had been just a babe in arms when he had last seen her. She had a shadowy way of walking. Too quiet. He thought it preternaturally so. She had either been training in dance or she had been practicing the sneak-footed tricks of thieves.

They entered the parlor where the Hargothe was offered and accepted a soft chair. Tea was brought, small words exchanged. Finally, the servants were excused, and the Hargothe was alone with his sister and niece.

His sister spoke first. "You have not come to apologize, I suppose."

"No." She would have to bring up his supposed transgression. "Your husband's death was not my fault."

"You tortured him with your mercusine horrors. What other cause could there be? Dunne Toost himself said that Hasnev's heart gave out."

"It is known that rotund men have weak hearts. But I didn't come here to argue this all over again. I came to offer you a deal."

"You sound like Marlow. But at least with him I know the exchange will be equitable. With you it's 'do what I say or die.'"

"You exaggerate. I am not unreasonable."

"Quinn," Juni said, "what your uncle means is that he is not yet prepared to threaten a Radiant. Go on, Tenn. Make your offer."

"I have bonded with a Beloved One."

Quinn rustled out of the leather chair she had been

slouching in. A sharp word from her mother stopped her from approaching the Hargothe.

Curious, he thought, reaching out to touch her mind. The probe was ever so light. He could hardly bring her to her knees and rip forth her thoughts if he expected his sister to cooperate. He didn't find anything specific, but she held a great load of animosity toward him.

"Congratulations," Juni said to him once her daughter had flopped back into her chair. "Did you pull off its tail yet? Or are you still setting fire to animals these days?"

The Hargothe let her taunts go. His past experiments had been very instructive. He didn't expect her to understand them. "My Beloved One was subsequently stolen by a demayne."

Quinn let out a shocked cry, but Juni just lifted her tea cup and blew on the hot liquid. The smell of easy black wafted across the Hargothe's face. Finally she said, "So Marlow stole it. That's what you're saying."

"Indirectly. That's why I need you to read the summoning so I can retrieve what is mine."

Juni set her cup down, the porcelain clicking onto its saucer. The Hargothe had not touched his. He didn't put it past his sister to poison him.

The outright refusal he expected did not come right away. He saw that as a good sign. "Why ask me at all?" she said. "Why not use your willshift to compel me?"

A stupid question. Willshift could make her move, could possibly make her speak a few lines. But to invoke the demayne summoning, she had to implore Kil's favor. The

Despised God would never grant it if the Hargothe used Juni as a puppet. That was why he couldn't touch her mind at all. She had to mean it when she read the words of summoning.

"I am not a monster, despite what you believe," he said. "I merely know that you will meet with success and I will not. Can nothing be done to sway you? Have you an enemy who needs a reckoning? Perhaps a servant stealing from your jewelry box? Allow me to investigate their minds and I will identify the culprit. All can be arranged. Merely name it."

Instead of the pause of consideration he expected, she simply said, "No."

"Now Juni, there is no reason to deny yourself the great boon I offer you. And why do so? Merely to deny me what I seek? That is not reasonable for one of your practical ambition."

"Do you dare to insult me in front of my own daughter?"

"Insult? What insult?"

"I know exactly what you mean by 'practical ambition.' Why can you not accept that my husband loved me, and that I did not rise to my position through the bedchamber, but through the power of my mind?"

The Hargothe raised his hands to ward off her indignation, which was attended by a very prickly heat emanating from her whole body. "Spare me, sister. I understand you need to make a show for your child, but let us be frank. You are in a weak position as a Radiant. Your title is at risk. The other houses do not see you as legitimate. They tolerate you because Her Enlightened Majesty once showed you favor by allowing your marriage. But they all see that as a warning to them, not as a sign of *your* worth. If you were to think about how power truly works, you'd see the advantages of having me as an ally. I can discover information through many means. The entirety of the Way of Til's network of Donse Masters is at my command. The Highest himself is practically my footman. Our alliance can go beyond this first minor favor I ask. We could work together, and together there is no office in the realm that is too lofty an aim."

"Quinn, leave us."

"Mother, you cannot—"

"Leave us!"

The girl left, but not without uttering a diatribe that she didn't think he could hear. But he heard it. And one name she uttered stood out in his mind, as if written in fiery letters. She had used the name Nax. So . . . Quinn knew Kila Sigh and the Beloved One he had renamed Ishmilla.

The Hargothe could not probe her mind from this distance, and he didn't dare attempt it before he had negotiated an agreement with Juni. He would have to bring her into his crypt for a discussion. What a strange connection, though. Clearly the force of destiny was guiding Kila Sigh back to him. The animal was important, for he believed the bond contained information useful for his plans. Once he understood it fully, perhaps any creature could be so bonded.

When the door to the parlor had clunked shut, his sister stood. "You are a horrid man, Tenn. You have been an embarrassment to me my entire life. I had thought you nearly dead, based on Marlow's reports. What transpired between you two that you can no longer rely on him?"

"Aside from summoning a demayne to steal my Beloved One? Simple. He conspired to have a girl stab me."

To his extreme irritation, Juni laughed. He even heard a distinct thigh slap. It took all his will to not unleash mercusine retribution on her.

But then Juni spoke in the cool tones of business. "I do not believe you will fulfill your side of any bargain once I've delivered on mine. That is why I will require payment in advance."

He feigned disgust, but motioned for her to proceed with her demands.

"First, I want my house Donse Master recalled to the Abbey and not replaced. I'll put it around that no respectable Donse Master wants the post."

"Done." The Donse Master assigned to her had been his pick. The man was diligent and obsequious, but he had not turned up the scandalous stories the Hargothe had hoped for. It cost him nothing to sacrifice the man. "What else?"

"Second, Highest Binel will discover my tithes have been prepaid for a ten-year. I am pious."

"Done." The Hargothe's own accounts could cover that a hundred times over. Coin was nothing to him.

"Third, you will assure that the Way does not obstruct Quinn from entry to the Garden in Ori's Home."

Talk about a scandal. The idea that a Radiant's daughter would study with those harlots was more than scandalous. It verged on outright heresy. Quinn had schooled with them at the Baths down the street, and that had caused no end of murmurs.

But to go to the Harlot's Home at the Garden was an entirely larger move. For it couldn't be mistaken for anything other than it was. "So, you do have your eye on the Raven Throne. For Quinn, not yourself."

"You make too much of it. I merely want my daughter to have an education. A *complete* education, unlike what she'd get with your order. And if a vacancy in the Citadel occurs, it is best for all that a qualified leader be at hand to step in."

Juni was cut from the same bolt of silk as Marlow, smooth and impractical. But let her have these grandiose illusions. Her fantasies were nothing to the Hargothe. She wasn't asking him to support any such claim for Quinn, should the opportunity arise. And if it did—*when* it did—he would sit upon the Raven Throne and accept Quinn's hair as her penance before bundling her off to the kitchens to scrape pots for a ten-year.

"I accept your terms," he said, "but you must read the summoning tonight. My Beloved One must be returned before I can pursue other objectives. I shall have Highest Binel send to you the required documents concerning your tithes, Dunne Hitch's recall, and the Highest's signed letter of recommendation for Quinn's entry into the Garden school of her choosing. You will come to my sanctuary beneath the abbey. I believe there is a chamber there spacious enough for the rites."

"It is agreed, brother."

He departed, smiling to himself as he boarded his carriage. Juni had gotten many concessions from him. Surely, she felt she'd won a great victory. But she had asked nothing of consequence at all. Now to prepare the burn chamber beneath the abbey. He had forgotten about the room until his fool servant had reported that Kila Sigh had climbed up the flue. He had acolytes cleaning it out now. The stones were being collected by others. He need merely prepare himself to confront the demayne.

That was not a simple undertaking. The one Marlow had sent to steal Ishmilla had been of the highest order. Such beasts were known as Yoznithan, and their access to the mercusine was beyond the bounds of human capability. Their bodies were said to be so infused with power that neither blade nor flame could harm them. Indeed, the only things that could do were blades and barbs of blood-quenched steel. But harming the beast was not in the Hargothe's plan. He merely needed to offer it more than Marlow had.

The binding of demaynic entities was a well-known source of power in the southern islands, where all souls were already blackened with evil. Doing such was a different rite, one the Hargothe knew well. His transformation into the seer he was had come from just such a bargain, albeit with a somewhat lower order demayne.

As usual, it relied on naming. All things demaynic did. With his reinvigorated body and his purpose solidly locked within his mind, the Hargothe did not fear the risk of contending with Marlow's Yoznithan lord. In fact, he relished the thought. Perhaps it would come to serve him even more loyally than the sycophants he currently suffered to live. Perhaps this demayne would become the first of many.

The carriage wound through the switchbacks of the Street of the Diadem, rocking gently as the driver steered the horses around the slower traffic. The Hargothe settled into the subtle world of the mercusine, feeling the contours of his own mind and then reaching out. Perhaps Kila Sigh was about. Perhaps Marlow.

The faint sparks within the Baths of Ori drifted past him. He noted the Voluptuary was in a similar state of meditation. She was much too distant for him to attempt any touch. And she was much too well trained for him to risk such a stunt.

The others were Sensuals of lower ability, and he had nothing but disdain for them. He considered brushing their minds with terror, but decided against it. Even one of weak ability might have enough experience to detect that it was he who interfered with their thoughts. He was not yet prepared for open warfare with the other Ways.

Besides, a more interesting spark was drawing his attention. It moved downslope, nearing the lowest reaches of Terriside. He recognized it immediately, for he knew the mind intimately. He knew every one of the lad's pathetic secrets.

Henley. Interesting that the Voluptuary had let the boy leave her control. She had made a practice of giving ones of great potential leave to come and go as they pleased. She was a wily old biddy, but he could not comprehend what game she played by doing so.

"Seer, we have arrived." His elderly servant was touching his shoulder. The Hargothe realized that the carriage had stopped.

"The lad Henley is in lower Terriside, near to the Divide. Send Dunne Qirl and man or two of the Watch to seek him out. I would have him with me tonight, for I require his power. See that he is unharmed, for I do not have time to wait for him to recover from injury. Dunne Qirl must take the stonebone heller. It will likely be required to subdue the lad."

These instructions were relayed to others as the Hargothe made his way to the crypts.

What the righteous required, Til provided. With Henley's power, the Hargothe would have much more to spare when he contended with the demayne that night

"Have Highest Binel join me in my chamber. I require use of one of the hellers in the reliquary."

He was answered with many "yes, Seers," and that suited him. Soon his title would change, and then these men would prostrate before him for the mere chance to speak his name.

What that name would be, he hadn't decided yet. But it would begin with Emperor. He saw now that Til's plans merely began with his ascension to power in Starside. There was an entire world of lost souls who needed the Hargothe's hard-handed guidance.

10

THE HARD WAY

The carriage had rattled by ten minutes before, but Quinn Peline waited for another five before coming out from the colonnade along the Gallery of Swile alongside the Street of the Diadem. The Baths were just a mile up the street from here, and Quinn was tempted to go speak with the Voluptuary about the Hargothe's visit with her mother. But she couldn't do that now. The Shadline Cloak had appeared and signaled his wish to speak with her.

She hadn't seen the Cloak for over a month now, since the day he had met her outside Radiant Hiolly's greathouse where she had been snooping one night. He and two other masked members had heard her speak the oaths right there on the Hiolly lawn.

The strictures of the order were few, but coming when called was one of them. As a novice, Quinn didn't want to get off on the left foot.

The location of their next meeting had been mentioned as

she'd left the last one. In this way, the Shadline often moved meeting spots and had no need for a permanent location. Fortunately, her destination was not far from here.

Quinn rested her hand on the hilt of her dagger and strode across the street and into the opposite alley. As this was Gristenside, there was no danger from bystreet bandits or curl-fever stray dogs. In fact, the alleys were as clean and airy as most Terriside streets.

Coming to the cellar pub called The Hard Way, she pushed into the dim realm of Gristenside Merchants. As the hour was still early, there were few patrons. Those present were sober-faced, bent over mugs of hard black tea, discussing business deals or gossiping about politics. Quinn continued through the establishment, not even drawing a glance from the proprietor who stood behind the bar wiping down quality glassware with clean rags.

She stopped and wrapped her scarf around her head and face, twisting and tucking her thick hair out of view, and allowing only a slit for her eyes. She tugged on her gloves.

The back room was not crowded. Only five people. Three men and two women. They were veiled, and every inch of skin covered. But gauging by the quality of the fabrics on display, members of every quarter were present. One man gave off the distinctive odor of the stockyards, while a petite, round-framed woman had the hunched posture of a grandmother at least a hundred years into life.

Without greeting, they motioned for Quinn to sit on the other side of the long table. She was not offered drink.

The Cloak wore black, as always. His only occupation was

Shadline business. He was a master swordsman, and his upkeep was supported by the dues paid by members. Quinn had no idea how much money the Shadline order had socked away in banks across the realms, but she knew that at least one hundred Cloaks operated in cities around the world. All of them were set up as minor lords, and none ever wanted for ready coin to pay bribes, buy supplies, feed a shadline down on her luck, or to buy property and businesses to serve as fronts for the secret business of the order.

"You know the Cheapsgate orphan called Kila Sigh," the Cloak said to her. He was of indeterminate age, eyes etched with fine lines, but his body strong and lithe. He never smiled, but his teeth flashed when he spoke, giving him a wolfish quality. She didn't know his true name. His accent was not Starsider, but she couldn't place it.

"I do know her, Cloak. I consider Kila a friend." It was the most diplomatic way she could phrase her concern. Coming out and blurting that she would stab him if he tried to hurt Kila would get her nowhere but dead.

"You have seen her blade. She is Shadline."

"I have seen Cayne. I intended to mention it to you when we next met." She was safe with that answer because as a novice, she had to wait to be contacted in order to speak to him. "She is also a merculyn of growing power and is sought by the Hargothe."

The Cloak hissed through his teeth and looked at the others. "The rumors are true, then."

"Does it matter?" Quinn asked. "The blade has chosen her."

"Her mercusine skills are a complication. The order does not usually interfere with the Ways of the Triumvirate."

Quinn didn't see that it mattered. Kila was not a devotee to any of the Ways. Not yet. "She belongs among our number. We all made oaths to the fraternity of the Shadline. We cannot leave her to the Hargothe."

"If she does not swear the oaths we have no true obligation to her. I approached her today in Cheapsgate. She assumed I was trying to swindle her." A rare flash of emotion lifted one side of his mouth. It disappeared as quickly as it had appeared. Quinn thought it might be chagrin.

He went on. "The stories about our order are usually a benefit in this regard. I appear before them and they recognize what I signify. They usually express great relief—else grim acceptance. It depends on the nature of the bonded blade. Some are practically a curse when in the wrong hands. But always the Shadline knows the blade for what it is when confronted with the truth. Kila does not."

"It has been in her family since she can remember," Quinn said. "Her brother carried it. Her father had it before that, and he possessed it a good long while. Perhaps its powers are not as obvious as your blade's."

The Cloak grimaced at Quinn's violation of etiquette. One did not discuss another's blade. But the Cloak's sword had an ostentatious power that was not secret even among those outside of the order. It coursed with flame when drawn from its scabbard, and it often chose to immolate its victims even as it cut their bodies.

One of the men turned his palms up. "Perhaps the blade

provides Miss Sigh with her mercusine power. There is a hammer in Vayle that does something similar, though it requires renewal through use as an executioner's sledge."

Quinn grimaced at the notion. Shadline weapons offered more than a keen edge that never needed a hone. Some required specific uses to keep the power active. Others, like hers, provided perpetual benefits without cost. At least, no cost she knew. Her blade, simply known as Black, kept her footsteps silent. It even seemed to mask her smell, for she had traipsed past sleeping dogs and them none the wiser.

The younger of the two Shadline women, who sported a rose-colored tunic and matching trousers, leaned back in her chair. Her eyes were veiled, but she was clearly looking at the Cloak. "If you had Kila Sigh in front of you, why didn't you just throw her over your shoulder and bring her here?"

Quinn blurted out a laugh that ended in an embarrassing snort. "One does not simply throw Kila Sigh over one's shoulder."

The Cloak frowned at her for her lack of decorum. "I do not make a habit of abducting members into our order. As I said, the stories about us are well known, and most naïve Shadlines are relieved to be contacted. The Shadline weapons are usually not so subtle in their powers . . . or their demands. But Quinn may be correct that long exposure to the blade has blinded Kila to its powers. For Cayne to have remained secret so long, its power must not be particularly obvious. And it is a wondrous lucky thing one of our own spotted it and knew it for what it was. Else it might eventually do Kila or someone else great harm.

"It's a knife. It's whole purpose is to do harm." Quinn immediately realized she should have kept her mouth shut, but another man started laughing. He was silenced by a glare from the Cloak.

"Intentional harm, yes," the Cloak said. "But Cayne may be a thirsty blade, and may seek out flesh more urgently the longer it has been denied."

Quinn puckered her lips and made a popping noise. "I didn't know that part. So it can just fly out of the sheath and stab someone?"

"Don't be ridiculous," the Cloak said. "A Shadline weapon can influence one's thoughts in subtle ways, make the holder do its bidding through long, constant pressure upon the mind. Just as Black led you to break into Radiant Hiolly's greathouse. Had you resisted, you might have attempted an even more foolish caper a ten-day later."

Quinn changed the subject. "I will speak to Kila. Once she understands that the Shadline order is real and that she needs training, I'm sure she'll speak the oaths. She may be a bit feral, but she's not stupid. Besides, she could use more order in her life."

"That is exactly what I summoned you here to ask."

Quinn stifled the burst of air that she'd nearly blown through her lips. When the Cloak "asked" one to do some-thing, one did it. The polite phrase was silly. But one also didn't call out the Cloak for being silly. He had enormous power, and could send you a thousand leagues to fetch a particular sort of onion if the whim took him. She had heard he'd done nearly that with the previous holder of Black. It took that man four years to complete the mission, but he'd apparently grown into his responsibilities as a result.

"If I may be excused," Quinn said, "I'll go find her. She often stays with some boys who tend an atlen barn in lower Terriside."

The Cloak nodded his assent and Quinn departed. This was not exactly how she'd planned to spend her day, but at least she was still looking for Kila. The mission gave her a boost of enthusiasm, too, so she hustled downslope to Terriside. And then—feeling somewhat silly—she ascended to the roofway. She didn't go as fast as she'd seen Kila run, and some of the jumps were much too far for her. But she made better time on the roofs than by winding down the Street of Sorrows.

When she got within sight of the atlen barn, she stopped to catch her breath.

And then she dropped into a crouch. For just beneath her, winding slowly along the alleys, was a group of the Watch lead by a Donse Master. They were heading straight for the atlen barn. And no coincidence. They had to be looking for Kila. If she was in there, she would be cornered. And Henley, too. The poor lad had come out of the cathedral looking like the fabled hermit of Craw Cavern. If he were retaken, she doubted he would ever see sunlight again.

11

KIL'S OWN FIRE

Drawing her blade, she ran and leapt, Black silencing the sound of her feet crashing onto the atlen barn roof. She knew the boys slept in a loft. She smacked the hilt on the tin roof. "Better get out of there. Donse Master coming."

It made no sound, of course. Black muted everything she did. Sighing, she sheathed the blade and thumped her fist on the roof. "Come out, boys. The Watch is at your door."

A mumble and a crash of something below was followed by the appearance of two cats through a rusted hole in the roof. One was a portly black fuzzball called Lop, the other an orange short-hair called Huff.

She knew Lop was Fallo's cat. She also knew it didn't do anything for free. She yanked a bit of bread from her pocket and offered it up. The cat sniffed at it then gobbled it down. Not five seconds later, the boys appeared.

"You've done it now," Fallo said. "Lop will be your friend for the next few minutes." The boys crept to the edge of the roof and looked over. Henley immediately slunk back out of view of the men on the street.

"That's him," he said. "The bearded Donse Master with the little wood stick in his belt. He's the one who caught me the first time."

Fallo flashed his thick black eyebrow and headed for a jump across the alley. Henley followed, cats arcing across behind. Quinn would never have believed the jump possible for such small animals. She brought up the rear and soon discovered the lads were not about to go slow on her account.

"Wait!" she called after them. "Where's Kila?"

Henley waited for her at the end of the next jump, standing by an overstuffed pad of burlap, put there for the very purpose of breaking a roof-runner's fall. Beyond him, Fallo dumped two coins into a tin pail. When Quinn landed and rolled to her feet, he jerked his head toward it. "Pay up or one day you'll get a flickbolt in your back as a gift."

"Where's Kila?" she prompted as she fished in her pouch for a copper plug. She didn't have anything smaller than a silver. She crouched by the pail. "Is there a way to open this bucket to make change?"

Fallo snorted and shook his head in disgust. Quinn didn't think it fair. His family had enough money to buy most of the lower slope. Henley's had, too, once.

"Kila wasn't with us," Henley said. He wore no look of humor or disgust at Quinn's lack of small money. She dropped in a silver plug and decided to stop in later to tell the building owner she had a credit account going on his rooftop.

"Where is she?"

She asked it to the wind, for the boys were already across the roof and launching themselves into air. Quinn pursued, now getting a bit annoyed with the lads. She had done them a good turn warning them of the approaching danger. The least they could do was answer a simple question.

The Donse Master and the guard were far behind, probably not even aware their quarry had fled. Now it became a chase to keep the boys in sight. She lost.

Discouraged and sick of leaping and landing so hard that her teeth jarred in her jaw, she climbed down behind the Yin Inn and proceeded up the street, wondering what she'd tell the Cloak. He would have to understand, she supposed. It wasn't her fault that Kila hadn't been at the atlen barn.

Her stomach soured. The Cloak would consider her failure to keep up with Fallo and Henley as a sign of poor physical conditioning. She had only trained with him once, and that had left her so exhausted and sore that she couldn't ride a horse for a week—or comfortably sit at the dinner table. Her mother had been mightily suspicious, but Quinn's excuse of having fallen down the stairs had kept her off the truth.

Quinn moseyed up the Street of Sorrows, absently looking in shop windows at the wares for sale. Nothing particularly interesting, for Quinn had more clothes and things than she had use for. Plus, she didn't particularly enjoy wearing skirted garments anymore. They made sneaking around unnecessarily difficult.

Still, that black cape there was of fine twill. It would give her that roguish look that the Cloak favored. It would keep the rain off, too.

Quinn became so caught up in how dashing she'd look in it, she didn't notice the boys standing on either side of her until she saw their reflections in the glass.

"Follow us," Fallo said. She did, winding into the alleyways that cut behind the main shops on this stretch of the Sorrows. They hopped onto refuse bins and forced her to climb back onto the roofway. They came to a rooftop garden, trellis and planters all bare. A skim of snow covered all in a lovely frosting.

"I don't know where Kila is," Henley said. "We were talking about coming to your house to ask about her, but we were worried your armsmen might put whipaxes through our necks."

That wasn't an unreasonable worry.

"So, the force of destiny has brought us together," she said. The cats appeared and found a warm spot by a chimney pipe. "I suppose I can tell you what I was going to tell her." She proceeded to relay all that she had heard of the Hargothe's conversation with her mother. She left out the part about Kila being a Shadline bearer.

"So you're saying the Hargothe is your uncle?" Henley's face darkened and Fallo's eyebrow bunched into a hideous "V" over his nose. The boy looked like a villain. If she hadn't known better, she would have avoided him—or used Black on his throat—just for the evilness of his countenance.

That bothered her. Ori favored many with beauty—Quinn

had been told she'd been gifted more than her fair share—but the Gentle Goddess also gifted hearts with beauty. Many did not receive both blessings.

Could an ill-favored man match the worth of a handsome one? Quinn knew at least a dozen scions of Radiants who could make girls giggle themselves silly with a mere rakish look. But she wouldn't trust a single one of them to guard a Winternight pie.

Then there were boys like Winstor Grett, a boy with an oddly proportioned body, a head too big, a nose too bulbous, and a torso so short it looked like his legs joined just under his ribcage. But he was not only smart, he was kind and funny and generous of heart.

In this, it seemed, Fallo had been blessed with character at total odds with his face. And now that the full ugliness of his face was aimed at her, she felt achy inside, for judging him and for keeping her relationship to the Hargothe a secret.

"Yes. He is my uncle," she finally answered. "I am not any happier about it than you are. I had never seen him before today. He asked my mother to help him summon a demayne. He claims one stole his Beloved One. That has to be Nax, right?"

"Demayne?" Fallo said, voice rising in pitch. "By Kil and the Muses Five, what is Kila up to now? Is she a demayncor on top of all the rest?"

Quinn looked for a place to sit, but the available surfaces were covered with snow. She sat on a ledge anyway, the damp quickly adding to the growing chill already in her bones.

"Kila is no demayncor," Henley said. "But I wouldn't put

it past her to go looking for one. Ragin once told me a demayne had come to their room in the novitiate's ward. It took Kila in a great swirl of green light and then she was gone. Kila must have sought one's help."

"Doesn't sound like it worked," Fallo said. He still hadn't relaxed his stare of death toward Quinn.

"I helped you get Kila and Hen out of the Abbey," Quinn said to him. "And at great expense to my reputation. Not to mention my allowance. I had to make a real contribution to the Way of Til to smooth things over for the disturbance I made. Thankfully, they never connected me to your part in it. Tell me why would I do that if I had any loyalty to my disgusting uncle?"

"Will your mother help him?" Fallo asked.

This was where it got weird. "She will. I know that look she gets when she thinks she's got someone in a weak position. She will have negotiated something fantastic. And if they came to an agreement, she will honor her part in it."

"Where is Kila now?" Henley asked.

Quinn was irritated by the question. If she knew, she wouldn't be freezing her arse off on this rooftop. But then she realized the boys had turned to look at their cats. Henley turned back to her. "Huff says Oly told him that Kila is heading to the Citadel with a Donse Master."

"Who?"

"Oly doesn't know. He's someone she's spoken with several times before. He has a hiding spot that makes Kila fade from Oly's mind. He likes it when she goes there so he doesn't have to hear her stupid thoughts."

"He's not a very nice cat, is he?"

Fallo and Henley both whistled at the same time. "Not at all." Then they both laughed. Fallo scratched the black thatch of hair on his head and gazed toward the Citadel. "Why would she go up there?"

"Tell Oly to ask her," Quinn said.

"He's not close enough to her to ask. And he wasn't curious enough to ask before she got out of range."

"Well, send him after her."

They laughed again, Henley's face turning bright red. Fallo had snaggly teeth, so when he laughed he looked like a painting of a nosg Quinn's father had once shown her.

"You louts are simply afraid to ask Oly to do what he *should* do."

"Afraid? Not at all," Fallo said. "But Lop won't do it for less than half an atlen, roasted and salted."

Henley nodded. "Huff said your idea is like trying to chew off his own tail."

What a peculiar expression. But Quinn understood. Everyone tolerated Oly's bad behavior. That left a simple answer. "I guess I'm going to the Citadel. Thank you, lads, for your help." She ran to the ledge and jumped. It was a bad leap, and she had to claw just to catch the roof edge across the alley. Her legs and body slammed into the brick wall, she lost her grip, and she fell fifteen feet to the ice covered alleyway.

Nothing broke. But she didn't think her knees would ever be the same. The boys dropped down next to her. Fallo took her elbow and helped steady her. Henley brushed her knees, which— strictly speaking—was a horrible breach of etiquette. But she didn't mind.

"And you call yourself a Shadline," Henley said. "I've seen one-legged chickens hop farther than that."

She gave him a cold glare, which earned her a deep reddening in Henley's cheeks. He mumbled an apology, which she accepted with a curt nod.

"I slipped," she said.

Fallo snickered. "I'll say." He rushed on as her frosty eyes turned toward him. "It happens to the best of us. Now about that plan of yours to go to the Citadel. Do you expect to walk up there and ask for Kila?"

"I didn't have a plan." She said it with more heat than it deserved. Once she'd heard herself, she shrugged irritably, finding her cloak a bit too tight around her shoulders all of a sudden. She was in an awkward situation. To please the Cloak, she needed to bring Kila in for the oaths, but to keep her freedom and her head attached to her neck, she couldn't barge into the Citadel making demands. "If we knew what she was up to, maybe we could figure out a more sensible course of action."

A shadow filled the end of the alley. Two men of the Watch turned in, flanking a gray-bearded Donse Master. The man held his short wooden rod out. Henley's body went rigid. Quinn caught him by the arm as he fell. Fallo grabbed the other.

They shuffled away, carrying Henley's weight between them. "Put the lad down," the Donse Master commanded. He stepped forward, rod raised.

Quinn's skin tingled. "You have no cause to attack this boy," she said in a voice she hoped sounded like her mother's. Imperious and not to be trifled with.

The Donse Master nodded for the Watch men to approach. They did so, swords drawn. So that's how it was, Quinn thought. "I am Lady Quinn Peline. You will sheathe your weapons, return to your commander in the Westbunk, and report yourselves for baring steel in my presence. And you, Donse Master, will return to the Abbey and await word from Highest Binel about your penance."

The guards paused, but the Donse Master merely laughed. "Take the girl, too. Kill the ugly one." The Watch men wore burnished breastplate and thick red cloaks that swept behind them as they flung out their off-hands to prepare for sword-work. Both had thick mustaches and corded necks.

Quinn and Fallo continued backward, dragging the immobile Henley after them, his heels scraping on the slick alley stonework. Behind them was the intersection with another alleyway.

There had been four Watch men at the atlen barn. Quinn guessed the other two were working their way behind them.

"Let's set him down," Quinn said. "I need my knife hand free."

Fallo helped her ease Henley down, keeping a sharp eye on the approaching men. They had the slow, wary steps of men approaching a feral dog they meant to put down. Not afraid, but wisely cautious lest they get bit.

Well, these men would feel Quinn's bite before she would let them drag her or Henley away. Fallo pulled a dagger from his belt. It looked like it hadn't seen a hone or oil in a century. He gripped it lightly, showing he had at least some training in its use.

Quinn wished she'd had more training than the one session with the Cloak. In truth, she was much more accomplished with flourishes, twirls, and spins than she was with outright stabbing and slashing.

She did understand the basic principle, which was to cause as much pain and blood loss as possible. But anyone would know that intuitively. The Cloak had spent most of their time teaching her to parry.

Her foe's swing came abruptly, from below. The upward stroke caught her by surprise, forcing her to lean away. Her heel caught on Henley's leg, spilling her onto her backside. The guard blurted out a laugh and stood over her, sword point pressing between her breasts. "Drop the blade, lass. I mean to take you intact. T'would be a shame to mar your lovely skin. But if you force me to defend myself, Dunne Qirl will be my witness that I had no choice but to lop off your head."

The problem with men like this, Quinn thought, was that they believed their own flawed logic. If he killed her—or even wounded her—his life was forfeit. A Radiant's daughter was not immune to the law, but her death at the hands of the Watch would never go unanswered by her mother. Even the other Radiants—no great lovers of House Peline—would demand his blood. The consequences to this man would be violent and swift.

But all of that would be no consolation to poor dead

Quinn. She lowered her knife to one side, pinching the hilt lightly between thumb and forefinger to show that she was not preparing a surprise stroke.

The moment had frozen Fallo and the other man. Both watched the tense moment of decision with quick flicks of their eyes. The Donse Master stood behind all, his wooden rod still raised.

The sound of boot-falls resounded in the alleyway behind Quinn. The other two guards were nearly there. She had been defeated. She had failed. And it looked like she was going to die, for in her oaths she had sworn never to relinquish her Shadline blade.

She set the knife on the ground.

The Watch man said, "Shove it away from you."

"Fallo, I'm sorry." She reached to the blade, shoved the pommel so that, instead of sliding away from her, it rotated in place. Catching it by the tip, she snapped her wrist, sending the blade spinning toward her opponent.

He had time to blink once, but the timing of the rotations was off. The pommel bonked into his eyebrow. Not the killing eye-shot she had hoped for, but it must have hurt like Kil's own fire, because the man recoiled, lifting his sword point from Quinn's chest.

She was already crabbing backward, out of range should he recover quickly enough to strike. He didn't.

Black had rebounded from his head and tumbled to the ground. It bounced from the pommel and twirled toward Quinn. It was Pol's brightest smile yet. Quinn snatched her weapon out of the air and leapt to her feet. She was peripherally aware of Fallo turning and jabbing at his opponent. The Donse Master was shouting orders to men approaching from Quinn's rear.

Her foe was swearing and pressing his free palm to his eyebrow ridge. A trickle of blood seeped between his fingers. He stamped his feet and bashed his hilt against his breastplate. His eyes were full of murder now.

Swords rang as they came out of sheaths behind her. She didn't chance a glance. The lumbering guard was winding up for a swing. Anger had overridden his training, which didn't speak too well of his training. She easily dodged a blow that would have severed an atlen's neck. Spinning, she ducked under his blow and shouldered into his flank. In the same motion, she brought Black upward, tip slipping just under the bottom of his breastplate. The Shadline blade easily parted the mail underneath and plunged into his abdomen. She gave a twist as she withdrew the blade.

Blood came out with it. She blinked, momentarily horrified by what she'd done. His elbow caught her head, dislodging any regret. She returned the favor with another upward thrust, this one catching him under the chin.

Black drove in as easily as slicing fresh bread. The man's body went rigid and he fell toward her. She backpedaled out of the way and he landed on Henley, who didn't move so much as an eyelid in reaction.

A cry arose behind her and was instantly cut off. The sound of bodies striking pavement followed. The Donse

Master was running the other way. Quinn turned and found the Cloak standing in the alley, his black cape billowing behind him. He held his Shadline sword at his side, the edges licked with red flame. The two guards who had been closing from the rear lay dead, both separated from their sword arms and their heads.

Fallo was retreating from his opponent, who swung with wild abandon as if trying to bash a nameday paper nosg apart to collect the rock candy inside.

Fallo leapt back with every swing, surprisingly agile for one of such lanky and awkward form. He didn't know the Cloak was watching. The Shadline master made no move to help.

Quinn made a face and motioned at the Watch man. When the Cloak didn't do anything, she gave him a perplexed look. "Are you just going to let him get carved up?"

"I owe him no protection."

Quinn darted behind the swordsman, who was now circling to put Fallo's back to the wall. She lunged and severed the tendons at the back of his knee. That put him on the ground. She stepped in, drew Black across his throat, and stepped back to avoid the splatter that followed.

Fallo wasn't so fortunate and got his face bloodied. He moved aside, wiping the man's lifeblood from his demonic visage. That's when he noticed the Cloak, who was studying him with great curiosity.

"Who in Kil's name are you?" Fallo said.

Henley stirred, no longer under the power of the Donse Master's mercusine relic. Quinn helped him sit up. The guard who had fallen on him had bled all over Henley's cloak. He made a face as he flicked blood from it. "That Donse Master was after me. I knew that would happen. I just thought I'd have more time."

"Why does a Donse Master want you?" the Cloak said. He was still looking at Fallo, his eyes unblinking. Quinn noticed his gaze was not on Fallo's face, but locked on the boy's rusty dagger.

"I am apparently a budding merculyn," Henley said, ruefully.

"Then you should go to the Garden and train. I would recommend against joining the Way of Til, however."

The Cloak lost interest in Henley's problem. He moved like a cat toward Fallo, not going directly, but sweeping in an arc, his eyes not once leaving the blade. "Where did you get that knife?"

Fallo raised it. "It's a long story."

"You will come with me and tell me your story in the minutest detail."

Because there was a stranger around, the cats had not come down from the rooftop to inspect the boys. Henley was throwing nervous glances between the Cloak and the alley entrance. Quinn leaned close. "You should go. I know this man. He is an ally. But he must discuss things of great importance with Fallo. I recommend you return to the Baths for the time being. Fallo and I will come to collect you. You can both stay at the Radiant's city-house tonight."

Fallo had an uncomfortable look on his face as he endured the intense scrutiny of a swordsman holding a flaming blade.

Quinn had been in this position once. She had come by Black through a very odd circumstance, just after discovering Elise Hiolly's murdered body in a hedge maze. The Cloak had come shortly after.

That Fallo's blade might be Shadline seemed utterly ridiculous. All the examples she had seen so far were exquisite weapons, the pinnacle of craftsmanship. His dagger looked the opposite.

Henley climbed to the roofway and disappeared. The strange standoff between Fallo and the Cloak had turned into a simple battle of gazes. A dawning of understanding was creeping over Fallo's face. He dropped his gaze to the dagger. "This thing? A Shadline?"

His hand went to his jacket, pressed on the breast pocket, as if remembering something in it that now made sense. He lifted his caterpillar eyebrow. "Truly?"

"We shall return to this morning's meeting room. Come, Quinn."

She went to Fallo and guided him by the arm. They didn't need to be hanging around dead guards when the Donse Master returned with more troops.

"This is a great privilege," she said to Fallo. "But do not expect it to be easy."

She caught up to the Cloak. He didn't acknowledge her. "You didn't know of Fallo's blade, either," she said. "That makes two Shadline blades that have appeared in Starside with no known history."

"You have learned to count. Impressive, Quinn. One day you may even learn to add. This new blade is a marvel, yes.

But I see naught but dire omens in it. The force of destiny moves all toward great changes. The Shadlines may soon be called."

"Called? By whom? For what?"

He didn't answer.

12

HER ENLIGHTENED'S FINGER

The carriage Dunne Marlow hired for his and Kila's ascent to the Citadel was not as luxurious as the one belonging to Quinn Peline's family. The leather bench was a bit worn and the curtains frayed along the bottom. There was no mercus sconce for light or heat, just an unlit whale oil lantern affixed to the forward bulkhead.

Kila didn't think much of the atlen birds harnessed before what was a rather wobbly hack. The birds were mismatched in color and size. The driver had to continuously shout for one to slow and the other speed up. He applied his whip to both, producing the wrong effects, and making for a side to side lurch that made Kila sick to her stomach.

The Street of the Diadem climbed sharply here. She peered out the window at the roofs of Gristenside greathouses now falling away below. If the hack came loose from its harness it would be a long and deadly backward roll.

The conveyance abruptly stopped and the birds squawked

and stamped. A Watch guard approached, spoke to the driver, and then waved them on. They passed through a stone gate, the portcullis drawn up permanently. There hadn't been an assault on the Citadel since the uprising against the first Enlightened, Duri LiMinluit.

That fact didn't matter to the next guard, an unblinking man of frozen violence. Kila barely saw him as they passed, and yet she shivered.

He was a member of Her Enlightened's personal Fell Guard, each man of which was said to be worth one hundred of the Watch. He stood like a statue, his helm plumed with blue atlen feathers, the cheek guards swooping, beak-like, to mask his mouth. His burnished armor gleamed in the cloudy daylight as if shedding a light of its own. But what drew most of Kila's attention was his great spear, the tip of which thrust a span above his head, tapering to a wicked point. That was what folks called "Her Enlightened's finger." As in, "You keep going on about bread prices, Her Enlightened's finger will tap your heart."

The driver spoke to the man, but he neither looked their way nor acknowledged the words with a response. The portcullis opened of its own accord and closed behind them.

They continued through a series of these gates, each watched over by a lone, unmoving member of the Fell Guard. "You'd better be right about this," Kila said to Marlow. "I don't think my blood would stay hot enough to ash these fellows if they so much as looked at me sideways."

"That's just as well. An attack on one of them is an attack upon Her Enlightened Majesty."

They entered a narrower section of the approach to the Citadel, where walls hemmed the carriage in on both sides. Huge bronze statues of naked men and women in poses of extreme combat stood atop the walls. Kila paid special attention to a heroine with a long braid over one shoulder and a bow drawn back to deliver an arrow into the eye of some unseen foe. Hiwonne. Her face was intent, but a hint of a smile curled her lip, as if she were enjoying this battle immensely. The fabled Hiwonne was one of Kila's favorites.

The final gate rattled shut behind them. The carriage turned a wide circle and stopped in a grand courtyard. A footman came forward to open the door. Dunne Marlow stepped out ahead of Kila. "I am Dunne Marlow, Donse Master to her Enlightened's small council. Please take me to my offices. My servant may wait for me in the kitchens. See that she has some bread and soup."

With that, Dunne Marlow was gone, ushered away by a stammering footman who was torn between his instinct to obey and total confusion. Obviously, nobody had told the staff to expect a new advisor to Her Enlightened Majesty. Another man—a boy really—came forward and beckoned Kila to come out. "Don't lolly, now. Step quick or stay here."

Kila climbed down. The sight of the Citadel from this proximity pulled a curse right out of her mouth. "Kil's member!"

The lad flushed. "A Donse Master has *you* in service? A foul-mouthed girl?"

Kila looked down her nose at him, which required tilting her chin quite high in imitation of him. "Dunne

Marlow is a worldly man. He prizes intelligence above refinement."

"Seems he is a poor judge of both. Come with me. I have better things to do than host lowborn pleasure-girls." Kila nearly punched him the gut. She thought better of it when her eyes skimmed across the two Fell Guards standing at the doorway where Marlow had just entered the Citadel proper. The lad didn't lead her that way. Instead, he crossed the court-yard and took an outer flight of stairs into an overheated chamber full of food smells.

Kila thought she had passed into Til's hallowed dining hall. There were at least five ovens, all at work with spitted hog, yearling doe, and countless chickens. Another oven held loaf upon loaf of golden-brown bread, spilling forth such divine odors Kila had to grab hold of her stomach to keep it from leaping out of her and laying waste to the world.

The boy pointed at a side room with table and chairs. It looked like a dining room for servants. She went in, took a seat, and waited. She was not disappointed. A sallow-faced girl in a white bonnet and apron brought a tray and set it before Kila. She gave Kila a narrow look but didn't say anything she might regret if it turned out Kila was important. Kila dove at the food like the Cheapsgate stray she was.

"What's in that odd bag on your back?" asked the girl as she was leaving. "I heard you were a Donse Master's pleasure-girl. Do you have slit-skirt gowns and unmentionable frocks?" She seemed quite curious and eager to see these scandalous items.

"I'm not a Donse Master's anything. I'm his attendant, and

that's all you need to know. I'm going to need fresh air once I've completed my meal. I'd like to climb part of the Eerie Stair and take a look at the panorama."

"Out the back. Look up. You'll see it. It'll be windy up there."

Of that, Kila had no doubt. She ate until the last crumb had passed between her lips. She stretched and patted her belly. The food had been worth the entire scheme to get here. But she hadn't come merely to eat. She had come for dragon scales.

The exit led to a walkway at the rear of the Citadel. The spires reached so impossibly high overhead that Kila realized they were higher than the Divide itself. She knew the carriage had wound up the side of a mountain, but to see these structures standing so proudly was to feel like a speck of nothing. She wondered if she'd finally get a glimpse into Moonside— the mysterious city on the other side of the Divide. She had once had a sort of raven's-eye dream about it, but the city had been hidden beneath a blanket of clouds.

The walkway curved around the foundations of the Citadel, splitting off toward smaller buildings erected all around it. She supposed these were servant quarters. There were no signs indicating what was what.

She didn't need any. The steps for the Eerie Stair were clearly visible from here. After winding through a narrow squeeze point where the mountain bedrock had split apart in some epoch long ago, she came to the bottom of the climb.

Just as she feared, there was a guard ahead, the unmistakable atlen plumes and cruel shape of Her Enlightened's finger silhouetted against a gray sky. She knew the man had spotted her already.

She didn't crouch back to hide. What this called for was bravado, she decided. She climbed as if the stairs belonged to her, not even stopping as she passed directly in front of his eyes.

He didn't stop her. She went up another dozen stairs, feeling the blast of wind sweep down from above. It iced her cheeks with one touch. The man didn't cry out, and he didn't throw his spear at her.

What was the purpose of posting a guard there at all? she wondered.

Turning back, she looked at him once more. From this angle she could see him more clearly. The way his boots melded with the rock told her all. He was a statue, carved there in such detail anyone who didn't know better would be fooled. Marlow had been right. The Fell Guard counted on assumptions to guard the Eerie. It made sense, too. Why spend so much manpower guarding a way almost nobody would attempt?

Kila smiled to herself and continued up. She couldn't see the Eerie yet. She had no idea what it looked like or how far she would have to go, but it would be high up. The Eerie was said to be directly opposite the windows of her Enlightened's spire-top apartments.

"A silly place to put your quarters," Kila said to herself, eyeing the great central tower. "Why would you want to live there? You'd have to climb hundreds and hundreds of steps just to get to bed."

But then Kila wondered if Her Enlightened would even bother to come down. Maybe she stayed up there for weeks at a time. Kila shivered at the thought. And the wind. She was glad for the seahound coat. And the boots, even though they made her feel she had tree stumps for feet.

She was also glad for the surprise meal Dune Marlow had demanded for her. From the short distance she'd already climbed, she knew the effort would cost every bit of the bread she had wolfed down.

From far off, like the whisper of a shadow, Oly's presence flittered across her mind. He was agitated about something or other. Nothing new. Kila wondered if Wen had received the same treatment from the surly animal. At the moment, Oly was too far from her to pass more than vague feelings. That suited her just fine.

She bent to the task of climbing, step after step. Each was carved from the bedrock of the Honor Mountains. This particular stretch was growing precarious, the steps no wider than her shoulders and the drop steep enough she would suffer many broken bones before she struck flat ground. She absently wondered if it would be better to die mid-fall or to leave Til's Realm in a grand splatter. She thought a conk on the head in the first few feet a much more favorable fate. No need to suffer more than necessary.

The steps were wondrously flat and even. Even the ages of wind and rain—and presumably the innumerable feet of dragon-tenders—had done nothing to wear down the rock. This was the work of ancient hands, the first race.

She came to the first tunnel and was displeased to see that

it penetrated directly into the face of the mountain. There were no lights inside. So here was a conundrum. She easily maintained the mercus mask, but now she needed mercus light.

How quickly would the Hargothe detect her? How fast could he dispatch men to come after her? An interesting couple of questions. She remembered the Fell Guards and the gates. Each required a visitor to stop and wait. The trek from the Abbey to the Citadel alone would take three quarters of an hour, even with strong atlens pulling a carriage. The Hargothe would send armed men of the Watch, and they'd likely recruit the Fell Guard into the hunt, claiming that Kila Sigh was a wild merculyn putting the whole Citadel at risk.

Or would they? If others got involved Kila might well be taken prisoner by the Fell Guard, and there would be no guarantee of her being turned over to the Hargothe. He might not risk sending such an obvious force after her.

On the other hand, if he did, they wouldn't need to ascend to the Eerie to fetch her. Unless she grew wings, she would have to come back down these very steps.

She didn't relish going into the pitch blackness, but she decided to explore it a bit before committing to revealing herself upon the mercusine.

Taking one final look at the open sky, she plunged in.

FORCE AGAINST FORCE

The burn chamber had been cleared of all the detritus of the dungeon and crypts. The Hargothe had ordered it carried out rather than burned, for the room smelled so strongly of soot and spoiled cabbage already he didn't think he could tolerate the additional smell of fresh smoke.

Now the acolytes were bringing him stones. None knew why he required them, and none dared question it. Each presented a stone. He felt them with his hands and mercus senses. When he found one acceptable, he instructed the boy to leave it on the floor.

He needed one more the size of an autumn pumpkin. Not a precise measure by any means, but he understood that the guidelines were more to provoke a sense of intentionality in the demayncor than to get the exact size correct. He rubbed his fingertips across the round granite stone the acolyte held for his inspection. Finding it acceptable, had the boy place it on the floor, then blurred the memory of the moment from the boy's mind and sent him away.

All was in order. Juni could place the stones in the correct configuration. She would complain, but she would do it.

The Hargothe always knew the position of the sun. He had several hours to wait before she arrived. Perfect. He would have time to work with Henley.

He returned to his crypt and was instantly aware of Dunne Qirl's presence. Henley wasn't with him. "You failed," the Hargothe said.

"The boy had warning of our arrival. He and two others fled. We cornered them, but a fight ensued. There was a Lady involved. She is the daughter of Radiant Junisa Peline."

The Hargothe surmised what had happened. Immediately after her dismissal from the parlor, Quinn had run off in search of Kila Sigh to warn her of her mother's involvement with the Hargothe. She had given young Henley warning. Mere chance, but had Dunne Qirl and his men been more careful, they should have still succeeded.

"There's more, Seer Hargothe," the man said. He was not a weak Donse Master, and his diligent study and loyal devotion had earned him use of the stonebone queller, which immobilized those with mercus potential. It would be useless against one of the Hargothe's training, but for a lad newly awakened, he would be frozen as if turned to stone. "Henley was accompanied by a lad believed to be dead. Fallo PiTorro. He is the eldest son of the caravaner, Tarek PiTorro. Fallo's caravan was attacked a while back. All were murdered and burned. Apparently Fallo survived and has been running wild in the streets since."

"You are avoiding something. I care nothing about caravaners and their sons." Not entirely true. Such men wielded great power and influence in Starside of late. "Speak to no one about the PiTorro lad. But do speak now of the subject you avoid. I can hear all in your voice."

"A black-cloak with a Shadline blade interceded to help the three youths escape us. Four men of the Watch were slain."

The Shadline didn't interfere with the Way of Til. That was an absolute. To do so would violate the black-cloaks' tenets and run counter to their interests.

Dunne Qirl continued, "He had a sword that ran with flame along its edges. Mercusine, surely."

The Hargothe had not thought of the Shadline in years. Doing so now raised his ire. All relics of the mercusine belonged to the Way of Til. That the strange order of blade-masters was tolerated was only because they were too powerful to be quashed. To save face many generations ago, Highest Rinfro had granted the Shadlines perpetual use of their weapons, blessed and mandated by Til. This presented to the world the fiction that the Way could reclaim the weapons at will. A total fantasy, and one that made the Hargothe clench his jaw so hard his head began to pound.

He had to deal with Dunne Qirl now. "Where is the boy?"

"The Baths."

A sensible move for the lad. He would be safe there. For now. "Post a man to watch the comings and goings there. I want that boy the second he steps foot outside that compound."

"Yes, Seer." The man bowed, robes rustling, and departed.

The Hargothe lay upon his bed, breathing easily and seeking solace in the mercusine. It was not unusual for things to take unexpected turns. Only the gods were immune to bad luck, and even they could not turn aside the force of destiny in every case.

He pondered the question of fate for a while. Everything he'd done and seen in his visions had guided him to this point. Yes, there had been many years of suffering. Most of them spent in this room, trying to escape the assault of a sense-filled world.

But one thing was clear: Til had placed him here for a great purpose. It wasn't to merely flare in power and then die. He was here to do something. Become something. Why else had he been given permission—and the hunger—to consume the powers of others?

A boy was a blade of grass before the scythe of time. But the Hargothe was a towering oak. Perhaps even a great forest. Those who lived around him were intended for his use.

"Til, why do you put these obstacles before me?"

He said it aloud, which startled him. He didn't believe Til had eyes and ears the way a man did. But saying the question helped him distance himself from it. He heard it as if someone else had posed the question to him. The answer came directly from the Theb, the holy book of the New Pantheon.

Til formed the world but did it not hold together. So he scooped up mortal flesh and worked it into the clay. And in doing so provided the world with a natural opposition, force against force. Life and death.

Scholars read it to mean that without strife and struggle, the world would lose cohesion. Life would have no meaning at all without conflict. Perhaps they were correct. Though well-read, the Hargothe didn't consider himself a scholar. He wanted to *do* things, not merely learn them.

And he had so much to do. In the scale of his ambitions, even Kila Sigh was a small piece. She was a waypoint, not a destination. The power she could give him was not what he wanted. He wanted what her power could do. He would form a new world someday, one with strict adherence to the word of Til as revealed by the Hargothe. The weak-willed and stupid citizenry needed his wisdom and protection, while the wicked needed purging.

And there were *so* many wicked people.

14

TELT

The unfortunate boy sat at the table in the back room of Hard Way pub, bent over a cup of ale and staring at his dagger, which lay on the table before him. "His name was Jikki. And he doesn't want anyone knowing where he lives. He gave me the dagger for a purpose."

"Which was?" the Cloak prompted. He sat across from Fallo, cloak hanging over the back of his chair. He wore fine but simply-cut clothes. Black, with black satin details. His sleeves did not have the lace cuffs most rich men favored. These were loose, and folded back to reveal a hint of his corded and veined forearms. He leveled his unblinking stare at Fallo and waited.

Quinn knew that stare well and was thankful not to be on the receiving end for once.

Fallo's single eyebrow had collapsed over the bridge of his nose. He didn't look angry so much as conflicted. Clearly the Cloak was asking him to break a confidence.

Finally, he nodded to himself, as if he'd solved the problem. "My father is Tarek PiTorro, the caravaner. He has hated me since my birth. He often told me that I shamed him, that I was unfit to be his heir. He said his legacy would be tarnished by my hideous face. He ignored me most of the time, choosing to focus his attention on my younger brother, Deni.

"When he told me to join a caravan to gain experience in the family business, I was thrilled. I sensed a thaw in his animosity. But it was a ruse to get me out of Starside. On the return trip the caravan was beset by raiders, everyone in the caravan murdered, and the wagons burned. I've been dead ever since. If you take my meaning."

"How did you escape?" Quinn asked.

"I can scarcely remember. I was in the center of the ring of wagons. The guards had taken position outside. They were slain. There was a parting in the flames. Clear ground and air appeared ahead of me. I ran. Later, two guards with hounds came to make sure all of us were dead. But I had deduced by then that my father was behind the attack, for one of the raiders was his axeman, Yilo Chuff. I retreated into the mountains where I found safety in a cave. And that's where I met the hermit, Jikki."

Such a horrific tale told with such nonchalance. Quinn felt immense pity for the boy. He was two years her junior, but his eyes seemed so much older. Now she knew why.

"Jikki had many strange and wonderful artifacts," Fallo said. "But the dagger stood out among them for its low quality. It was precious to him. I didn't know why. He wouldn't explain it. He merely bade me return to Starside with it and show it to someone. He claimed that this person would recognize it."

"And did you do as you promised?"

"As well as I could. The individual lives at the Citadel and isn't in the habit of taking meetings with strange young men bearing daggers and tall tales. But a servant there took the blade to the individual in question and then returned it to me. I was to keep it."

Quinn found that she was leaning forward, her forearms braced on the table, her ale forgotten. Curiosity was taking control of her body. If the boy didn't tell her who he had gone to see, she didn't think she'd ever be able to sleep.

The Cloak said, "If anyone understands secrets and promises, it's me. Do not disclose what you've sworn not to. But it is clear that the blade belongs to you now. This Jikki person may have lived her entire life—"

"*His* entire life," Fallo said.

"—his entire life in order to be there for you. The force of destiny guided this blade to your hand. It is a great responsibility and privilege. You must take the oaths and join the brotherhood."

Fallo eyed Quinn. "If there are more 'brothers' like Quinn, count me in."

Heat rose to Quinn's cheeks and she grinned. "You don't lack for confidence, do you?"

"When one lacks all other charms, confidence is all one has." He picked up the dagger and rubbed his thumb across the rusty and pitted flat. The nicks in the edges were rounded, evidence of much use even in its dulled state. "I don't have a hone. But I don't really want to sharpen it. The blade is like me."

The Cloak beckoned Fallo to return the blade to the table. When it was lying flat, the man pointed at the dull edge. "You need not tend to the edge, nor should you attempt to remove the rust. A Shadline weapon does not require such, for they are imbued with power that makes them exactly as they are. For reasons I cannot fathom, the makers chose to make this blade look like a ruin. Perhaps it is to make enemies underestimate its power . . . the way people underestimate you. But before I can allow you to leave with it, you must take your oath."

"And if I refuse?"

"I will have to kill you."

Quinn gasped and spilled her ale as she jerked away from the man. He had made no such threats to her. And she'd known the name of her blade from the start. It had told her, right into her mind.

Memories of that moment of bonding made the tiny hairs on her arms stand up. It had been painful and strangely pleasurable.

"I like that you speak plainly," Fallo said. "So many others talk in riddles. I sometimes think the Voluptuary doesn't truly know anything the way she's always talking about Kila-this and Henley-that and the stirrings of dark forces are making the whole city shiver. You merely say, 'Oaths or death.'" Fallo smiled. "What do I have to say?" He drained his cup and stood. "I, Fallo PiTorro, swear not to stab anybody who doesn't have it coming."

The Cloak didn't find this funny at all, but Quinn did. She

said, "I don't remember that part, but I like it. Can I add that to my oath?"

The Cloak ignored her. Standing, he took up Fallo's dagger. He closed his eyes and said, "This blade's name is . . ." His eyes popped open, and he nearly fumbled the weapon. He gripped the hilt more firmly. "This blade's name is Telt." He swallowed before rushing on. "Speak the words: I am Fallo PiTorro, bearer of Telt. I pledge my blade and my honor to the service of the Shadline brotherhood."

Fallo repeated the words, his voice cracking, eyes wide. Quinn could barely concentrate on the vow-speaking, for her mind jounced all over the name of Telt. There was not a single person in Starside who had not heard the legendary name immortalized in song.

The verses of "The Lais of Mayla" were so ingrained, they occupied the same part of mind as "Nameday Blessings" and "Puppy in the Pantry." The Lais were of Til's daughter, Mayla. About her birth and death, which happened within seconds of each other. In the aftermath, Til slew the dragon who had killed his daughter. But a tooth fell from the beast before the rest of the beast vanished into smoke. That tooth was stolen by men and split into three shards. These were forged into weapons. One was called Telt.

Fallo was done speaking. The Cloak was as wrong-footed as Quinn had ever seen him. He slumped into his chair and stared at the blade in Fallo's hand. The boy held it away from his body as if it were a snake.

Quinn drank what little unspilled ale remained in her cup. The liquid was warm and bitter on her tongue. "Does this mean that the other two blades are real? Shinane and Skeye?"

The Cloak blew out a hard breath. "If so, that makes four previously-unknown Shadline blades. With Kila's and this one showing up so closely together . . ."

Quinn wasn't sure if him not finishing his sentence was better than if he had. The Cloak was not often at a loss for words.

"So what is Telt's power?" she asked, rubbing her elbows. An odd chill had swept into the pub. "The Lais only say the blades were made, not what they do."

The Cloak tilted his head in a sort of shrug. "It didn't tell me, but the name was clear and bold, not whispered like yours. No, these dragon blades are something new, a type of Shadline I've never encountered before. And perhaps that makes sense, given what they're made from."

Fallo grunted and let out a nervous laugh. "You don't honestly believe this is made out of a dragon's tooth, do you? It looks like iron."

"Much of it certainly is. Dragon bone is mostly hollow. I've heard it likened to a bee's honeycomb, or a sponge from the seabed. To be forged into that shape, it would have required an iron filling and outer cladding, the bone once again serving as a sort of skeleton. My friend, you bear a legendary blade. There is much honor in it, and much respon-sibility."

Fallo snickered. "I think you like saying that too much."

"I like speaking the truth, as do all good men. But I take no particular joy in lecturing you. I merely repeat myself to emphasize a point. Your life changes henceforth. The order of the Shadline may require you to fulfill your oath in ways most others are not asked."

"For instance?"

There was no response. The Cloak abruptly stood and whipped on his cloak. "I must meet my superiors and inform them of events. I will return soon. Expect to be called to your training then. It will not be easy. In the meantime, beware the pull of the blade's influence on your thoughts and desires. It is in these impulses we become aware of what a blade's purpose is. Without a strong will, a Shadline bearer can be driven to self-destruction, for such an artifact expects to be wielded by a master strong in his or her own purpose. The blade can be your ally, but only if you do not let it be your master."

The Cloak flowed into the shadows and was gone, leaving Quinn and Fallo sitting in silence. Finally, Fallo clicked his tongue and got up.

"Where are you going?" Quinn asked. She felt that they should discuss what had happened and what it all meant. But Fallo seemed to have shrugged it off.

"To the Baths. I want to talk to Henley and Ragin and see what we're going to do about Kila."

"What do you mean? She's at the Citadel. What *can* be done?"

"Oh, she's climbing to the Eerie. I forgot that you don't have a cat to talk to."

Quinn hadn't seen Fallo's obese black cat since they'd left the alley in Terriside. "What did Oly tell them?"

"His words were: 'That idiot is going to the Eerie.'"

"Why would she go there?"

Fallo waved a hand irritably. "Why does she do anything she does?"

An excellent question. And one for which Quinn did not have the first answer.

15

SHADOWY AND SINISTER

The Eerie Stair was as famous as the Citadel and about as well understood. Which meant that common knowledge was informed by legend and hearsay rather than direct experience. And so Kila was astonished to discover so much of the Stair was contained within the mountain.

Aside from the chill, the tunnels reminded her of the thinnie tunnels. Not the most welcome association.

For instance, this section was not ascending at all but was a level stretch of hewn tunnel, lit by occasional penetrations in the ceiling. She stopped in one splash of gray light and sought a glimpse of the sky. There was none. The shaft was round, as if bored by a great carpenter's drill. But however far the light had to travel to reach these depths, it was far enough to mask the opening. Only a stream of cold air told of an outer world above.

Kila was thankful for these shafts, for they gave her just

enough light to see by, even in the bleakest stretches. She came to the end of the tunnel, where a stone-block arch opened into another of the endless winding staircases. Up she went, growing vaguely dizzy as the tight spiral went 'round and 'round. The steps here were not carved from the bedrock, but were instead placed upon a winding iron frame. The design was clear. The builders had bored this vertical shaft and then assembled the stair in sections. The treads were metal, too. None of it showed the slightest speck of rust. Only dust.

The walls were smooth, too. Mounted into the rock was a smooth handrail of steel, for which she thanked the gods. Her breath plumed from the chill, the same cold that made her nose run. But this was countered by the exertion of the climb.

Her footsteps rang on the treads, sending up dull and short-lived bell tones that resounded in the hollow shaft. Her clunky boots made her feet feel thick and unwieldy. Kila couldn't imagine attempting this in bare feet, though. The cold worsened the higher she climbed.

As she topped the stairs and came into another tunnel, she was greeted by a swell of light and an opening ahead. The gurgle of running water filled the short tunnel. She came into a great cavern, one wall missing and open to reveal a magnificent vista.

A stream of water poured from a brass pipe thrusting from the near wall. Clear and sparkling, it tumbled into a shallow pool contained in a hewn rectangular section of the floor.

The floor itself was smooth and polished, though sections of it were hidden under drifts of snow blown at the opening. Kila went straight to the water, for she had brought none with her. She tested the depths of the pool and found it only a hand deep. She stepped into it, knowing her boots would keep the water out. Putting her lips to the falling water, she drank. Icy, and bit metallic, the water was nonetheless delicious, and it soothed her throat.

She drank her fill before stepping back onto dry ground. The first thing she noticed was a complete lack of dragon scales. Or any other sign of animal occupation. There were not even birds' nests. What she did find surprised her, for such a thing had never been mentioned in story or song.

Set close to the rear wall of this mountainside cave was a dais, and upon it a magnificent throne. It was carved from black granite and polished to a deep shine. The stone was flecked with silver, making it look like a starry sky. The left armrest had crumbled away, leaving a jagged portion.

Kila approached it, wondering who had once sat upon it. Surely some king of the lost race of builders. But why here? She hadn't passed a single side chamber. There was no sign of dwellings here.

Shrugging deeper into her seahound coat, she went to the ledge where snowy floor gave way to empty space. Never one to shy away from the edge of a long drop, Kila was neverthe-less more cautious than usual as she approached. Planting a foot a few inches from the edge, she leaned forward, aware that a strong gust could be the end of her.

She didn't expect to see much but a mountain slope, but was greeted with a gut-squeezing drop. The face of the cliff angled just slightly away from her, but from her perspective it was vertical. An unmeasurable distance below lay a field of enormous boulders. Farther out, more mountains, their peaks white. Heavy cowls of ice hung from a cliff-face opposite her, shadowy and sinister.

Far below, trees fringed the lower slopes, and daylight glimmered from a distant waterfall not yet frozen to stillness by winter's breath. She glanced back, looking for an exit. This was not the Eerie, but merely a stopping point along the climb. Trouble was, there was no other tunnel or staircase leading from the chamber.

She started to worry that she'd missed a side passage, or perhaps had fallen for one of Marlow's tricks. She recalled the Eerie faced the city. But from here she couldn't see any of Starside. That meant she was facing west. There had to be more to the climb. The thought drew her eyes up, and she caught a glimpse of a ladder scaling the cliff. That lead her to the far right side of the drop, where a narrow path led to a platform carved into the mountain side.

The iron ladder began here. It climbed straight up, narrowing until it disappeared in a haze of cloud. Kila rubbed her hands together. "What fun."

She knew never to look down. That always made one's head swim. It seemed the human mind was born with an aversion to falling. The rungs were not connected to any vertical braces on either side, but were instead bent at the ends to thrust into the rock. They were solid, if a bit thin. And slick.

The thing that bothered Kila most as she climbed was the lack of rust on the rungs. It spoke of things mercusine. But who was there to sustain the effect? It reminded her of the cellar wall in Marlow's jewelry shop cellar.

Kila had met the most powerful and knowledgeable merculyns in the city, and she suspected they wouldn't have the foggiest idea how the rungs stayed pristine.

Whoever had built this ridiculous ascent to the Eerie, they must have had reasons for the manner of its construction. A very disturbing thought occurred to Kila as she climbed and held on through gusts of shearing wind.

The approach to the Eerie was dangerously exposed here. Not because they couldn't build an inside stair like the ones she'd already climbed, but because the dragons had demanded an outside approach.

"Because *they* can fly," she said. Certainty filled her with a grim respect for the builders. They had reached some sort of peace with the beasts, and part of it meant approaching in a manner that prevented all stealth. A dragon could leap from the Eerie and swoop down to inspect anyone who approached. If they didn't like the looks of them, one flash of fire and a girl would be a crisp bit of ash floating over the mountains.

All this begged the question of how Her Enlightened Majesty kept the dragons in her service. Not that any were available to do much for her, since they were never here. The last one to have flown over Starside had come before Kila's birth. Her father had spoken of it with awe in his voice. "Noxianthenes soared around the Citadel spire. He made three circuits, shrieking his greeting to the Enlightened. He spewed flame three times. It was said to be the dragon's manner of salute. Then it beat toward the Eerie and was never seen since." Father assumed the beast had departed Starside on a moonless and cloudy night. "Where he went, and on what mission, is known only to Her Enlightened."

If it had been anyone other than Father, Kila would have called it a sailor's song and forgotten it. But Wenton Sigh did not lie. He'd rob a man, but he wouldn't lie to him.

The rungs were now caked with ice. Kila had to brush each one clear, grip it, then test her weight on it. She made the slow climb, falling into a steady rhythm that took her ever-upward.

The wind buffeted her, stung her face until her eyes watered, and froze her lashes together when she blinked. She was so deep in the meditative tedium of pain and exertion she didn't realized she'd reached the top until her hand probed for a rung and found open air.

Giving a hoarse cheer, she pulled herself onto the flat landing and rolled onto her back. Her breath heaved and her arms burned from the effort of the climb. It hadn't been the pulling, for her legs did most of the work. It had been her grip on each rung, holding her onto the side of the mountain, that had utterly fatigued her.

She wiped the rime of ice from her lashes and sat up. The ladder had led to yet another tunnel. She crawled deeper into it to get out of the wind. Needing a rest, she opened her pack and dug out a bit of dried beef and a hunk of bread.

"Well, Naxie," she said into the emptiness inside and outside herself, "you can't say I didn't do anything for you. Wherever you are, I'm coming."

She didn't usually talk out loud to her lost cat, but in that moment she needed the reminder of why she was doing this ridiculous thing.

Marlow had better be right about the weight of dragon scales. She couldn't imagine climbing down that ladder with much extra weight on her back. Actually, she couldn't imagine climbing down at all.

Best not to try imaging it. Father had always said that thinking about suffering was a sure way to double your pain. The only thing that made him more disgusted was complaining about past suffering, which was—he claimed—to indulge in excuses for not getting on with the present.

Shaking out her aching forearms, Kila trudged down the tunnel. To her relief it was not a long walk, and it didn't lead to another set of stairs. She had arrived at another great cavern open to the world outside. Even as she entered the space, she knew for certain that it was the Eerie. Not because she could see the tip of the highest Citadel spire and the Ansin Ocean hazing far off in the distance, but because there was a dragon there.

16

INSIDIOUS DESIRES

Lady Quinn Peline left Fallo at the entrance to the Baths. It was a short walk from there to the Peline greathouse. She used those minutes to compose herself.

Her mother knew nothing about Quinn's Shadline affiliation. What Quinn had to do now was tell her and then ask some very difficult questions. She found Radiant Peline in the parlor, enjoying tea while a young footman named Fandy played a droning tune on the nyckelharpa.

It was far from the usual work for a man in such a position, but he happened to be quite skilled. Mother exempted him from other duties whenever she called upon him to play.

Quinn could not discuss anything with Fandy in the room, so she poured herself a cup and joined her mother on the rose-colored settee facing the performer. Her mother didn't offer a smile, but she made room for her daughter. Together they sipped and listened.

The fact that Mother was "lazing," as she would call it, said a great deal about the state of her mind. Clearly, she was not happy about the situation with the Hargothe.

When the song ended, Quinn stood. "Thank you, Fandy. I need to speak alone with the Radiant."

"Stay, Fandy," her mother said. "Play 'Her Eyes Borrowed My Love's Glow' or the one with the dog who loses his tail." Mother didn't look at Quinn when she said this. She was in a worse mood than Quinn had suspected. Obviously, she knew that Quinn was going to question her about helping the Hargothe.

But she didn't know that Quinn knew what the Hargothe wanted the demayne for. Easily remedied. "I know what your brother wants," Quinn said over the rim of her teacup as Fandy started up a song.

To her credit, Mother didn't react. She continued with her tea, nodding her head in time to the tune. When Fandy had completed the song, she gave him a silver plug and sent him away. Once the doors were closed, she came to stand next to Quinn at the window. The slate-colored sky hung low over the city, drapes of ragged cloud scudding by on hard easterly wind. It looked like it would snow at any minute.

"What do you think you know?" Mother could wield her stare as directly as a whipaxe blow to the forehead when she was out of patience.

"Your friend the Voluptuary pulled me into a favor. As a result, I know that the Hargothe is desperately searching for a girl named Kila Sigh. She is a friend of mine. The thing the old man seeks to recover from the demayne is something he stole from her."

"I cannot see that it matters what he seeks or how he got it. I have negotiated beneficial terms for both this house and you. Once I have completed the task, you will be free to go to the Ori's Home at the Garden."

Quinn laughed. "I'm not going to the Garden."

"Yes you are. I'll hogtie you and hire a longshoreman to bundle you into a cargo hold if I have to. The future of this Radiancy rests upon your shoulders. I will not have any more children. Our position is weak enough as it is. You will never attract a husband of enough worth to lift the house in status. That is my curse upon you. So we must not rely on marriage. You must learn to manage our estates and build wealth and influence in more honest ways. By working for it."

Talk of marriage was always upon Mother's tongue. There had been a brief time when an agreement had been established between Mother and House LiMillar to marry Quinn off to a lesser LiMillar cousin. But then the boy had died suddenly. The LiMillars hadn't offered up any of their other boys, which had sent Mother into a rage. Quinn hadn't ever met her betrothed, but Mother assumed that there must have been something wrong with him. Since then she had maintained a special animosity for the LiMillar family. Quinn wasn't fond of them, either, but for different reasons.

"Whatever the Hargothe's plan is for Kila Sigh," Mother said, "it is no concern of mine. I will carry out this task and you cannot stop me."

"I don't want to stop you," Quinn said. "I just want to get

Kila there so she can recover what's hers."

"If the Hargothe wants her, then she'd be better off leaving Starside. Who is she? I'm not familiar with House Sigh."

How Kila would laugh to hear that. "She's an orphan from Cheapsgate." The reaction this revelation provoked was worth the whole tense conversation. That a Lady of a Radiant's house was fraternizing with such a lowly person was pure scandal.

But Mother surprised her by quickly shifting from outrage to squinting suspicion. "The Voluptuary pulled you into this? For a Cheapsgater?" She rubbed her elbows and moved away from the window. "I owe much to that woman, for all she speaks in riddles. She can make a dinner menu sound like revelations from the Theb. What did she say about this girl?"

"She called on me to help her and her brother when they were in dire need. The boy has since died. I did not know him. The girl is strong in the mercusine, and the Voluptuary has been trying to convince her to stay as a novitiate to train. But Kila is more leather than silk. Rules, in particular, tend to chafe her more than most."

Mother twisted her lips in consideration. "I like the sound of this Kila Sigh. I should like to meet her. What is it that the Hargothe stole from her?"

"Believe it or not, a talking cat."

Rather than scoff, as Quinn had expected, Mother moved back to the settee and sat. "Oh, I believe it. I was just verifying the truth of Miss Sigh's tale. My brother told me he had acquired a Beloved One. Tenn has sought such a creature nearly his entire life. Marlow and I rescued several of them from his experiments back when we still lived at the plantation. And it does not surprise me he stole it from someone else."

It was Quinn who ended up stunned with shock. "You've seen cats before?"

"They were common enough in the country. They kept the mice and rats in check. The workers considered them good luck. Father didn't hold much with Donse Masters, so their hatred of the animals didn't infect us out there. One doesn't see a Donse Master that far from the city anyway. They prefer to hew close to bulging purses and well-stocked larders. The souls of lowly planters and rock-pickers are not worth that much to them."

"You agree, then, that Uncle Hargothe must not get control of Kila's cat?"

"I said no such thing. And never again call him 'Uncle' in my hearing. I know you seek to provoke me, but let's dispense with that ploy. I hate his rotten bowels and make no mistake. But I'll strike a deal with Kil himself to secure your future and that of this house. It is pointless to discuss anyway. How do you think you will get this Kila Sigh person into the abbey, much less into its dungeons?"

Quinn was not about to tell her mother that she had helped two boys do just that recently. "I'm not asking you to do anything except delay. I know where Kila is, but it's going to take her a while to get back here. Whatever you need to do, do it slowly. Kila will find a way there. Just don't come between her and the Hargothe, and certainly not between her and the cat. She will know you are my mother, but if you try to keep the cat from her she will kill you."

"If she shows up, the Hargothe will have her. I think she will be the least of my worries."

"Listen to what I am telling you. Kila Sigh may be small and young, but she dropped Highest Binel to the floor with a thought." Or so Fallo had told her. She knew the hideous boy exaggerated sometimes, but Henley had confirmed the tale.

Her mother didn't offer any more arguments, but instead changed the subject. "Unless you plan to go riding, please take off those jodhpurs and put on something more becoming your station. And for Pol's Love, put that wretched blade out of sight. What husband would have you for a wife if he had to fear being stabbed in his sleep?"

"Any man who fears my blade is not worthy of my bed. And I'm much more comfortable in trousers than those stupid gowns you want me to wear. Kila and I have that much in common." More than that. Both were Shadlines. Both had lost their fathers young. Both liked to sneak and steal.

Quinn straightened and shrugged her shoulders. No, she thought to herself, that last thought was Black's influence on her. And maybe the trousers were, too, she realized. She had never preferred trousers prior to coming into possession of the blade. She had to be attentive to such things lest she become subject to the blade's more insidious desires.

She had done the best she could with her mother. And now that it came to it, she saw no advantage in confessing she'd become a Shadline. The next thing to do was get word to Kila. Whatever the fool girl was doing going to the Citadel, she needed to get on with it and get back.

"Please Mother, whatever you're doing for the Hargothe,

do it slowly." She didn't wait for her mother to respond. When the time came, she counted on her mother to instinctively do as she asked. That was a power children had over their parents. They manipulated them even when the parent thought they were ignoring such efforts.

In less than ten minutes she was in the Baths. She found Fallo, Henley, Ragin, and the cats in the novitiates' ward library. A great fire burned in the hearth. The boys were slouched in overstuffed leather chairs, staring at nothing and adding a general glumness to the silence. Henley, in particular, looked like there was no hope for tomorrow.

Quinn sympathized. He was trapped by his own power, for the mere capacity for mercusine powers drew Donse Masters to him like flies to dung. She had been born into a strange prison, too. Nobody had asked if she wanted the responsibility of carrying on the Radiancy. Nobody even knew if she was capable, and yet it was expected.

"Where is that cream-colored skunk?" she asked.

Without looking up, Fallo said, "Oly's stomping around the kitchens and annoying the cooks. Lop is mad at him because now the cooks are withholding their treats. They don't like it when Oly jumps on the countertops and steals chicken bits. They think all the cats have bad manners."

"Lop couldn't jump that high if she wanted to," Henley said.

"True."

"I need Oly to come with me to the Citadel," Quinn said. "I need to tell Kila what's going on with the Hargothe and my mother."

Fallo grimaced. "The likelihood of him helping you is equal to that of the Voluptuary dancing naked at a Tilsday service."

"My mother is doing something to help the Hargothe bring Nax back."

"Hmmm. Oly does want Nax back," Henley said. "I'll ask Huff to tell him."

Being in the presence of people who spoke to animals was chilling. Even though Quinn was fascinated by the animals, she couldn't shake the bias against them she had been raised with. She wondered if she would have been so intrigued with them if not for Black's influence upon her. Perhaps there was some benefit to the blade's darker leanings.

"Oly says he isn't going to walk that far," Henley reported.

"I'm Lady Peline. I will fetch a carriage. We only need to go far enough to get Oly in contact with Kila."

"He says she is very far up."

Quinn considered the timing. Her mother was going to the abbey at nine bells. That gave her a couple hours to find Kila and bring her back.

Once Kila had recovered Nax, Quinn could drag the recalcitrant girl somewhere to meet the Cloak and speak the oaths.

"Tell Oly to meet me out front."

Fallo stood up. "Should we go with you?"

"I can't go," Henley said, face glum and body slumped in the overstuffed leather chair.

"Neither can I," Ragin said, equally sullen. "The Voluptuary ordered me to stay with Henley. No offense, Hen."

"Don't call me Hen, Keel."

"They have an odd relationship," Fallo said to Quinn. "I'll go with you. In case, you know . . ."

"Are you saying I can't handle myself?"

"I didn't say that. It's just, things are strange. One never regrets having a friend when the unexpected happens. And believe me, when Kila is involved, a weird occurrence is a given."

Quinn needed a moment. The impulse to be offended had come on stronger than the boy's comment had warranted. He had been with her in the alley. He'd seen her fight the Watch men. The Watch man had merely caught her wrong-footed, otherwise it wouldn't have been that close. But surely Fallo wasn't saying that she couldn't handle herself. Besides, he was right about the wisdom of having a friend along when things got tense.

"If it comforts you, then gather what you need and come along," she said coolly. "But I'm leaving now."

Fallo grinned, showing jagged teeth. "Everything I own is on my person," he said. He held out a hand, pointing to the door. "After you, Lady Peline."

His mocking manner simultaneously amused and infuriated her. She *was* a Lady, after all, and his superior in society. He ought to show greater respect and deference. And he most certainly ought not ogle her so brazenly. Conscious of his eyes on her, she pulled her cloak more snugly about herself. But even then, she wasn't sure if it was to conceal—or reveal—her curves.

17

LUCKY TO BE INCIDENTAL

The library felt very small to Henley, despite how large and empty it was in the wake of Fallo and Quinn's departure. The fire didn't seem to heat the air, and its flickery glow reminded him of the great dining hall of his father's greathouse.

What a sorry state he'd fallen into. It burned him not to be free to help Kila, though there was little he could do. But if he had gone, he would have drawn the wrong sort of attention.

Ragin didn't look any happier. He had taken a vow to be Kila's partner in study here at the Baths. The two had even briefly shared a room.

Henley could tell by the look on Ragin's face that the vow was the least of the things pulling Ragin after Kila. He was quite obviously smitten with her. As Henley had been—for a day or two—after they'd become friends. But he'd quickly realized that Kila would not settle for someone like him. Henley was practical, like his father. Kila was a reef he had no intention of foundering upon. Besides, he was at least a year or two younger than she.

But Ragin was just her age. And he came from a family that still possessed a great fortune. If things could be sorted out between him and his horrid father, perhaps Ragin could provide a life for himself and a lively young woman. But it wouldn't be Kila Sigh, Henley thought. She was Dem-Kisk.

Henley shivered and moved to stand before the fire.

"Kila and I climbed up that chimney," Ragin said. "I haven't had a moment of happiness since."

Escaping the Baths was not one of Henley's problems. It didn't make him feel any better about his predicament. But the need to leave weighed on him fiercely. He had been held captive before, albeit in a smaller cell. But that had birthed in him an incredible desire to be free—to go and do what he wanted.

That was not to be. Not until he mastered this cursed mercusine power that had infected him like the thinnie plague.

"Ragin, come with me," he said, the idea and the words rising in him at the same time. "I'm going to run for the docks and buy passage out of Starside. I'm going to the Garden, where the Hargothe won't be able to touch me or even feel my presence. I'll learn what I need to learn, and then I'll sail west. I'll never come back here. Let the others worry about Kila and the doom she's going to bring to the city."

Ragin didn't answer. There was a scuff on the tile behind Henley. He turned to discover the Voluptuary had come in. Ragin still sat on a chair, face now a bit abashed for not warning Henley of her arrival. Henley supposed that the wily woman had signaled for Ragin to remain silent.

"Voluptuary," Henley said, nodding with respect ingrained by long years of training in etiquette.

"I am relieved you are going to the Garden," she said. "Ragin will accompany you. I anticipated your eagerness to leave us, so I have bought berths for you upon the packet ship *Flyer*." She handed him a small pouch. "Coin for your admission fees to Ori's Home. Beware the dockside men who will claim to guide you. They are acolytes of Til, placed there to mislead new arrivals into the Way of Til. If you make that mistake, you will soon be delivered back to Starside. In chains."

"Madam Voluptuary," Ragin said. He was standing, and trembling. "I strenuously object to being sent away. Kila Sigh is my partner. I so vowed in your presence. To abandon her would be to my shame. Do not order me to leave. I beg you."

"You have never understood that vow. I say yet again your vow was to Ori, not to Kila. To be her partner in all things does not mean you must follow her off every precipice from which she chooses to throw herself. The path you were to take together as novitiates was one of learning, not adventure. And do not allow yourself to think Ori is blind to your circumstances. I keep you from running into senseless danger by forbidding you to leave. Now I protect you and guide your development by assigning you to attend Henley on his voyage and studies at the Garden. It is my prerogative." She pointed a finger at him. "You will go. Besides, you need distance from Kila. You're besotted, and that makes for poor judgement."

"Besotted? I am not!"

"Ragin," Henley said, "denying your affection is more embarrassing that admitting it. Spare us the discomfort of hearing your denials. You make fools out of all of us otherwise. In this I agree with the Voluptuary. You would do well to come with me. Besides, you do not want to be here when things get worse. And believe me, they will get much worse."

The Voluptuary raised an eyebrow at his prediction, but she did not contradict him. Nor did she question the source of his certainty. And she didn't need to. She was a wise and intelligent woman—surely she could see that doom approached for all of them.

"I have one more task for you both," she said. "It will not be pleasant, but it is necessary." She made a twitch with her fingers, and Finta Sahng stepped from the shadows between two book shelves. The ancient healer held the end of a chain in one gnarled hand. It dragged with a metallic rattle across the tiles behind her.

She called softly and pulled on the chain. A dark, slumped form lumbered forward, a deep hood concealing the figure's head and face. The chain rose to the opening of the hood, presumably to fasten to the person's neck. The sight of such treatment of any man would have horrified Henley. But to see Finta holding the chain made him swear.

The Voluptuary said, "You will escort this man to the Garden. Once there, you will turn him over to those better suited to looking after him. Yes, the chain and collar look brutal and wrong, but it is necessary for his safety and that of everyone around him."

Fascination drew Henley forward. There was something familiar in the man's stance, the way his great, all-concealing cloak draped from his ham-sized shoulders. A flare of firelight, caused by a sudden spark from the logs, glimmered from eyes set deep in that darkness. Henley didn't need to see more to know who it was.

"Where did you find him?" he asked.

"Yiqa discovered him in Terriside, trying to break into a vacant jeweler's shop. A great fortune that she did, for he bore a great hammer stolen from a blacksmith."

Intended for Kila's skull, no doubt. A flush of guilty heat rose in Henley's chest as he wondered if it would not be for the best if Yples had succeeded in killing her.

"Why a jeweler's shop?" he asked.

The Voluptuary frowned, but offered no answer beyond a slight shrug.

Finta handed him a leather satchel. "Feed him one dose of the bolus every morning, and one at bedtime. Do not miss a single dose. Make him prove he has swallowed it. If he refuses, force him. Get a handful of sailors and tie him to the mainmast if you must, but get the bolus down his throat."

"Surely a man must be treated with more dignity than this," Ragin said. "Even one sick with madness would benefit from more compassion."

The Voluptuary nodded. "Saying that does you great credit, Raginalt. But you are wrong in this case. He is quite mad, and like you, he needs great distance put between himself and Kila Sigh."

"Why? Who is this man?"

Henley gripped the bag of drugs Finta Sahng had given him. "It's Dunne Yples, the man who taught me that Kila is Dem-Kisk."

At the words, the man drew back his hood. His eyes widened and he looked all around. "Dem-Kisk," he rasped, throat unable to muster more volume since he had ravaged it with his endless ravings in the cell next to Henley's. A line of drool dangled from his lips. "Thinnies to flames."

His eyes locked onto Ragin. He pointed a trembling finger at the lad. "You. You were there. Dem-Kisk. Tell them. Tell them. Thinnies to flames." He stumbled forward, fists clenched. It seemed he battled the drug that kept him weak and docile. Finta watched warily.

All at once the fire faded from his eyes and he fell into a confused stupor, panting and looking confused. Finta drew his hood back over his head, concealing his pathetic and flaccid face. What a terrible long fall he'd had from his post as a Donse Master to the houses of Gristenside Radiants.

Henley suddenly felt a bit better about his own sorry state. "I don't plan to become a novitiate," he said. "I must be forthright about this. I go to the Garden merely to serve my own interests."

"I have prepared introductory documents you can provide to the Voluptuary there. I am also arranging for a fast carriage to whisk you to the docks. I do not want the Donse Masters getting a whiff of you in time to snare you. To assist us, I've asked Finta to prepare you a draught to dull your mercusine sensitivity. It should conceal the depth of your abilities. Hopefully, the Hargothe and his more sensitive Donse Masters will think you are a minor new awakening. They will dispatch someone to seek you out in the morning. But by then you'll be gone."

Finta presented Henley with a small vial of black liquid. "Drink. It will make you sleepy. The effects will last a few hours. By then you will be well beyond the Hargothe's reach."

Henley didn't require any more convincing. The burden of looking after the madman was annoying, but he saw true compassion in it. The Way of Til would simply give the man over to the Hargothe for draining. Perhaps in time Dunne Yples might be cured.

"Won't kidnapping a Donse Master raise tensions between the Ways?" Ragin asked. His posture told of someone bracing for a long argument. He didn't want to go, and he didn't plan to. But Henley knew that he would lose the argument. Ragin was a rule-follower. Like Henley had once been.

"Astute," the Voluptuary said. "That is why you must keep his hood up when you arrive at the Garden. He studied there many years ago, and it is certain someone would recognize him if they saw him."

"And what about Huff?" Henley asked.

"He will be welcomed. Prejudices at the Garden are not the same ones as here in Starside. But beware, for though the Garden prizes study and knowledge above all things, people are people. Flawed, venal, and often rash. Most will never have seen a bonded cat. Take care that they do not make you the subject of lifelong research."

"Give me the leash," Henley said. His chest felt made of stone, though his heart thumped harder than usual. He would do what was necessary. One foot in front of the next. A long path to freedom was better than no path at all.

He popped the cork from Finta's vial and swallowed the thick and bitter liquid. It was oily and clung to the back of his throat. The effect was immediate. A total numbness of the mercus and the senses. His vision grew darker, his hearing muffled. In all it was a pleasant feeling, for it numbed his fear, too. "You should have made some for Ragin. His heart is breaking."

"Someone must stay alert," the Voluptuary said. "It falls to Raginalt to bear more than his share of pain. That is life."

Henley called to Huff. *We are leaving.*

Where are we going?

Somewhere safe.

Sens Renna hustled in, her placid face flushed from exertion. "All is prepared. The carriage awaits."

Ragin accepted a satchel from the blond novitiate girl, Darya. "Warm clothing for the journey," she said. "And your things."

Ragin accepted another satchel without enthusiasm. He looked especially pale, his light hair turning a fiery orange in the firelight. "I protest."

"Your protest has been noted," the Voluptuary said. "You are going."

Henley had not said goodbye to Fallo. Just as he hadn't had a chance to say goodbye to Wen before he'd died. Or to his father. He owed his survival to Fallo. And they had become the best of friends. But Fallo would understand. He didn't need Henley anyway.

He gave Dunne Yples' chain a light tug and strode out of the library. Ragin trudged after him. Huff joined the procession, stalking along the wall and keeping nervous note of the many feet coming along behind.

They were soon in the carriage and on their way, atlens pulling for much more speed than was safe in the city. The carriage wobbled and swayed every time the driver took them around the sharp turns of the switchbacks.

"I woke up this morning thinking it would be a normal day," Ragin lamented. "Had I known I was bound for a sea voyage, I would never have gotten out of bed." He did look miserable. But Henley didn't feel any responsibility to cheer him up. There was nothing to be cheerful about until the ship cleared the harbor. And even then, it would be two months at sea. A refreshing voyage for Henley, but he had a notion that Ragin had never been to sea despite coming from a shipping family.

Finally, he said, "Henley Mast and Raginalt Keel, setting off on a sailing ship together. Just as our fathers did so long ago. I read a history once that claimed time was a wheel, the world a great tapestry where heroes are born, fight, die, and then are born again. Perhaps we are part of that."

Ragin snorted. "What makes you think we're heroes? I just get bossed around no matter where I go. If it wasn't my father, it was my brothers. Now it's the Voluptuary. I don't remember any of the heroes of the Time Wheel being bossed around."

"You have a terrible memory then. Don't you remember the woman who was always tugging her braid and being furious with the three heroes?"

Ragin let a mournful smile curl one side of his mouth. "Yes. I suppose I do, now that you mention it. But we aren't like those boys. We're incidental to the story."

"Kila Sigh pulls people into her chaos, Ragin. Believe me, I know. It was my urge to go looking for her that got me caught and imprisoned. Consider yourself lucky to be incidental. And if we are truly favored of Pol, we will hear of her battles a long time hence, after they are all resolved." He leaned back in his seat and closed his eyes. The drug Finta had given him was making him sleepy.

"Why does what's good for me have to hurt so keenly?" Ragin said softly.

Dunne Yples moaned and rattled his chain. A soft whisper came from deep in the hooded darkness shrouding his face. "Dem-Kisk. Thinnies in flames."

18

HARNZYNE

The dragon lay on its belly near the entrance of the Eerie, its scaly tail curled around its resting body. Despite its mass, it didn't obstruct the great arched opening beyond. A dozen its size could land and launch at the great mouth of the cavern.

Kila's boots scuffed the snow-strewn floor, sending up quiet footsteps that echoed in the enormous space. It was at least as vast as the thinnie cavern beneath Starside. The ceiling arched up and up, so high Kila wondered if mercusine forces were required to support it.

The dragon was either asleep or dead. It hadn't moved at all since she'd entered. Either way, she didn't plan on approaching it. She was here for scales, and she didn't know how dragons felt about thieves. She assumed they didn't much care for them.

Considering the difference in size between her and it, she hoped her presence didn't rise to the level of awareness.

Perhaps she was like a mouse to it. You never knew one was in the room with you unless you spotted it scurrying from corner to corner.

Taking inspiration from such lowly rodents, Kila clung to the back wall as she crept, eyes dividing their attention between her search for scales and the dragon itself.

The cavern was empty except for a rack of shovels and rakes. She supposed mucking out the Eerie was a tough job, if infrequent. The beasts were supposedly intelligent and quite self-sufficient. No need for food to be brought here. Besides, such would be impossible. Nobody was going to climb up here with a goat on their back.

She had imagined the Eerie darker, more natural than this cavern. Though the walls were jagged rock, and the opening was not perfectly smooth, all was formed with enough symmetry that it did not appear natural. This cavern had been made for its purpose.

The floor was only dusted with snow this far back, but if there had been dragon scales here, they'd already been scavenged. She quartered the floor, each pass taking her closer to the beast. It had not so much as twitched the tip of tail. Surely it was dead.

From this angle the creature had a cat-like quality, though its features were nothing like a cat's. But the posture—fore-limbs tucked close, head resting on the floor—gave the impression of a cat curling into a ball for warmth.

She wished Nax could see it. Kila knew that Nax would have approved of the beast. Nax liked dangerous things.

The closer Kila drew to the beast, the more its sized

impressed her. Even lying on the floor, its ridged spine sloped up to twice her height. The head alone was the length of a horse. It could probably eat one in two bites. The great nostrils were permanently flared, and three curved teeth were exposed on each side of its mouth. The eyes were closed, lidded from above and below.

Like the scales she had seen in Highest Binel's bedchamber, this beast's were a range of colors. It all depended on how the light struck them. They flamed with reflected daylight. But the body didn't move. Not even a hint of breath lifted the ribcage.

"It just curled up and died," she said to herself. What a boring death for such a magnificent beast. But upon further reflection, what other death was there? It would take a mighty monster indeed to slay a dragon.

Its presence here was a stroke of luck. Marlow had assumed the place was filled with shed scales. That was clearly not so. But Kila did have an entire dragon's corpse to loot. She approached it slowly, taking in its size and imagining the wonder her father must have felt seeing such a creature in flight. It scarcely seemed possible for it to stay in the air. Its wings were folded so tightly to its body they had to be impossibly thin.

The scales ran in brickwork fashion, one overlapping the seam of the two below. She drew Cayne and tapped the beast's flank with the pommel. A dull cracking nose rose and echoed. Flipping her hold on the hilt, she tried to wedge the blade-tip under a saucer-sized scale. If she could pry it up a bit, maybe she could cut the attachment tissue.

But even the keen edge of her supposedly Shadline blade would not slip under the lip of the scale. She braced it and smacked the pommel with her palm but succeeded only in scraping her blade across the surface of the scale, sending up a flash of blue sparks.

That was interesting.

"Is it made of metal?" she mumbled. The scales didn't look metallic so much as like iridescent shell. But she had never heard of steel on shell creating sparks.

She absently twirled Cayne as she considered the problem. Scales came off somehow, otherwise Highest Binel wouldn't have any. If the beasts were like birds, maybe they molted. A fat lot of good that would do her with a dead dragon on her hands. She began a slow circuit of the beast, looking for any scales that had begun to lift. She stopped just in front of the dragon's enormous snout, marveling at the regal lines and ridges of its brow. The whole look of the face spoke of intelligence. And not the mere alert attention a well-trained dog could display. This looked wise. She could well imagine the terror it could instill in girl or beast if those terrible eyes were locked on one's own.

She completed her circle around the beast, noting with sickening fascination the length of the talons protruding from the bird-like toes. It was a predator whose entire purpose was to hunt, kill, and consume. Sort of like a cat.

And that led her thoughts back to Nax. This mission had failed. Unless she could pack the entire dragon in her satchel, she was going to have nothing to pay Flaumishtak.

Frustrated, and at a loss for what to try next, she went to

the ledge and took in the view. She was in too foul a mood to find any joy it. The perch allowed her to look down at the Citadel, down at the Divide. And even to the other side. That did break through her frustration. For there was Moonside, the hidden and legendary twin to Starside. There was no way to get to it unless you were a bird or Her Enlightened Majesty. The view wasn't particularly revealing, for the entirety of Moonside lay hidden beneath a sea of black and blue clouds. The surface roiled like storm clouds, hinting at great currents of air rising and falling. The Divide obstructed much of the city, but Kila saw that the seaward edge of Moonside was also walled off. No hint of docks or any other access to the water. To the north, the clouds met the shoulders of the mountains. "Like a bowl of cloud stew," she said.

Her eyes started to burn and her lip quivered. She knew how eagerly Wen would have taken in this view. Here she was, unable to enjoy it and her brother had never gotten a chance to see it.

Sniffing, she looked away from the hidden city and traced the Street of the Diadem through Gristenside to Dunne Medow Cathedral. It was so tiny from here. She noted how ill-fitting the Cathedral was to its surroundings. It had obviously been added to the city by those who came after the original builders. The Street of Sorrows continued downslope through Terriside, finally ending at the Cheaps. The gate was not visible from here, but the towers on either side thrust up like toy fortifications. Beyond hung a low black haze, the combined chimney smoke of the shacks of Cheapsgate.

You see now how far one can climb and yet not rise. The

voice spoke into her mind. Not Oly, not the Hargothe. Not even the demayne Flaumishtak. This was a new voice.

Kila spun, looking for the source. The dead dragon still lay curled in its cat-like position.

"Are you speakin' t'me?" she said to the beast.

He will not speak to you. Not while you are bonded to the Beloved One. Dragons respect such bonds as sacred.

"Where are ya? Come out an' lemme see yer face."

That will not be possible. You must come to me. I have told you before, but you are forgetful.

Kila got control over her posture, which had slouched into a fighting stance. She sheathed Cayne and shook out her arms. "How 'bout ya get outta my head an' speak with yer voice?"

I would love nothing more. But you would not hear me. Even if you dropped your mercusine mask. Turn around, look at me.

Kila turned, again facing out to open air. She didn't know what she was looking for. "What are ya? A bird?"

You are the Raven, not I. Look. The window on the spire. Do you not see the kerchief I wave?

Kila squinted and shielded her eyes from the gray of the sky. The Citadel stood like a part of the mountain itself, but the foundations gave way to beautifully proportioned walls and towers. A central spire, directly in line with the Divide, rose to a round top, drawn up to a point. But lower, tiny hints of windows dotted the wall. In one, near the top, a flutter of white. It could be a kerchief. Or it could be the flap of a gull's wings. It drifted away from the window, curling and flying on the circling wind.

"Did you just drop it?" Kila asked, not raising her voice above a whisper.

I did indeed. I have long desired to speak with you. I still would like to meet. But your mind is clouded and forgetful. I do not understand why.

With growing certainty, Kila realized she was speaking to Her Enlightened Majesty. Who else in the Citadel could communicate so? Not even the Hargothe would be able to invade her mind while she was blocked from the mercus.

Have you collected all that you require from my Eerie?

"No. Not a single free dragon scale to be found. Too many thieves got here before me."

Surely you don't think I leave them lying about. They are precious.

"I was told that someone used to fetch 'em from here . . . And now that I think about it, by Kil's heavy fist, I wager it was you." Kila wondered if Marlow knew his previous source for dragon scales had been Her Enlightened herself. She doubted it.

Dealing with demayne is unwise. How many scales did you agree to?

"One thousand."

Silence followed. It was so prolonged, Kila began to think Her Enlightened had simply decided she was too foolish to bother with. But then a response came. *I shall ask Harnzyne. Perhaps he will feel generous.*

"You mean . . ." Kila turned at the sound of a rumble behind her.

A wash of hot air blew past her, ruffling her hair and

engulfing her in a sulfuric stench. The dragon no longer rested in its comfortable ball, but had rolled onto its belly. The head lifted. And then lifted higher. The gem-like amber eyes stared down the length of its snout at her.

It stretched its wings, unfolding them to several times the length of its body. The limbs trembled at the full extension, like a cat coming awake after a long afternoon slumber. The wings folded in and the creature came onto its feet. The eyes never left Kila, and she sensed a wariness in the beast's manner.

Kila's guts felt very watery as she endured the glare of those intense and predatory eyes. She had no escape except to fall thousands of feet down the cliff behind her. Her hand went to Cayne. The dragon froze, its unblinking eyes flaring. She froze, too, realizing it might insult him to brandish a blade.

Kila left Cayne in the sheath and held her hands up. "Just instinct, uh, Harnzyne. Didn't mean any offense."

The beast lowered its head and sniffed the air, tasting Kila's scent. With slow, lumbering steps, it moved aside, then slumped back to the floor and curled up once more. As a final dismissal of Kila's existence, it drew one wing over its head to cover its eyes.

Kila scurried to the spot it had vacated, for it was mounded with scales. A thousand and a thousand more. She scooped them up, noting the warmth still in them. "Thank you, sir dragon. I'm in your debt."

She picked one up, astonished to find it lighter than an equal sized scrap of paper. And just as thin. Thinner even at the edges, which were razor sharp. The surface was hard and smooth, like porcelain. She thumped it against another scale, producing a sharp click.

Just like Highest Binel's scales, these were roundish, polished, and aswirl with color. She did press her finger into it this time, but it did not sink into the illusory depths.

The dragon huffed and adjusted its hind legs. The motion snapped Kila out of her awed stupor. She started stacking scales like dinner platters, noting that a set of fifty was not much thicker than a stack of ten.

She stuffed them into her satchel, no longer bothering to count. She scooped and collected scales until there was no room remaining in her backpack, estimating it held at least four thousand. When at last she cinched the straps closed and hefted it onto her back, she was astonished to discover no appreciable weight added to the pack.

"Thank you, Majesty. Thank you, Harnzyne."

Do not thank us yet. One can pay a demayne and still discover she is deeply in debt.

Kila could not think that far ahead. She had what she'd come for. Now she merely needed to get back to the Citadel and find Marlow and make him summon Flaumishtak.

As she left the Eerie, she cast one glance back. The dragon slept, and snow began to fall outside. The wind rose and howled in the cavern. A desolate place. She was happy to leave it behind.

19

____

TALONS OF AIR

"She got what she was after," Her Enlightened Majesty said as she turned away from the window. She pulled the window shut and twisted the latch.

The icy wind that had whipped in did not seem to bother her. Marlow had retreated to stand as close to the fire as he could without singeing his robes.

After a long delay, he had been shown in and told not to speak to her until she addressed him first. What he had discovered was a slim young woman, facing away from him, staring out an open window. At one point, she had waved a kerchief into the air and released it.

All he could see of her now was her lovely blue gown, empire waisted, skirts draped to pool around her feet. Her black hair tumbled in sheets and intricate braids, which themselves were woven into looser braids.

He had seen a many a Radiant's daughter with such braids, but none approached the intricacies of Her Enlightened's.

Marlow imagined the woman had hairdressers who did nothing else but twist and weave her hair each morning.

Still she had not turned to face him. From the position of her elbows, he guessed she was clasping her hands in front of her, a pose of calm consideration.

He didn't know what his brother had told this woman, but in Marlow's last—and rather harrowing—confrontation with the Hargothe, the bastard had mentioned he had secured a position for Marlow on Her Enlightened's small council. Marlow was taking quite a risk showing up to claim it.

"Your brother spoke carefully about you, Dunne Marlow," the woman said. "It was good fortune for me that he is blind, for when he mentioned your name I surely revealed my feelings on my face. As it was, I merely accepted you on a trial basis."

And then she did turn. Marlow understood now her hesitation to face him. "Maeda? What are you . . . are you . . . ?"

"I am. I always have been. A pity I couldn't tell you. I am not much of a thief, in truth."

He had purchased dragon scales from her many times. Always meeting in a Terriside tavern, and her always shrouded in a hooded cloak. He would hand over a pouch of gold skillets, and a day or two later a bag of scales would show up at the jewelry shop. She'd introduced herself to him, claiming to have been to the Eerie. Well, this explained how she'd known the way was unguarded.

"I haven't been able to contact you for over a year," he said, laughing softly. "I am running low on my own stock of scales."

"*She* has awakened. I cannot come out into the city now. I must act with great caution. Unlike you."

Dunne Marlow felt a bit dizzy, the room now a bit too hot. He moved away from the fire and sank into a chair. His mind couldn't assemble two rational thoughts in a row. He thought of all the meetings he'd had with her as Maeda. And her knowledge of why he wanted dragon scales, and even the damning details of the Way of Til he'd revealed to her.

"You wear her queller," she said, nodding at the ring. "You are a skilled talker."

"And she is a skilled merculyn. This ring was wasted on her. I had to part with my queller recently."

"The Hargothe destroyed it. I felt it release. A pity. But you are correct about her."

She kept referring to Kila. Not by name, but she clearly knew who she was.

"I am curious why you agreed to have me here if you knew who I was. And what I do." He saw that she held a small figurine. A jade carving of a fish. She worried its surface as she sat in the chair opposite him. It was only then he realized the enormous breach of protocol he'd committed by sitting in her presence. She didn't seem to mind, so he stayed seated. How many beers had they enjoyed together? Enough that sitting across from her now felt familiar. Easy.

"Your brother is not the only one gifted with the occasional glimpse of things to come. I've seen you by my side, in victory, since I was a little girl. As for your dabbles with demayncy . . . the worlds of the mercusine web are innumerable. To name one of them 'hell' is to say that this world, too, is the hell of some other realm. Have you not travelled through the Derslin Wheel you discovered?"

Again she had caught him off guard. He'd thought the Derslin Wheel his secret. Keeping his composure, he said, "No. I have not discovered the method to it. But Kila did recently, briefly."

This didn't appear to surprise Her Enlightened Majesty, who merely nodded. "Of course she did. And good of her to learn the masking technique. The Hargothe is a troublesome figure in the turning of events. The force of destiny is strongly at his back."

"And so, too, is it with Kila Sigh," Dunne Marlow said.

Her Enlightened didn't respond, but instead let his words sit there in opposition to hers. The meaning in her silence was profound. For she acknowledged that two powerful figures were moving in the world, both with the force of destiny behind them. There could only be conflict henceforth, with very destructive consequences.

"What will you do?" he asked, needing to fill a silence too heavy with forebodings to bear.

"As much and as little as I dare," she said. "I have summoned Kila to me three times now. Perhaps this time she will come. Her memory is clouded, and her dreams are protected. Only just now, with her in my direct line of sight, was I able to reach her awake."

"You could help her. Kill the Hargothe, give her—and all of us—room to prepare for what Kila is to become."

She rested her hands on her knees and leaned forward. Marlow thought she looked no older than twenty-five. Impossible, for she had reigned for three decades. She was truly beyond time. "And what do you imagine she will become? Dem-Kisk may be nothing worse than a plague, or it may be a cataclysm such as they experience in the western mountains, where entire peaks explode with fire and rain molten rock upon the surrounding countryside. Maybe she will lead an uprising against me, or perhaps she'll bring down the Triumvirate and put up herself as the godhead of the world."

She leaned back and sighed. Her eyes were dark, and the lids dusted with a smoky color. Her cheeks were lightly rouged, too, he now noticed. Subtle artifice. He observed her hands. Slim fingers and prominent tendons at her wrist, but not a spot of discoloration. Her skin was as smooth as a young woman just entering her second ten-year. She had a placid expression, much like the Spinsters of Pol wore. Though she didn't much look like his beloved Spin Hetta, she reminded him of her. Just as Kila did. She had a wisdom about her, a worldly knowing not attributable to age, but merely from the habitual expression such understanding placed upon one's brow. He sensed in her an acceptance of the world as it was, no matter how disappointing it may be.

"You didn't answer my question," he said. "Why not kill the Hargothe?"

"Do you think me so stupid that I would not use that solution were it open to me?"

Marlow started to protest, but she waved him to silence. "I must stay out of the fray except to watch it. And only when the side of the gods becomes clear will I act. Kil stirs, Til snores, the goddesses move their pieces upon the edges of the board. It is not within the sight of mortals to understand the game. Do you know who spoke the prophecy of Dem-Kisk, Dunne Marlow?"

Being a scholar only in what he could use, Marlow hadn't the slightest notion of who had made up the incomprehensible verses of the doom prophecy. He answered with a shrug. "No. If it is prophecy at all."

Now she smiled. "A blaspheming Donse Master? What next? A Spinster sell-soul? But I understand your skepticism, I do. There is no sense in the verses of the Dem-Kisk prophecy. If it is a warning, it fails on its face, for what does it warn against? Perhaps it is the ravings of a madwoman and Dem-Kisk was merely a word she picked up from the ancients. 'Red grass,' it means in their language. Did you know that? I didn't think so. You should visit Misen-Tine some time. There are such astonishing frescoes there you wouldn't believe me if I described them to you. But you won't go there, will you, Dunne Marlow? You are not the sort to go plunging into the dark caverns beyond Starside. You merely reach for influence and power. Is that not why you asked your brother to secure a place for you on my small council? Perhaps you seek to enrich yourself into the bargain. I care not."

Marlow's body went stiff as a force outside of him squeezed from all sides. It constricted such that he could barely draw breath. His legs extended until he was rigid as a board, his shoulders pressed to the back of his chair, his heels on the floor.

Her Enlightened Majesty rose and stepped around his feet so that she could bend at the waist and press her nose close to his. Her eyes flared with reflected firelight, and he saw in them the ferocity she kept so well-concealed. "I expect to be betrayed. I do not worry about it. Someday someone will kill me, as has been done to all the Enlightened who have come before me."

She drew a slim dirk from the sleeve of her gown, the edge keen and ever so bright. She placed the edge to his throat. "I can kill you, shove you through yon window, and have Harnzyne eat you before you strike the ground. Blink if you understand."

He blinked.

"Do not be the one who betrays me. Serve me, my interests, and my empire. Do that and nothing else and you will never want for my loyalty in return."

Though he was quelled, it didn't prevent her from using the mercus as an outside force. This paralysis was not a will-shift, but something totally new. She had taken hold of him with giant talons of air.

The dirk had vanished, presumably returned to her sleeve. She again held the jade figurine of the fish. Was it a heller, perhaps? He wasn't going to ask. Not now. And though she had revealed herself to him just now, he took comfort in it. She could just as easily have killed him as warned him. That meant she saw value in him. That was good.

"You can't kill him, can you?" he said, voice tremulous despite the audacity of his statement.

He was rewarded with a genuine grin. "I can. I could also lift every Cheapsgater out of squalor. But I don't do either thing. Why? Because in both cases I have seen futures of greater ruin than if I let his evil and their suffering continue." She let out a long breath. "It's a wonder that so many Radiants scheme to take the Raven Throne from me. If they knew the burdens I bear they would pray such responsibility never came to them."

"So, you are capable of killing him, but you don't because of a vision."

"I have never had a councilor with a tenth of your nerve, Marlow. Your impetuous mouth may be what I need, but it may also condemn you. Beware, I am patient . . . until I am I not. Now, off with you. Kila Sigh will be needing your help. She has her dragon scales."

Marlow's cheeks went cold and his palms clammy. How the woman knew such detail was beyond his understanding. But it showed her power. And as much as she had showed in this meeting, he guessed she had vast reservoirs yet untapped. She may not be all-knowing, but nothing he had seen discounted her title of "Enlightened."

"I will do all you ask," he said. And he would. She had pulled from him a true respect. She didn't couch her intentions in obtuse moral codes. She did as she did for her own purposes, unexplained, but enlightened by her vision.

"Hurry," she said, finally releasing him from her mercusine grip. "Kila descends quickly."

20

SUSPICIOUS OF GIFTS

Kila had reached the throat of the final tunnel when Oly's voice came to her mind. She'd felt his nearness growing since descending from the Eerie. All he sent now was, *Faster.*

I'm going down the steps toward the Citadel now. Where are you?

She could feel Oly's irritation fully now. He had to be close. She felt the fullness of his belligerence. He didn't want to be there, and he didn't want to tell her anything.

Something happened to make him jump. Kila flinched in involuntary sympathy with his sudden surprise. *What's going on?* she demanded.

Lop jumped on me.

Fallo with you?

Yes. And this Quinn person. They are all annoying me. Lop says I have to talk to you or she's going to jump on me again. She eats more than you do.

Why are all of you here? Did the Watch round you up? The Westbunk was just below the Citadel. The Watch was head-quartered there.

No. The Hargothe is going to summon your demayne friend and reclaim Nax.

Kila picked up speed, boots shuffling in rapid thunks as she went down the Eerie Stair. Her thighs burned with the effort, and every inch of her flesh felt rubbery with exhaustion. She passed the statue of the Fell Guard and skirted along the rear of the Citadel. A few servants were hustling by. They gave her sharp looks but didn't try to stop her.

She felt Oly's presence even more clearly now. She followed it like a hound on a scent. In this case, a noxious scent. She came around a corner to the main courtyard. This was where she and Marlow had arrived. She didn't see her friends or Oly anywhere. But she did recognize the two regal blue atlen in harness before a carriage with a Radiant's crest on it.

She marched straight to it, opened the door, and found Quinn sitting across from Fallo. Oly lay on the floor, Lop's body nearly engulfing his. Both animals looked up as she entered.

"Oly is telling me as little as possible," Kila said.

Quinn paused a moment, taking in Kila's cold-weather gear. "Boots, no less. Next we'll have you in one of my dinner gowns."

Fallo waggled his brow as he envisioned the sight of Kila in a gown. Considering his sly leer, he was picturing it in too much detail. She sat next to him, giving him a not-so-accidental jab in the gut with her elbow.

"I made a bargain to get Nax back," she said. She paused and slumped back, relieved to finally be off her feet. "I came here to get the payment. All I need now is to get to Dunne Marlow so he can do something for me."

"It may be too late for that," Quinn said. "The Hargothe came to see my mother. He has struck a bargain with her to assist him in retrieving his bonded Beloved One."

Oly and Lop let out mournful mewls.

"Why was the Hargothe at your house?" Kila asked, dreading the answer.

"He's my uncle." Quinn rushed on before Kila could erupt. "I had never met him before. My mother hates him."

"She hates him so much she's helping him."

A knock on the roof came from the driver. "Shall we go, Lady?" he called.

"Wait," Kila shouted back. She parted the curtains and peered at the entrance to the Citadel. "Whether your mother helps the Hargothe or not doesn't matter if I can have Marlow summon the demayne first. I have the payment."

Quinn's voice was low. "I doubt we can make it through the all gates before my mother arrives at the abbey to meet with the Hargothe. I don't know what's involved, but whatever it is, they'll have a lead on you and Uncle Marlow."

Kila stared at Quinn. "*Uncle* Marlow?"

The Radiant's daughter held up her hands helplessly. "I didn't know you knew him. Besides, we haven't seen him much since his scandal with that Spinster." She did look genuinely distressed about her kinship with these men.

Sensing a thaw in Kila's irritation, Fallo said, "Wouldn't it be best to simply let the old corpse and Quinn's mother perform whatever dark rite is required and hope that the Hargothe *does* get Nax back? Then you simply go in, burn him to a crisp, and Nax is free to come with you."

"I can't kill him. Yet." If it had been that easy, she would have done it already. But Huff had warned her that the Hargothe's life was inextricably entwined with Nax's now. If he died, so did she. That was why she'd had Marlow summon Flaumishtak in the first place. She could get both Nax and bond back only by paying the demayne his thousand dragon scales.

"There's Uncle Marlow," Quinn said, pointing out the window.

Kila opened the door. "Get in, Marlow. We have to fly."

The disgraced Donse Master came running, heedless of the odd stares of the onlookers milling about the courtyard. He climbed in, nodded to Quinn as if he'd expected her to arrive. "I understand you were successful, Kila. Let's see."

Kila removed her pack and loosened the straps. She opened the flap and pulled forth a stack of scales. "It wasn't quite as easy as you said it would be."

Marlow shrugged. "But you have them. By the way, Her Enlightened Majesty wishes to speak with you."

Quinn squawked and Fallo gasped. But Kila merely rapped on the roof and shouted for the driver to get a move on. The carriage began its rattling journey downhill.

She eyed Marlow with suspicion. "Quinn says that your sister is helping your brother summon Flaumishtak."

Marlow winced. "Don't speak that name aloud outside the Derslin Wheel, girl. Do you want Kil's eyes upon you?" He turned to his niece. "The old man came to see Juni, did he? I didn't think of that eventuality. She hates him more than I do. But she can read the rites. Uncanny affinity for all things demaynic. I'm surprised she hasn't bonded a cat already. Perhaps she would have if the Hargothe hadn't been killing them all."

Kila flopped back in her seat and tapped her toes with impatience. "We must summon Flaumi—the demayne—before they do. I have the payment. I won't have come all this way for nothing."

Marlow nodded. To Kila's astonishment, he opened the carriage door and leaned far out to shout instructions to the driver. He finished with: "And do not slow. Run your mother down if you have to!"

The driver responded with a whoop and the crack of his whip. The blue atlens shrieked and the carriage picked up speed. The gates flew by, and Kila noted they must have opened long before the carriage had reached them.

"She's making sure we are not slowed down," Kila said.

Marlow flicked an eyebrow and scratched his chin. "It would seem so."

"Who?" Fallo asked. His hand rested on the hilt of his crummy dagger.

"You'll like this, Fallo," Kila said. "As Marlow mentioned, Her Enlightened Majesty has taken an interest in me. She even asked her pet dragon to move aside so I could scoop up scales. I don't trust her one bit."

Kila had always been suspicious of gifts. People didn't do favors for strangers without selfish motives. Surely the dragon scales would cost her something eventually. But she would worry about that once she had Nax back.

Lop mewled and Fallo leaned toward him. His eyes flicked up to meet Kila's. "Lop says Henley is leaving. For the Garden. He's boarding a ship now. Ragin is with him." He frowned at his cat. "Henley had another run-in with a Donse Master trying to nab him off the street. Quinn and I stopped it." He reddened a bit, spoiling what was obviously an egregious lie. "I guess he decided that the only way to feel safe was to leave. But why go to the Garden?"

The destination didn't much surprise Kila. She had felt a bit of Henley's power when he had helped save her from Dunne Yples. The Hargothe wasn't ever going to give up looking for him, just as he would never give up seeking Kila. "I'll miss him," she said. "But maybe he won't have to stay away too long. I don't plan to let the Hargothe go on breathing for much longer. Then I'm leaving, too."

"You can't leave," Quinn said. "You have responsibilities." She eyed Marlow and said nothing more.

Kila supposed she was still on the Shadline kick. Clearly, Quinn was used to getting her way all the time. Being a rich daughter of a Radiant must be nice.

"Don't worry about Henley, Fallo," Kila said, ignoring Quinn's comment. "Once I have Nax back, I can figure out how to get rid of the Hargothe. He can't get to me while

I'm masked to the mercus. But I can get to him." She patted her satchel and grinned. "I'll send Flaumy after him if I have to."

Marlow shifted uneasily. "It won't be as simple as that. If, er, Flaumy believes he can strike an even more lucrative deal with the Hargothe, he will simply refuse to strike one with you. Never forget that demayne are not human. They have entirely different notions about what constitutes a deal. And they do nothing that does not serve their interests."

Kila buckled the straps on her pack. "Dire words coming from one who consorts so readily with them."

"I know what I'm doing. And I know when to let a particular demayne rest. But you do not. I can see it in your face. Heed me in this. I will summon him this last time because it is necessary to complete your bargain. But I will not do so again."

Kila folded her arms and absently jabbed her toe into Oly's hindquarters. The cat spat at her and turned his back toward her. "And will your sister stop summoning him? Am I going to have to keep watch for Flaumy coming for me for the rest of my life?"

His lack of an instant denial didn't sit well with her. She had seen the magnificent power of the beast, had witnessed him do things with the mercus she couldn't even begin to grasp. She had seen the bodies of those who had fallen to the demayne's attacks. One girl had been headless.

Quinn had her blade out. She absently twirled it over her knuckles and then flipped it into the air. A sudden lurch of the carriage made her miss her catch, and the blade thunked, tip first, into the floor of the carriage. And not an inch from Oly's nose.

Sucking air through her teeth and offering Oly a chagrinned apology, Quinn plucked up her blade and returned it to her belt sheath. Oly merely slitted his eyes and turned his head away from her, too. Fallo snickered nervously and shook his head. He mumbled something about a mummers' farce, but since Kila's senses were deadened by her mercus mask, she didn't hear the whole of it. Lucky for him, she supposed.

"We're not going to make it in time," Marlow said.

A glance out the window showed Kila they were passing the Baths. They still had much of Terriside to wind through, then the fifteen-minute walk through darkness to the Derslin Wheel.

"Stop the carriage," Kila said. "We have to do the rite at the Baths."

Her three companions shouted their indignation and thoughts about her sanity all at once. But Marlow was right: they were not going to make it.

"Where else can we do it?" Kila said. "Unless you want to set up the stones on the street. I'm sure the Watch patrols will be very interested to observe that little show."

"The Sensuals will never allow me into their Baths, much less perform a demaynic summoning. They'd bind my ankles to my wrists and deliver me to the Westbunk in a manure cart."

Kila smacked the roof of the carriage to get the driver's attention. "Stop!" she called. The driver responded by cursing his birds and yanking them to a wobbling stop. The sound of the brake lever scraping on the wheels sent a tooth-shattering squeal through the carriage.

"If not the Baths, where?" Kila said. "There's no point in racing to the jewelry shop if we're going to be late."

Marlow parted the curtains and looked to see where they were. He clicked his tongue. "Well, there's always my sister's house."

Quinn gasped, but followed it with a sharp nod. "Yes. But not in the house. Mother would kill me if something happened to one of the staff. We can set up in one of the barns. That'll work, won't it?"

Marlow shrugged and held out his hands. "It'll have to."

This time Kila leaned out the door and ordered the driver to turn around. This close to the Baths, they had only a minute's ride to get to the greathouse of Radiant Peline.

As the wheels crunched over the fine gravel of the long drive, Marlow was ticking off items they'd need.

"Rocks?" Quinn said. "All you need are rocks?"

"And light. And I wouldn't mind a cup of whiskey."

"I'll arrange it," Quinn said. "But you'll have to select the rocks. There are many to choose from in the gardens." The carriage swung to the rear of the house. Having a Donse Master along didn't make up for the sorry and suspicious state of Fallo and Kila. No way was the driver going to get chewed out for delivering such ragamuffins to the front entry.

That suited Kila fine. If she ever started being admitted to the front entrances of greathouses, she'd know her life had taken a very serious wrong turn.

As they poured out of the carriage, Dunne Marlow told

Fallo to come with him to fetch rocks. Kila headed straight for the atlen barn with Quinn.

The driver was ordered to stake the birds out in the front lawn for the night. Kila thought the poor man had swallowed his tongue, but he eventually knuckled his brow and said he would do as asked.

"Hold on, Naxie," Kila muttered as she raced to the barn. "I'm coming."

21

A MEMORY LIKE A BOOK

All was arranged. The burning chamber was empty, the stones were placed, the book of summoning rested atop a lectern the Hargothe had men fetch from a musty storeroom. Incense burned in gilded dishes arranged around the periphery of the room. And to the Hargothe's delight, the smoke went straight up the flue so he didn't have to endure the odor beyond a faint taste in the air.

The only element missing was his sister. The Hargothe paced, hands clasped behind his back. Juni was always late, and while patience had never been one of his main strengths, the delay wasn't without some benefit. One did not simply summon a demayne.

He heard Juni's approach, mostly from the scuff of his elderly servant's shoes on the stone floor of the hallway. But there was a trepidatious quality to the noise of her breathing, betraying not only fear but intentional sloth. She was stalling. And no surprise. Whenever Juni sensed that a person wanted something done with alacrity, she would become more deliberate and take longer pauses. Why? Because she didn't like being told what to do. She was as bad as Marlow in that regard.

She entered and paused to take in the preparations. The Hargothe turned to face her, aiming his eyeless sockets at her. He kept his admonishments to himself, knowing lectures on promptness would only make her more stubborn and slow. Perhaps, when this business was concluded, he would take some time with her mind to make her more amenable to his commands.

"Welcome, sister."

"Just like the plantation days," Juni said. "Except there's no Marlow here to guide us."

"He isn't needed. The words are in the book. Read them and I'll speak with the demayne."

She went to the lectern. A sour smell rose from her. Nerves. Her breath shook in her chest. The Hargothe was tempted to brush her mind with urgency, but feared that any intrusions might alter her will enough to spoil the invocation.

"This rite does not include the naming of the stones," she said. "I will have to do that first." It wasn't worth saying. Of course she would have to name the stones, else the demayne would walk right from the circle, grip them by their necks, and drain the blood and souls from their bodies.

Juni began a circuit of the stones, starting with the pumpkin-sized ones. She mumbled under her breath as she granted names to them. There was nothing mercusine in what she did, but merely mundane inventions of names. One stone she called Pol, as was customary, if a touch superstitious. The Goddess of Luck was so capricious she was just as liable to spite you as reward you for such efforts. The next was named Ori, for the supposed protections she provided. As far as the Hargothe was concerned, the Goddess of Love and Wisdom was a fraud. An appropriation of Til's qualities in order to create a separate concept of female divinity. Absurd. The mere existence of woman was the result of Til's rage at mankind for forsaking his Word in the first days.

He let it go. Juni needed to conduct the naming, and whatever nonsense she preferred made no difference to him. The remaining stones got diminutive names, like the ones you'd assign a dog or a preferred horse. The chief requirement in the naming was that the demayncor remembered them all. And that the demayne could not know them.

"I will make the circuit two more times," she said. "I want to make sure I remember which stone is which." A reasonable thing to do. For an idiot. Juni had a memory like a book. She likely didn't even require the tome he'd brought down from the library. This notion that she might not remember the names of the stones was a ridiculous effort to delay.

The Hargothe said nothing lest she slow even further. For all the years she'd lived, she had not matured past the ten-year-old child he'd left at home when Father had sent him and Marlow off to the Abbey to become acolytes.

To calm his growing irritation, he stopped pacing and sank into the subtle world of the mercusine. He was immediately drawn to a familiar spark. The boy, Henley. He had moved from the Baths of the Harlots and gone east—so far east he had to be in the furthest reaches of Cheapsgate. His spark was muted. But the Hargothe had spent so much time with it, he would recognize it anywhere.

He reached out to touch his elderly servant's mind, thrusting terror and urgency into it. The old man arrived in the burning chamber, breathless and wheezing. "Seer, what is wrong?"

"I instructed you to have men posted outside the Baths should Henley leave them. He has, and yet the boy has not been apprehended."

"But that is not possible. Our acolytes followed a carriage leaving the Baths. It went to the Citadel. They saw the young Fallo PiTorro through the window. They assumed his friend went with him."

"Wasn't Dunne Qirl with the watchers? Surely he could feel the lack of mercusine potential in the carriage. Surely he would have recognize Henley's spark."

Inside, he raged. Dunne Qirl was relatively strong in the mercus, but he might have missed Henley's departure, dulled as the boy's spark was at the moment. He must possess a queller of some sort.

"Why did Fallo PiTorro go to the Citadel?" he asked.

"I don't know, Seer. He was in Radiant Peline's carriage."

Juni stopped her mumbling and came to join them. "Who was in my carriage?"

"You weren't aware that someone from the Baths had taken your carriage to the Citadel?" the Hargothe said. "I thought we had struck a bargain, Juni. What game are you playing at? Are you betraying what we do to Her Enlightened

Majesty? Do you think she would have me thrown into chains?"

"Don't be silly. We've struck an advantageous bargain. I wouldn't jeopardize it by sending Quinn to the Citadel to report you. She is likely just showing her friend that she can get to the front courtyard. Children like to boast and impress each other."

The Hargothe turned to his servant. "I expect Henley retrieved from Cheapsgate and returned to the Abbey. Dunne Qirl should not return without him. Understood?"

"Yes, Seer Hargothe. I will see to it immediately." The old servant bustled off, muttering imprecations about Dunne Qirl and the failures of the men set to watch the Baths.

Juni watched the man retreat, a thoughtful stillness in her breathing. For the first time in a long time, the Hargothe regretted having put out his eyes. Juni sometimes betrayed her thoughts in the way she held her mouth. He had to settle for listening to her breathing and her heartbeat. She was still nervous, but the quality of her anxiety had changed. Likely she was worried about her fool daughter.

This would be a good time for studying her through Kila's powers. The Hargothe had never had much success with physical world manifestations of the mercus. He could create light and use smell to charm. But those things were superfluous to an eyeless merculyn who could just as easily force a feeling directly into one's mind.

But Kila could see metal, even if it was hidden from view. He had marveled at that ability when he'd discovered it in her memories. It hinted at how she had managed to ash the thinnies. If he could study Juni's blood, would he see it rising to her cheeks with shame? Or perhaps flushing her limbs in preparation for flight?

Alas. He couldn't perform Kila's trick with seeing metals.

"Please continue, sister. I mean to have what is mine and then to be done with you. It is in both our interests for you to proceed more quickly."

She returned to her circuit of the rocks, speaking each name and bending to touch the stone. The Hargothe returned to his meditation, watching the mercusine web, feeling the ebbs and flows of power as it coursed through Starside. Somewhere out there, Kila Sigh hid from him. He would have her soon. And then he would turn his attention to larger aims.

Much larger aims.

22

BREAKER OF BAD BITS

The servants would never keep this a secret. For one thing, Quinn had never had a Donse Master as a guest before, much less one known to have been caught up in a scandal with a Spinster of Pol. Second, her demand to have braziers brought from the gardens into the barn had caused a flurry of activity among the footmen, most of whom had assumed they were off duty for the night. And so they had to hastily dress and hustle about the gardens to heft the heavy stonework posts and bronze bowls into the atlen barn.

Finally, the atlens now in the front yard had started to squawk their complaints, rousing responding cries from atlens at the next greathouse over. Only now had things begun to quiet, and the final footman had been kicked out of the barn.

Surely, the servants would talk. But there was nothing to be done about it.

The straw had been swept clear of a large circular area in

the middle of the floor. Fallo and Marlow had placed the various required stones in a shape Marlow had called "the Crown." And it did indeed look like a crown, the largest two stones' positions as jewels atop the two prongs thrusting up from the brow. Kila squatted in the corner, thumbnail between her teeth. She looked haggard in the firelight, which painted everything a reddish orange, and sent wavering shadows to the peaked ceiling.

Cold air blew through seams in the siding, making the air crisp. Quinn's breath fogged in the stillness as she stomped her feet and rubbed her hands to stay warm.

Somewhere to the east, Quinn's mother was facing a similar arrangement of stones. Quinn struggled to picture it. Her mother had never mentioned having any experience with summoning demayne.

The cats were nosing around the ring of stones, tails high. While everyone else acted nervous, the cats were merely curious. They were said to be infused with demaynic spirits themselves, so maybe the prospect of seeing another demayne appealed to them. Quinn was not so sanguine about it. On several occasions, she discovered that she had drawn Black. It comforted her to have the blade in hand, though what use it would be against a demayne she had no idea.

Probably no use. Though the Shadline blades were mercusine, and stronger and sharper than the mundane weapons of the world, they were not ever discussed as especially powerful against agents of evil.

"You'll put your eye out if you're not careful," Fallo said, sidling up next to her. He, too, had his crummy looking weapon out. But he wasn't putting it through any flourishes. He merely used the tip to pick at the dirt under his thumbnail.

When Quinn did not rise to the bait, he pointed his dagger at Kila. "What do suppose is going through her mind?"

"Nax. Killing the Hargothe." Quinn bobbled her dagger and only succeeded in catching it at the last moment before it struck the floor. "What else does she ever think about?"

"Single-minded focus was my father's greatest attribute, too," Fallo said, nodding. "Unfortunately, he focused his hate on me. But you know what? I would much rather be the focus of his ire than hers."

Quinn shivered. Kila looked particularly small and young at that moment. But the girl watched Marlow with such intensity Quinn wondered if she was in mental communication with him the way she could talk to Oly. "She doesn't suffer fools, does she?"

"Henley is convinced she's Dem-Kisk." It was the most serious tone she had ever heard from Fallo. And indeed, his face was drawn tight, eyes troubled. He looked less monstrous in this light—more exotic, like a painting of a storybook trickster.

"Her willingness to deal with demayne is not a good sign," Fallo said. "I understand why she's doing it. I would do anything to retrieve Miss Lard-fuzz over there if somebody stole her, but I'm not rumored to be the destroyer of the world. A little demaynic dabble on my part is merely stupid. But her doing it . . . ?"

This conversation was doing nothing to ease Quinn's growing apprehension. She decided to change the subject.

"My mother wants me to go to the Garden. I told her I can't. My oath to the Shadline takes precedence over all other responsibilities. But maybe it isn't such a bad thing Mother has negotiated this permission with the Hargothe." She looked pointedly at Kila.

Fallo clicked his tongue and grinned. "Ah, you think she could go in your place, like 'Lina for Nanci.' Hate to be the breaker of bad bits, but Kila looks nothing like you. She's blond, too young, and"—He eyed Quinn's bosom—"a bit too boyish."

Quinn looked away to hide the redness in her cheeks. "Irrelevant. Nobody at the Garden knows my appearance."

"And you think Kila will simply agree to sail off to the Garden under your name? If she were caught posing as a Lady —which is preposterous on the face of it—she would be dragged to the Citadel and thrown from the highest window."

That was a problem. Solvable, Quinn thought. "Henley and Ragin will be there. They could guide her through some basic etiquette. Besides, the Garden would be a place of solace for her."

"And what about her duties as a Shadline? I thought you were supposed to drag her before the Cloak and force the oaths from her."

True. But once Kila had sworn her oaths, Quinn believed the Cloak would see the wisdom of getting Kila out of the city. "The biggest obstacle will be convincing her to go. She may need to be compelled."

"You're suggesting we tie her up and throw her aboard a packet ship? That won't end well for any of us."

He had a fair point. But Quinn believed she also had good points. And if her mother believed Quinn was at the Garden, then Quinn could disappear on Shadline missions without her mother ever knowing. The scheme was a bit selfish, but it was also in Kila's best interests.

Marlow finished whatever he was doing. He'd spent the last quarter of an hour walking from stone to stone, placing his hand on them and muttering to himself. Despite Kila's verbal prods, he would not be hastened in this aspect of the ritual. Probably good to be careful in matters like this.

Marlow rubbed his hands together. "It's time for the summoning."

Kila straightened and hefted her backpack of dragon scales. "What happens if both you and your sister are doing this at the same time?"

"One of us will fail."

"That's it? Nothing happens?"

"If we're lucky." He closed his eyes and removed a ring from his finger. After a deep breath he said, "Do not interrupt me. I have to do this from memory. Do not enter the circle." He began to chant in a language Quinn recognized as of the ancients. She had never taken to it, as the consonants all rubbed together in her ears like dissonant notes on a nyck-elharpa.

Marlow spoke the syllables with ease. Kila watched, brows low over her eyes. There was no fear there. Just determination. And more chilling to Quinn. Rage.

23

THE NIGHT IS CHILL

A light breeze curled across the waters of Brinsto Bay, icy and fresh. The sailors crawling over *Flyer's* decks and up in the rigging didn't seem to notice. Most were barefoot, but they all wore wool coats and thick knit scarves. Henley admired the skill and purpose in all their movements, for he knew at what cost such ability had been earned.

He only wished they would move faster. The disgusting black liquid the Voluptuary had given him was wearing off. His heightened mercus senses were breaking through the numbness.

"Don't worry yerself too sorely, Master Henley," a man said behind him. "We'll be upon the waves in the clack of a capstan."

Gooseflesh rose on Henley's arms. He'd given his name as Kent. He turned, ready to fight, but found only a smiling weathered face, mostly toothless. "Shunny? Is it really you?" he said. "I thought you died on *Nightskirl*."

"Pol smiles," the old sailor said. "Rescued from the waves just afore m'last ragged breath." He leaned toward Henley and put the back of his hand to his mouth. "I watered m'trezz with m'tears when I heard you'd burned, laddie. Truly, I did."

Shunny had been a mentor to Henley during his sailing days aboard *Lark*. Those tough days had instilled in him a love of the sea and an appreciation for the skills of men like Shunny. It took a force of will not to embrace the man. But doing so would do Shunny no favors. It wasn't seemly for sailors to fraternize with passengers on a packet ship.

Misreading the cause of Henley's anxiety, Shunny said, "If Hackworth Keel himself shows up, I'll brain 'im with one of yon belaying pins. Mark me fer Kil's own if I don't."

Ragin was standing ten paces aft, holding Dunne Yples's chain. If he heard Shunny's threat he didn't show it. "That's Ragin Keel. He's a friend now and estranged from his father."

Shunny eyed Ragin, eyes narrowing with suspicion. "If you say so, Master Henley, but with yer father crisped, I do feel a bit o' responsibility fer yer safety. He was a fair man and we had very few weevils in our biscuits. Better'n on this ship, an' it be a goodun."

The bosun shouted at Shunny to get to work, so he scurried off, nimble as a man thirty years his junior. The sight gladdened Henley, but he could not keep from watching the activity dockside. There wasn't much happening there now, the cargo having been loaded already and the longshoremen wandered off to their favorite trezz dens. The tumbling mass of Cheapsgate clung to the edge of the city like a barnacle, and now that darkness lay upon the world, was only lit by furtive lamplight in tiny groupings. Most Cheapsgaters didn't have the coin to buy fish oil for their lamps.

By contrast, *Flyer* was festooned with lanterns, some hanging from the main yards, others mounted along the rail. Still others stood atop the quarterdeck where the great spoked helm wheel was. As the mercus-numbing drug wore off, Henley heard more of the curses coming from able seamen aloft. He also smelled the taint of the Sourwater Inlet that ran along the other side of Cheapsgate.

He walked aft, keeping an eye ashore. He knew better than to ask the captain to hurry, but he couldn't help but move closer to the helm and eavesdrop on the man's instructions.

Captain Vernon Itello was a fat man in a great wool coat that swept to his knees. He wore a somewhat ratty uniform hat that looked like a cast-off from a city Watch officer's dress uniform. He kept his hands behind his back and spoke in a deep rumble to his second in command, who repeated his instructions to the bosun. This protocol was more like Her Enlightened's Navy in manner than the rough and tumble trezzer Henley had served aboard.

"Carriage coming fast, Captain," called a man high on the mizzen mast. He pointed inland, toward the city gate known as the Cheaps. The bosun screamed for the man to keep his eyes on his task and leave the shore to the shoremen.

Alarmed, Henley climbed part way up the ratlines

ascending to the mizzen yards. From here he could see better. Sure enough, an atlen-drawn carriage was tearing down the main merchant lane. Since *Flyer* was the only ship preparing to leave, he had to assume the carriage carried a last-minute passenger, or more likely, a Donse Master sent to take him to the Hargothe.

There was no sign that the captain intended to push off anytime soon. He could hear the rumble of the carriage wheels over the cobblestones and the grunt and squawk of over-worked atlens. Ragin was looking at him, concern pulling at his pale face. Henley motioned for him to take Dunne Yples belowdecks.

It certainly wouldn't do to have the approaching Donse Master recognize Dunne Yples by his mercus abilities. The carriage appeared and screeched to a stop alongside *Flyer*. No sooner had the wheels stopped turning than a familiar Donse Master leaped out, brandishing a short rod. Henley dropped from the lines and put his back to the low rail.

The captain didn't notice, but his second-in-command, Lieutenant Jiles, surely did. The young man had his hands on his hips, brow furrowed. He had the permanently angry face of one surrounded by incompetents. Considering the skill on display all over the ship, this said more about Jiles's poor temperament than their abilities. He stared at Henley, suspicious and judging.

The Donse Master called to the captain. "I demand you put ashore the lad, Henley Mast. He is a runaway acolyte of Til."

The captain ambled to the quarterdeck rail. "Henley Mast is dead, Donse Master. And even were he not, the Way of Til has no authority to command me when I stand on the deck of my ship. Begone. The night is chill and growing chiller."

Henley wanted to stand up and cheer, but he was worried the Donse Master would paralyze him with his mercusine relic. "Captain, do you truly wish to deny the will of the Father? Think, man. When you return here, do you want to be afoul of the Way?"

"You threaten me, do you? I shall note that in my logbook. Goodnight to you, sir. I shall not humor you further except to say no boy by the name of Henley Mast is aboard my ship."

"He is! I can sense his mercusine spark."

That was unfortunate. Sailors didn't like or trust merculyns. They considered them bad luck. Many eyes went to Henley as he cowered by the rail. But the captain didn't look at him. And aboard a ship, the captain was father, king, and god. "Perhaps you indulged too deeply in your evening trezz, Donse Master. I recommend Critt Sanglo's establishment if you need a bed. Ask for Greta! She'll keep you warm."

The ship erupted with howls of laughter. The captain shouted orders to cast off, which were relayed by Lieutenant Jiles and then echoed again by the bosun. Soon the ship was in motion.

Henley remained hidden. The Donse Master shouted curses and came very near to blaspheming as he slandered the captain's mother and sisters. But soon the sails were bulging and the brig began to lumber over the waves. With each passing moment, Henley felt the tension seep from his shoulders.

By and by he discovered the captain had come to stand before him. "Up, lad."

Henley obeyed. As a paying passenger, he didn't have to follow orders beyond what was necessary to keep out of the way. But the captain carried himself in a manner that commanded obedience. And given what he'd done for Henley, Henley was ready to climb the foremast and work in the rigging.

"I knew your father," the captain said. "I wish I could do more than simply keep his sole heir out of the Til's-boys' grip." He offered his hand and Henley took it. "Come, lad. I have a nice bottle of port in my cabin just aching to be opened. Would your other companions care for a thimble-full?"

"Depends on how badly you hate Hackworth Keel."

"Oh, there be no bottom to those depths, lad. I assure you."

Henley grimaced. "Well, that's a problem, because my friend is Hackworth's youngest son."

The grin drained from the captain's round face like a fast out-flowing tide. "A Keel? Aboard *my* ship?"

Henley raised his hands to forestall the oncoming squall of rage. "He's not like the others. He saved my life when my father's house burned. He saved my life as surely you saved mine just now. I swear it."

The fury on the man's bushy brow didn't subside, but with a grudging nod he said, "Tell no one else. Tell the lad to stay in your cabin. If asked about his resemblance to Old Hackworth, tell the sailors Hackworth might be his father, but that he was raised a bastard in the Baths."

Henley couldn't imagine Ragin agreeing to that, but he nodded respectfully. "I'll tell him. But I think when you hear my story you'll be inclined to overlook his parentage. The other man with us is very ill. He has been made insensible by medicines to keep him calm. The chain is for his own protection."

The captain's face softened, but the difference was one of jagged rock worn smooth. It was still rock. "The Sensuals do much good for those who otherwise would suffer the cruelty of the street. Just see that this man does not interfere with my crew and their duties."

Henley went down to the cramped cabin he was to share with his companions. Two bunks folded on iron hinges from one wall. During the day they could be stowed to make room for dressing, or simply for one to sit at the tiny desk built into the bulkhead. The ceiling was low and resounded with the footfalls of men on the main deck. A single window, no larger than Henley's head, penetrated the hull over the desk. In the middle of the room stood an inconveniently placed support beam. A great iron hook thrust from one side, by which a hammock would be slung, providing the third bed.

Henley found Ragin lounging on the top bunk and Dunne Yples sitting on the edge of the bottom one. He had his hands folded in his lap. With his hood up, he appeared to be a man deep in prayer. All that belied that impression was the rasp and gasp of his breath through his slack lips.

The prospect of caring for the man over the coming two-month voyage brought back the shoulder-scrunching feeling of being trapped. Also, bitterness. Why did he have to be burdened with this additional responsibility when he already had so many troubles of his own?

"I'm going to the captain's cabin for a while," he said to Ragin. "He has no love for your family, it turns out. If anyone asks if you're a Keel, he wants you to say you're Keel's bastard, raised by the Way of Ori."

Henley braced himself for the inevitable explosion, but to his surprise Ragin simply shrugged. "That makes sense. More honorable than the truth."

"Dunne Yples will soon be due for his next dose of Finta's drug," Henley said. "I don't know if he eats it easily or if it must be forced down. If you have trouble, come find me. We must not let him start raving about Dem-Kisk around sailors."

Seamen were the most superstitious men alive. One whiff of Dunne Yples' madness and the men would start conspiring to throw him over the side. Ragin only blinked at him, then turned to face the wall, pulling a thin blanket over his shoulder. Henley couldn't blame him.

He backed out of the cabin and headed to the captain's stateroom at the end of the narrow companionway. The ship pitched and rolled as the swells grew longer and deeper. Henley had to brace a hand on the wall to keep upright. He would get used to this, he told himself. A man could adapt to almost anything.

There wasn't much consolation in the thought. He didn't *want* to get used to it. Perhaps he would only be happy once he got used to not wanting anything at all. He was certain such an adaptation would take longer than a two-month voyage. Perhaps he'd never arrive at such peaceful indifference.

Maybe life henceforth would be a rough and unwelcoming sea.

24
______

HER TRUE NAME

Kila dropped her mercusine mask, allowing the smells and sounds of the world to sweep into her awareness. Smoke from the braziers tinged the air with more acrid sting than they did warmth. But their purpose was light. The flickering, open flames cast long, dancing shadows against the walls and ceiling. The fiery glow lit Dunne Marlow's face a deep red and bloodied his teeth as he curled his lips to enunciate the strange words of the summoning.

She had heard him do this once before, so she knew that the chant would go on a while before anything happened. But whether from her own impatience or the actual duration, this time it seemed to take much longer.

And that worried her. Had Marlow's sister and brother already succeeded in summoning Flaumishtak?

She didn't know what she would do if Marlow failed. But another, more sickening, fear had begun to creep into her thoughts. If the Hargothe confronted Flaumishtak to recover

Nax, the old man would almost certainly die. And then so, too, would Nax.

Fallo and Quinn had come to stand with her, their faces made lurid by the same eldritch light as lit Marlow's. Quinn, lovely and fierce. Fallo, hideous and intense. They had come to the Citadel to warn her of the Hargothe's plans. That was true friendship. They would both be much better off running as far from her as they could, like Ragin and Henley had done.

Oly slunk along the far wall, ears alert, tail and spine low. He sent a constant flow of agitation at her, but thankfully no commentary. He wanted Nax to return as much as she did.

Lop was nowhere to be seen. Probably sleeping, or maybe sneaking to the kitchens to nick a snack. There was no sign of mercus power in what Marlow did. He merely spoke weird phrases, very repetitive ones, and kept his eyes focused on the center of the rock formation.

Kila closed her eyes, feeling the mercus now as a tingle in her hands and feet. Somewhere out there was the Hargothe. He could feel her, so she should be able to search for him. But she didn't know what she was looking for.

Frustrating.

She wondered if her presence had intruded into his mind when she had unmasked herself just now. Maybe that would distract him. Or maybe she had simply lit a lantern for Donse Masters to come capture her.

"Let them try," she mumbled.

"What?" Quinn said.

"Nothing. I was just thinking about—"

She fell to the floor, mind erupting in light. A cacophony

of shouts filled the atlen roost, and the rattle of armor and buckles accompanied the boot-stomps of Watch men. From their midst appeared a thickly-bearded Donse Master. He held a short wooden rod in one hand. His eyes were aglow in the radiance of the braziers.

Two of the Watch approached Dunne Marlow. Kila could not see him, for she was frozen into absolute immobility and facing away from him. Even her eyelids failed to blink. Her eyes stung with dryness.

The Watch stopped short of arresting Marlow, for they saw he was engaged in dark practices. Fallo was warning them all that a demayne would soon appear and eat their spines.

The intruding Donse Master ignored all this. "Forget Marlow," he barked, never breaking eye contact with Kila. "This girl is all we need."

Quinn interposed herself between Kila and the furious Donse Master. "I am Lady Quinn Peline. You have already set armed men against me once today. When the Radiant hears of this, you will have much to answer for. She has the confidence of the Hargothe."

This drew the Donse Master's attention. There was a small moment of uncertainty in his face. But it disappeared as he returned his attention to Kila. "It is of no consequence. I could have you put in chains and thrown into a Cheapsgate brothel as a comfort girl for all the sailors ashore. Kila Sigh is all that the Hargothe desires, and I will present her to him myself."

Quinn drew her blade and crouched. "You will have to kill me first."

"And me," Fallo said, his grotesque face made ferocious by a curled lips and brow so deeply scrunched over his nose he could be the demayne Marlow was trying to summon.

The sound of Marlow's chants continued even as the men of the Watch commanded him in nervous tones to desist. Kila struggled to keep panic at bay. Her total vulnerability evoked an animal-like impulse to fight. To escape.

What she needed to do was breathe. And it seemed breathing was the only movement remaining to her. The rod in the Donse Master's hand had to be a mercusine relic of some sort. She remembered Henley speaking of being captured in this very manner.

She brought metals into her vision. Her friends' blades glowed darkly, the brazier bowls brightly. The armor and swords of the Watch came alight with the reddish hues of iron alloyed into steel.

Kila sought the iron in their blood. She would kill them all if she had to. First the Donse Master. His heart appeared to her and she added to its mercusine light. The man clutched at his chest.

Fallo darted in, slicing at the hand holding the rod. Quinn lunged to drive her blade into his flank. Outside of Quinn's vision, Marlow cried out.

Watchmen shouted. Grunts and curses filled the barn. "Mask yourself!" cried Marlow, his voice torn with agony.

Kila sent more glow into the now-wounded and reeling Donse Master.

"Kila Sigh, mask yourself!"

Men began to scream. Fallo and Quinn's faces went green

with demaynic light. Both stumbled away from the array of stones, their ferocity replaced by terror. Kila's mercus extinguished. The wooden rod in the Donse Master's hand began to smoke. The man cried out and released it.

Instantly, movement returned to Kila's limbs. She scrambled to keep her balance. She turned to the stones and discovered Flaumishtak had returned to the realm of humankind.

Kila searched for Marlow. She spotted him prone on the opposite side of the crown formation. Watch men lay around him, two headless. Others were running from the barn. Flaumishtak strode among the bodies. His hooves were shrouded in green fog, but they clopped like horses' feet upon the hardpacked earthen floor.

The stink of burnt hair swirled in the air. His enormous head turned this way and that, hair sweeping back and fading to wisps of smoke at the ends. Two and a half spans high, the beast's head nearly brushed the rafters. Eyes like orbs of flame took in the cowering and wounded Donse Master, who mumbled prayers for Til's intercession between gibbering sobs. The beast's slash of mouth curled at one side, a smile full of evil intent.

Flaumishtak raised a clawed finger and beckoned to the quivering Donse Master. "A tiny morsel," he said to himself as the Donse Master took stiff steps toward him. Kila recognized the effects of willshift even though she could not see the mercusine.

Fallo and Quinn were slowly circling to get behind the beast. They held their daggers forward but looked like tiny children sneaking around an adult who neither cared about their meaningless blades or their mischievous game.

The bearded Donse Master betrayed terror only by his eyes, which were so wide he looked almost comical, like the scandalized grandmother in the mummers' play about the soldier and her twin granddaughters. This expression vanished in an instant when the demayne placed his great claws upon the man's head and, with a twist, ripped it from his shoulders.

Kila looked away. Her friends froze, determination wavering. Kila couldn't blame them, for only a fool would approach a demayne who had just decapitated a man with its bare hands.

More shocking than the total lack of blood was the ongoing activity on the Donse Master's face. His eyes looked all about, and his mouth moved, forming silent pleas. He was, quite obviously, still alive.

His body slumped to the floor and did not move. Flaumishtak brought the man's head close to his own, then turned it to whisper something in his ear. Kila was glad for the dullness of her senses, for she never wanted to know what words the demayne spoke. The Donse Master's eyes squinted shut and his lips parted in a soundless scream. Then all at once his features went slack.

Flaumishtak flung the head away and it rolled into the corner, bearded face fixed in a look of permanent horror.

Now the demayne turned his attention on Kila. *Ah, Delicious One,* he spoke into her mind. *Do not fear me so. I would never squander you for such a momentary flush of pleasure.*

"Stay back," Kila warned, drawing Cayne. "You and I have a deal to complete."

Deal? I do recall something about that. It's been an age. The demayne cocked his head, as if hearing something Kila could not. *Another summons? Interesting. Perhaps there is more sustenance in the offing for me.* He stepped back into the ring of stones. *I sense you have your new Beloved One near. Perhaps he would join me willingly. The spirit of this one resonates more harmoniously with me than the other.*

He was speaking of Nax. He also spoke of Oly. "I'll trade you Beloved for Beloved," she said.

A flush of approval came through the bond from Oly. The cat wanted to go with Flaumishtak.

Go, then, she sent. But Oly being Oly refused.

"We struck a bargain," she said to the beast. "One thousand dragon scales in return for Nax and the bond. I have my payment. I demand you honor your end of the bargain."

Hmm. That does sound familiar, but I do not know any Beloved One called by that name. He raised a fist and the swirl of green rose around him.

Kila lunged, prepared to climb on his back and go wherever the beast went. But other arms caught her up and lifted her from her feet. Reflexively, she lashed out with her blade. It struck home, but merely clicked, as if striking stone.

The demayne vanished in a haze of mercus green, leaving behind fading fog of its unearthly stink. Kila pulled Cayne back to strike again. Marlow had stopped her from going. He shoved her shoulders and she fell backward.

"Do not kill me, Kila Sigh," said Dunne Marlow. He held

his hands out, haggard face full of command. "I just saved your wretched hide. Had you gone along willingly, that would have been the last any of us would have ever seen of you."

With the disappearance of the demayne, the mercus flooded back into Kila's awareness. With it came her vision of metal. Her fury was so great that her friends and Marlow blazed with the iron in their blood.

Marlow held the wooden rod the dead Donse Master had used to paralyze her. He held it forward, his threat clear. "Be calm and count yourself lucky I was able to restrain him from killing us all. I had to give him Dunne Qirl and these poor men of the Watch."

A soft hand touched Kila's elbow. Quinn. She urged Kila to lower Cayne. "Listen to him. I know he can be a bit greedy, but I believe him when it comes to this."

Kila sheathed her blade and looked at the ritual stones. It had all been for nothing. "He's going to strike a deal the Hargothe, isn't he? I thought demayne had to honor their agreements."

"They do," Marlow said, lowering the rod. "But no law-speaker in Starside can weave words more artfully than a demayne. Tell me exactly what he said."

"I reminded him of our bargain. One thousand dragon scales in return for Nax and the bond. He claimed not to know any Beloved One by that name."

"Clever," Marlow said. "And obvious at the same time. Flaumishtak knew that Nax was not her true name. Had you asked for another subject or object in the world, and he would not have been able to squeeze loose from his bargain. But name a cat what you will, that is not its true name."

"But why is he trying to get out of the deal? I have a thousand dragon scales."

Marlow looked truly sympathetic as he tucked the wooden rod into the sash around his robes. "It means he wants to keep Nax more than he wants the scales. That speaks to the incredible value he places on her."

Fallo blew out his cheeks. "You're giving Lop delusions of magnificence. Now she's demanding we summon a demayne to fetch a lamb shank for her." The cat in question had waddled to sit upon Fallo's feet.

Oly was nosing around the exposed—but bloodless—neck of the dead Donse Master.

"Flaumy said he heard another summons. He was eager to go. That has to be the Hargothe." She went to fetch her backpack. She had endured too much to give up. "I'm going there now."

Oly, you can stay or come with me, but get away from that body.

Quinn stepped in front of her. "Think before you act. For once."

Fallo mumbled something about there being more chance that Lop would eat a carrot. Kila threw him a glare, but he merely shrugged.

"What is there to think about?" Kila said. "The only way to get Nax back is to confront the demayne."

"Wait, Kila," Dunne Marlow said. "Quinn is right. The Hargothe would not summon a demayne if he truly thought there was a risk to his own neck. My sister faces much, much more danger. She has never summoned a wily beast like Flaumishtak before. She doesn't have the experience required to put the needed restraints on his actions."

"Then what makes you think the Hargothe will be safe? Flaumishtak blocked me from the mercus. He'll do the same to the old man."

Marlow considered this, but finally shook his head. "Tenn will expect that move. He'll be prepared for it. Had you been properly trained, the demayne would never have been able to do that to you. No, my brother knows how to keep his skin safe. At least long enough to strike a deal with him."

"What could he offer that the demayne would want?" Kila said. "Ten thousand dragon scales?"

"Maybe you," Fallo said softly. A chilling thought, but Kila didn't believe it. The Hargothe would never let her go. And from the way Marlow spat, he didn't believe it either.

"What does a demayne want more than dragon scales?" Quinn asked into the silence.

"What does anyone want?" Fallo said. "Freedom."

Kila noticed Oly was back by the dead Donse Master. She moved toward him and drew her foot back in a warning. She would never actually kick him, but he didn't know that.

He scurried away, sending skin-crawling sensations across her back and neck. He completed his mental assault with a hiss.

"The Hargothe wouldn't set a demayne free," Kila said. "It would kill everyone in sight and then come for me."

"He wouldn't grant it total freedom," Marlow said. "But

he could offer well short of that and still give Flaumishtak unprecedented freedom to move among the people of this city. The Hargothe may even see advantages in the chaos that would create. The lives of the citizenry mean nothing to him. The power he gets from the cat must be very great indeed."

That puzzled Kila. She had been bonded to Nax and noticed no difference in her mercusine abilities, nor had they decreased when Nax had been stolen from her. But perhaps that was from her lack of training. Maybe there were benefits to the bond that were only apparent when one had achieved the Hargothe's mastery. In any event, she didn't care much about why the Hargothe had stolen Nax. She just wanted her back.

"None of this is reason for me to hide," she said. "I want to be there when Nax returns. I have to—"

"You can do nothing, Kila," Marlow said. "You go there and you will become a toy for either the Hargothe or the demayne. Even with all your power, you will be no match for them, untrained as you are." Marlow scanned the barn, taking in the dead. Five men. "You would do well to lie low. Go see Her Enlightened Majesty. Be patient. And most of all, be cognizant of your responsibility. You are the most powerful merculyn in an age, perhaps the most powerful ever born. Whether you are Dem-Kisk or not, you can do great good for the city or you can be its doom."

"I didn't ask for any of this!" Kila shouted. Cinching the shoulder straps of her backpack tighter, she dodged around Quinn and headed into the night. She would accept no responsibility that kept her from Nax. She had lost Wen, so there was nobody left to keep her from doing what she wanted.

Fallo and Quinn trailed after her. She began to run. They kept pace. As they reached the kitchen entrance to the greathouse, Kila moved to go past it and head to the long drive to the Street of the Diadem.

Quinn grunted. "For the sake of all that's good and holy, at least let me call Hagle so we can ride to the abbey. If you run the whole way, you'll be too tired to even do something stupid."

Kila stopped and waved for Quinn to do as she wished. Fallo was a blob of darkness next to her. He didn't speak. But she realized he had not said anything to discourage her from going.

That's because he knew what Lop meant to him. As useless and greedy as the fuzzy black cat was, it filled a gap in Fallo's heart. He knew what horror it would be to have that rent open.

He nudged her with his elbow. "After, we should leave the city."

"And pay our fare with dragon scales?"

"Not by sea. By land. We go through the Moriterren Pass and then through the mountains until we reach Jallisea. From there . . . anywhere." He sounded so serious, almost achy with his desire to leave Starside behind. "But before we can do that, you have to do something." He dug in a pocket and pulled forth a white card. He handed it to her. If she had not been flush with the mercus she never would have been able to make out the elegant hand in which the message had been written.

Tell Kila Sigh to come to me, it read. *The gates will open for her.* She turned over the card. The royal sigil of the Raven-in-flight was embossed on it. The card was a bit stained and the edges bent.

"How long have you had this?" she asked.

The sound of the carriage approaching drew her eyes, but Fallo simply reached for the card. He put it back in his jacket pocket. "A while. But that particular message is fairly new. I'll explain later, but I've come to learn that her instructions are worth following."

The atlens squawked irritably for having been put to harness again. Hagle hunched under his thick parka and an extra heavy blanket of sailcloth pulled over his head and shoulders. Quinn opened the door from the inside and beckoned to them to enter. From the barn came Lop and Oly, loping and signaling to their bonded humans that they were getting on the carriage or else. Marlow didn't appear. The carriage began to roll.

"Just going to walk in the front door?" Fallo asked Kila.

Kila smiled, a grin full of knife-edged menace. "They won't do this in the cathedral. Not even the Hargothe is ready for that scandal. They'll be in the dungeons or near the crypts."

"There are a lot of Donse Masters between the front door and the crypts," Quinn said. "And after last time I doubt they'll let me trick them with promises of large donations."

"We're not going in through any door at all."

"What?" Fallo said. "Are you going to dymense us in?"

Kila frowned. "What does that mean?"

Fallo's brow waggled. "Apparently that I know more about

the mercus than you do. Dymensing is what the demayne did when he vanished in a swirl of mercus green. At least, that's what the Voluptuary told me it means."

"No mercusine tricks needed," she said. "As long as you're not too afraid of heights."

For some reason this didn't have the effect Kila had hoped for. Quinn unsheathed her dagger and grinned with excitement. Fallo merely arched one side of his eyebrow and leaned back. "Where you go, I go, Kila Sigh. Til help me."

Kila snorted. Til hadn't helped her yet. She wouldn't count on his help now.

25

A BITTER MORSEL

The Hargothe had patience thrust upon him over the many years of his solitude in the crypts. The quality was not natural to him, and now that he had the strength to stand upright—and withstand the assault of the world upon his heightened senses—he had lost what little patience he had developed.

Yet here he was again, reliant on another. It burned his soul. Juni stood at the lectern now, reading and re-reading the words of the summoning. The Hargothe knew the language of the builders as well as anyone, but in this context they were nonsense, a string of words all preceded by "Come, if it pleases Father Kil."

Yes, the Hargothe thought. Kil's power was great in the world because of the weakness of man. The Hargothe would invoke Kil's power whenever required.

Juni's voice rose, words coming faster now. Not a spark of the mercus illuminated her, and there was no stirring upon the mercusine web emanating from her or the stones. It was demaynic magic, adjacent to the subtle world of the mercusine. If anything troubled the Hargothe about what Juni did, it was his blindness to its effects.

The spark he did feel was Kila Sigh's. He dared not leave the burning chamber during the ritual. And he didn't want to summon any of the acolytes or servants who would inevitably gossip about what they saw. For the time being he'd have to leave Kila be.

He felt the approach of the demayne, a haze of mercusine, like a fog. He knew from his experience before putting out his eyes that a haze of green was even now materializing in the Crown formation on the floor.

The beast was coming.

Juni's voice stayed steady. She knew that any wavering of confidence would open her to danger. Demayne did not relish being called when they were restrained under the names of the stones. They were sly beings, and the slightest misstatement of the rite might give them an opening through which to slip their restraints and come more fully into the world.

An incautious demayncor might find himself possessed by the summoned entity, hostage to its whims. Many believed the storied murderer, Olyle the Eviscerater, had been demayne-possessed.

The flood of mercusine power that came into being stunned the Hargothe. He could not imagine holding such raw power. Even Kila Sigh did not yet shine so brightly. He focused his attention on his mental wards. He was prepared to defend his own access to the mercusine, for blocking him from it would be the first instinct of a demayne.

The smell of singed hair and exotic spices filled the room, as did the throaty rumble of the beast itself. The Hargothe reached for its shape, using his mercusine senses. They painted a portrait of something hulking and vaguely man-shaped. It was clothed in rich, thick fabrics. The sound of its breathing was of particular note, for it was not at all like a man's breath. The nasal passages were too wide, the lungs too vast. It reminded him more of a horse's breath, and it even snorted in a bestial manner.

Juni had fallen silent, but the Hargothe knew she was engaged in a mental conversation with the demayne. He waited, forcing himself to keep his hands clasped before him, head up, eyelids open. No one who saw him would think him the slightest bit apprehensive. And truly, he wasn't. Eager, yes. It was time to offer the demayne something he knew it longed for. He merely needed to place the necessary limitations on it so that when the time came there remained a realm for the Hargothe to rule.

Juni must have completed her own negotiations, for the beast turned to face the Hargothe, its hooves making a hard clops on the stone floor. "You wish to bargain." A simple, declarative statement. Direct.

"I do, demayne. No doubt you recall coming to my chamber and appropriating my Beloved One. Kila Sigh and my brother, Marlow, made a deal with you to do so. No doubt you arranged it such that the price was impossible for her to pay. That was wise."

"Flattery is unnecessary, Tenn. Make your offer."

That the beast knew his name was a shock. He doubted Juni had told him, which meant that Marlow had. Oh, how that man was going to suffer someday. The Hargothe was tempted to offer Marlow to the demayne at that very instant. "Return to me my Beloved One, and I will grant you more freedom in this world than you have ever enjoyed before."

A sigh, no different than a horse's. "Continue."

"Five kills per day. No Donse Masters, no men of the Watch. The Citadel, too, is off limits . . . for now."

"You offer too little. But give me Kila Sigh and I will ask nothing else."

"What? *That* girl? I'll admit she is strong in the mercus, but why not ask for Her Enlightened Majesty? Or perhaps the Voluptuary?" He was, in fact, considered offering them to the demayne, but that would be dangerous for him. If they had wards set, they might trap the demayne and finagle the Hargothe's name out of him.

Her Enlightened Majesty certainly would have such precautions. Besides, the Hargothe wanted to attend to Her Enlightened's downfall in a more personal fashion. As for Kila Sigh . . . she was out of the question. The demayne certainly knew that. This was his opening salvo, a bargaining position.

"I'll give you seven daily kills, one of the Watch every tenday." A bit of fear in the Watch might serve him well, for the citizenry would soon notice the rash of murders in the city. The Watch would begin arresting anyone who came under the slightest suspicion. The people would lose trust. Her Enlightened would lose favor as she failed to step in and help. It was marvelous.

"Ten kills per day," the beast said. "And I care nothing for the Watch, or any other distinction among men you make. A man is a boy is a girl is a woman to me."

"In that case, I'll give you ten, provided you take five per day from the slums of Cheapsgate."

Her Enlightened Majesty had allowed that pit of depravity to stew for far too long. And why? It would be nothing for the Watch to set fire to it. Let Til draw into his arms the worthy, and Kil sweep up the ash of the remainder.

Demaynic murder would soon create riots among the stupid and filthy Cheapsgaters. Maybe then Her Enlightened would send in the Watch to do what should have been done following the first uprising against Duri LiMinluit.

"It is agreed," the demayne said. "Name the Beloved One you wish returned."

The Hargothe pursed his lips. He had not expected this question. He wondered how many of the spark spirits this creature had collected. "You know quite well which I want. I call her Ishmilla. Kila Sigh called her Nax."

"I do not know a Beloved One of either name."

The Hargothe struck, lashing out with mercusine horrors into the beast's mind. The effort met with the mercus equivalent of a stone wall. The Hargothe could no more access the demaynic mind than he could travel to its otherworld home.

Fuming, he folded his arms and squeezed his own elbows. The wheeze of his own furious breaths came especially loudly to his ears. The experience reminded him of confronting older boys when he was small, before he'd had the slightest glimmer of mercus awakening. That feeling of helplessness against brute strength had kindled a rage in his breast that had never been extinguished.

The beast huffed a horsey breath of impatience. "If you cannot name what you wish returned, I don't see any reason to remain here. You bore me."

"Eleven kills."

"But kills have no value to you. Do you not see? It costs you nothing to give what requires no sacrifice of heart, or even effort of body."

"He's right, Tenn," Juni said.

She must have gloried in being able to side with a demayne against him. She would come to regret that someday. How he would revel in the moment when she realized her agony was her own doing.

The beast had lured him into this weakened bargaining position so expertly he formed a grudging respect for it. Not that he didn't intend to consign it to a special hell of its own once his power had grown sufficiently.

So, it wanted more than permission. It wanted sacrifice. For what reason? Did a demayne draw sustenance from the suffering of others? Or did it enjoy merely bringing the powerful of this world into check through its leverage over them?

It kept asking him to name the Beloved One. Interesting detail there. Perhaps if he could divine what name it had given to his Ishmilla, the beast would be forced to return her. Demayne did live by a weird sort of contractual code. But divining a name was the same as guessing the name. An impossibility.

It was back to negotiating. "You require a sacrifice, then I give to you my own brother to do with what you will." The burn chamber filled with a roar. The Hargothe covered his ears and could not refrain from wincing. Only once the roar had quieted did he realize the demayne had been laughing.

"A disingenuous offer, Tenn. You feel nothing but enmity for your kin. Spare me offers of this sort. Present an offer in good faith or say nothing at all."

The Hargothe saw now why the demayne had opened the negotiations with a request for Kila Sigh. With the name loophole as leverage, the demayne had figured it could demand far more than some violent freedoms. So now the Hargothe was pinned between block and the whipaxe. What did he have that he was willing to part with?

What did he value? Only what he required for his plans. To sacrifice any of it was to put his plans in jeopardy. Kila Sigh would be a source of immense power to him. Surely the demayne understood that. Besides, he craved the flavor of her mercusine flow. He had indulged in it before, and the thought of handing her over to this beast made him sour with jealousy. She was his. His.

Same for the boy, Henley. A powerful lad, if only a fraction of what Kila could become.

But he was the answer. While the Hargothe felt the same sort of jealous ownership of the boy, he didn't absolutely require Henley for his plans.

He wouldn't cough up the concession easily. He thought

he might get more from the exchange than his beloved Ishmilla. "I give you Her Enlightened Majesty, my beloved sovereign. Any wards she might prepare would be nothing to you. I simply require also that you teach me the mercusine trick of dymensing. And when you have drained her, that you bring her remains to me. For study."

For display in the cathedral. He'd hang her upside down and robed in harlot's scarlet. He personally would damn her in the sight of Til as a witch.

"You think me a fool, do you?" the demayne said. Its hoof struck stone with an impatient stomp. But it didn't vanish, which told the Hargothe that it was intrigued by the turn of the negotiations. "Of all the humans in this city, she is the one I desire most. But I dare not collect her. You know this, of course."

"Nevertheless, consider her yours. If you choose, you may go after her. And it *is* a great sacrifice to me, for she figures greatly in my plans."

The demayne didn't answer this claim for a few moments as it considered. "I feel that you speak a partial truth. She is part of your plans and losing her to me is a sacrifice, but not a great one. Increase your offer."

"I cannot include Kila Sigh. To do so would be to sacrifice the entirety of my plans. Unless you would grant me an equal weight of her mercusine reserves . . ."

The demayne huffed and snorted. The Hargothe couldn't tell whether it was humorless laughter or mere disgust.

It said, "I have never granted the slightest spark to a

mortal. The mercusine belongs to the gods. Demayne harvest what we can for ourselves."

Feeling more strongly footed in the dickering, the Hargothe now made his concession. "There is another merculyn who I could spare, grudgingly. He is untrained. You could perhaps keep him alive until he has come into the fullness of his power."

"I know of whom you speak. I feel him upon the mercusine, though he fades from Starside with every passing moment. I would know his name."

"Are we agreed, then? You will give to me the Beloved One you took from my chamber, and reveal to me the art of dymensing. In return, I'll grant you release to claim the boy, Henley, to use for whatever purpose you desire."

"And all you offered prior. Eleven kills per ten-day. Her Enlightened Majesty should I decided to pursue her."

"On the condition you return her body to me when you are finished with it. The Abbey and Citadel are off limits for your kills."

"Remove the restriction of the Citadel, else I cannot claim the woman."

The Hargothe felt this last demand was merely negotiating for a sense of balance and not due to any particular need of the demayne's. In all, it was a much dearer deal than he had anticipated, and one fraught with risk. But he felt righteous in his actions and sure that the force of destiny was with him.

Still, he paused.

Something was pulling at his attention. A strange scrabbling noise coming from above. He had a moment's revelation before the demayne began to laugh. One by one, three presences dropped from the flue above the room. They landed, catlike and tense. He smelled atlen dung on their feet.

"Don't call me Delicious One, Flaumishtak!" came Kila Sigh's voice. "You will find I'm a bitter morsel."

The demayne laughed. "I am delighted that you finally joined us. It was boring me to continue stalling the negotiations with the Hargothe."

Juni was chomping with fury. "Quinn Harlow Peline! I don't know *what* you have gotten yourself into this time." Juni sounded like the scold she was. But it didn't surprise the Hargothe to learn that his niece had taken up with Kila in this caper. There was something wild and unnatural about both girls.

"And who is this who joins us?" he said as calmly as he could. "Our erstwhile merculyn and her band of brigands? Is the third your sickly brother?"

"Brother, yes. Sickly, no." The answering voice did not surprise him at all. He'd long known that the supposedly dead Fallo PiTorro had taken up with Kila. What did surprise him was the odd swirl of darkness that surrounded the boy. A void of mercusine, as if he were masked just as Kila was. But this was an external shield, not of his making. He didn't possess the slightest spark, but someone had granted him a weird absence. The effect was to make him utterly invisible within the Hargothe's sense of the room. Even his words seemed to come from all directions at once.

Each of the three intruders eluded the Hargothe's senses in different ways. He could smell and hear Kila, but she was absent upon the mercusine. PiTorro emitted all the senses, but the Hargothe could not pinpoint from where they originated. And Quinn was utterly silent, though he knew where she was through his sense of the room. Clearly, each had some mercusine interference. He had to assume that Quinn and PiTorro bore mercusine artifacts, quellers of different sorts. As sizable as the burn chamber was, it felt cramped with all the bodies now occupying it.

"I agree, demayne," he said. "I accept your deal."

A brightening of mercusine was followed by the return of a familiar presence. A voice came to him, hateful and accompanied by thrills of horror that scurried down his spine. *Let me go!*

Welcome, Ishmilla.

26

A GOLDEN LIGHT

Kila's voice rasped in the echoey chamber. "Nax!" The chill in the burn chamber stung her cheeks. Flaumishtak emanated a cold as deep as midwinter dawn. The smell of burning hair and other, sweeter, things was not as present to her as it had been in the atlen barn. This close to the Hargothe, she hadn't dared to risk dropping her mask.

Instead, she backed away from the walking corpse-like man. She found herself near Radiant Peline, a woman of middle years who wore a luxurious belted coat with ruffled blouse and wide-legged trousers beneath. Her hair was just like Quinn's, dark and thick. The two could have been sisters. Radiant Peline looked at Kila with a blend of suspicion and interest.

The demayne stood in the Crown of stones. It had been pure luck that the formation had not been centered beneath the chimney flue, or all three of them would have landed inside of it. According to Marlow, that would have put them completely at the demayne's mercy.

But all of this was peripheral to the object of her focus: Nax. The slim gray cat looked well. She stood near the demayne, crouched warily, ears forward and tail flicking. Her amber eyes were locked on the Hargothe, and her mouth parted to emit a soft hiss of hatred.

"Naxie," Kila called again. The cat looked at her, let out a mournful mewl, then retreated to hide behind the demayne. A rustling in Kila's backpack reminded her to free Oly.

She removed the pack and loosened the straps. Oly hopped out and spat at her. *You delayed so I would suffer.*

Next time I'll drop you down the chimney.

Oly responded with a flush of indignation that made Kila's chest go hot.

"Come now, Beloved One," Flaumishtak said to Nax. "You are returned to your bonded one. Do not by shy."

"I have a trade to offer," Kila said. She was aware of the Hargothe edging closer to her, one slow step at a time.

Flaumishtak looked at her. The flaming eyes flared, and the odd, bulbous nose twitched. She got the impression he was sniffing the air to test her scent. "Speak your trade," he said.

"Oly was bonded to my brother, who has since died. Oly bonded to me, but neither of us wants this to continue. Oly would willingly go with you if you return Nax's bond to me."

"Intriguing, but I do not know any Beloved One of that name."

"It matters not," the Hargothe snapped. "The animal is mine and is not this demayne's to barter away. We have struck a deal on that matter just now. So you, my dear, have arrived too late. Furthermore, I granted the demayne eleven kills per ten-day. I see two possible victims present, though I would ask him to spare my niece."

Radiant Peline moved in front of her daughter. "I control this summoning, and I forbid the murder of my daughter."

Fallo stood next to Quinn. Both had their daggers in their hands; both stood poised to fight. Kila dumped the scales from the backpack. "There you go. At *least* a thousand," she said. "I have delivered payment. Honor our agreement."

"Simply name the Beloved One. Must I repeat myself a thousand times?"

"Her name is Nax. The Hargothe calls her Ishmilla. She is the cat who stands behind you in the ring of stones."

"But what is her name? Do you expect me to merely trust that she was once bonded to you?" The beast laughed and beckoned to Oly, who approached the stones with slow caution, stopping frequently to test the air. Something was off in the demayne's manner. He was insisting she use some unknown name for Nax. But he had struck a deal with the Hargothe. Why didn't the beast vanish and begin killing all over Starside?

Kila could only guess that it wanted to enjoy her frustration. But on second thought, she considered the beast's apparent fondness for the cats. He had obviously kept Nax well during her time with him. "Just grab the cat and let's go," Fallo said. "Worry about the bond later."

Kila sent to Oly, *Tell Nax to come to me.*

Oly didn't reply. He was looking up at the demayne, his body now gone absolutely still.

"Quinn!" the Radiant snapped. "Leave this place. Walk straight out. Ignore anyone who tries to stop you."

"I'm not leaving without my friends," Quinn said. "And I wouldn't have to be here if you had done the right thing and refused to help this crusty old man."

"I did it for you. So you would be free to go to the Garden."

"I'm *never* going to the Garden."

Kila kept an eye on the Hargothe. He kept trying to sneak closer to her. She wondered if he thought getting his hands on her would help him break through her mask. She moved closer to Flaumishtak. Trusting the stones to hold him took more nerve than leaping across a wide alleyway on the rooftops, but she had to get closer to Nax.

Oly, tell Nax to come to me.

She can't. Flaumishtak won't give her permission.

Kila tried a new tactic. *Ask Nax what name the demayne wants me to use.*

"Send my Beloved One to me," the Hargothe said to the demayne.

"She is terrified of you," the demayne said. He seemed irritated by this.

"Nevertheless, she is mine. We agreed you would return her to me. Compel her."

"I would, but I am being restrained."

The Hargothe spun on his sister. "Why are you interfering? Allow the demayne to fulfill my bargain!"

"I need your assurances that you will do as we agreed. You have granted this beast kills and did not restrict it from killing me and mine."

"That is not my concern."

Kila could barely track what was happening. Clearly, Radiant Peline was in control of the demayne while it occupied the circle of the stones. That was good. "Radiant Peline," she said. "Tell the demayne to turn the cat over to me."

The Hargothe seethed, thin lips spraying spittle as he spun on his sister. "Have a care, Juni, for you come close to breaking the summoning. If you prevent the demayne from closing the deal, you may violate the restraints the stones provide."

Radiant Peline looked ghastly in the brazier light, and her confusion was obvious in the drawn look of her eyes and cheeks. Her daughter was tugging on her cloak and telling her to help Kila. The demayne watched, a sharp-toothed grin splitting its slash of mouth.

Oly, what is Nax's name? Kila sent to Oly.

It's Nax, you idiot. Oly stepped onto a stone, then slipped across the line and into the circle. The bond between him and Kila ceased to exist, as if severed by a blade. His presence, which had never fit her mind, released. The moment was both a relief and a ripping away of something essential. Kila dropped to her knees, the room swimming in her vision. The mercus mask she'd held so easily vanished.

The Hargothe struck like a snake, his agility a shock to all who witnessed it. He clamped a claw-like hand onto her head.

The eel-squirm of his mind penetrated hers. She recoiled, but he held with surprising strength.

I have you now.

Reeling from the hollowness of Oly's vanishing, Kila could not keep track of what the Hargothe was doing. The sensation of a thousand fingers wriggling into the nooks and crannies of her consciousness made her scream with revulsion.

Quinn was shouting something, and Kila saw her raise her dark blade to charge. The young woman was yanked back as Fallo hooked his arm around her throat and pressed his own rusty blade to her neck. His strange face was twisted in a wooden snarl. His limbs went stiff and trembled as he fought his own actions.

Quinn drove her elbow into his gut, but he didn't flinch.

The Hargothe was willshifting him, forcing him to hold Quinn back.

Kila gasped to see how strong the Hargothe had become. For even as he assaulted her mind, he controlled Fallo's body. His greedy probings continued even as he wrapped a boney arm around Kila's waist and drew her into a reverse embrace, one hand still on her head. He had taken away her physical strength, leaving her helpless.

You possess such power still? his voice curled into her mind. *You gave me so much, yet you are utterly renewed. An infinite source for me. And Flaumishtak is correct, so delicious!*

The last time he had intruded into her mind she had been able to cling to Nax's presence. That had given her the strength to endure what the Hargothe did. Now she had no such refuge.

Flaumishtak laughed, his rumbling, throaty mirth resounding in the chamber. Quinn sliced at Fallo, driving her blade into his thigh. His face writhed as he fought both Quinn and the Hargothe. Radiant Peline drew back, face horror-stricken. Nax's cries rose as if from far away.

Vision blurring, the world darkening, Kila saw Oly resting comfortably in Flaumishtak's huge arms. The cat's eyes squinted at Kila, dismissive and disdainful. Fallo finally lost his grip on Quinn, and she slashed at his other leg. He fell back, body stiff as a plank. His head struck stone and his body went limp.

Quinn rushed at the Hargothe, blade raised for a killing strike. But Kila knew it would do no good. She had tried to stab the man once before and had discovered him protected by a mercusine ward that made his flesh hard as stone.

Even that didn't matter, for Quinn stumbled to a stop and froze a pace away, arm still raised high, face frozen in a snarl. The Hargothe had simply moved his willshift to her. Seeing this, the Radiant screamed in fury.

Kila closed her eyes, feeling like a leaf flying on a gust of wind. She would come down when and where the whims of the Hargothe took her. At the moment, he was pulling at her reservoir of the mercus, the molten-hot flow searing her. She knew better than to try to ash him, for he would simply absorb her power more quickly.

Kila sought metals. Their glow flared all around. As a passive skill, the vision didn't require her to use the mercus so much as notice it. The Hargothe probed deeper into her mind. A familiar tickle brushed in her consciousness. For a second she thought Oly had decided to renew his bond. It felt ill-suited to her and all wrong, like a shirt too tight under the arms.

There it is, came the Hargothe's voice.

It wasn't Oly seeking to establish the bond, it was the Hargothe. If he did, she would never be free, even if she could escape this chamber. Even if she remained masked, he would always know where she was.

Squinting, she stretched her mercusine awareness to Cayne, still sheathed on her thigh. Her hands could not move, so she focused all her attention to feel the shape of the hilt, as she had done with the window latch outside of Highest Binel's quarters.

The mercus raged in her as the Hargothe sapped it. He used her own power to strengthen the noose he had slipped around her mind. She felt it tighten. Without knowing how, she shied away. The words "I'm not willing" popped into her mind. She repeated them. The tightening bond slowed.

"Oly," she called aloud. "You promised Wen you'd look after me." The words barely escaped her lips, for she seemed to have no breath. A great weight clamped around her chest. Her fingers curved, seeking the pommel of her blade though they were nowhere near it. Even such a tiny movement took enormous strength.

Relax, Kila Sigh, the Hargothe said into her mind. *Submit to the inevitable.*

Nax screamed and hissed. But the sound was closer now. Kila opened her eyes and saw the little gray at the edge of the circle of stones. Flaumishtak looked on with blazing eyes.

Quinn remained frozen, lips curled back in a permanent snarl.

The Radiant Peline was looking from her daughter to the Hargothe to the demayne. Her face held nothing but anger. Kila felt the mercusine firmness of Cayne brush her fingertips, just as she had remotely felt the window latch. She didn't dare try to force it or she'd lose it.

Surrendering to the nameless world, Kila finally grasped her blade with mercusine fingers. With a thought, Cayne leapt from the sheath, ringing like a bell, and rose to float in front of her face. The black steel absorbed the light, though it emitted its own strange glow of mercusine violet.

The Hargothe's noose tightened more securely around her mind. Constrained by the Hargothe's embrace and mercusine probings, she could only sense the Hargothe's body through her mercus perception. She squeezed her eyes shut to block out all distraction. Only the glow of metal filled her mind. The violet of Cayne, the red of the iron in everyone's blood. Quinn's body was a blazing statue a pace away. Fallo's blood spilled onto the floor. Radiant Peline's limbs flushed in preparation for attack as she stooped to pick something off the floor.

The brazier stands flamed with coppery light, and deep within the stone of the chamber walls ran veins of metals like the filmy star-cloud seen on moonless nights.

Cayne's hilt firmed in her mercusine grip. She sent the blade at the Hargothe. Cayne became a streak of violet, a lightning strike across the color-storm of her vision. A clank resounded in the chamber and the Hargothe cried out.

Cayne ricocheted from his skull, encountering the impossible hardness he maintained under his skin.

Quinn fell forward, suddenly freed. She screamed and mentally thrust with her dark blade. It scratched across the Hargothe's back, rasping and sparking as his mercusine armor deflected the edge.

The Radiant followed her daughter in, Fallo's blade now in her fist. She grunted as she thrust the tip at the Hargothe's neck. A sharp ping resounded and her blow glanced off, the blade's dull edge nearly catching Kila's ear. The rusty blade gave off a mercusine tone, like a brass gong, as it passed.

With a mental scream, Kila sent Cayne in again, arrowing for the Hargothe's chest. Suddenly the claw-like grip on her head released, and the noose he sought to slip onto her mind frayed and dissipated. The draw on her mercusine powers stopped, and the effect nearly blinded Kila as the rush threatened to consume her.

With the return of her power, Cayne flew to her. The blade had come home, leather wrapped hilt pressing to the hot flesh of her palm.

Kila straightened, shrugging her shoulders and sucking in a deep breath. She turned to find the Hargothe slouching away, his hands over his head to ward off another blow. Quinn was circling, feinting and slashing in quick strokes. Her mother moved to block the passage out of the chamber. But she was watching Kila, mouth open with disbelief. Kila stalked closer, now flush with enormous energy. Her scalp tingled with power, and her blond locks flew about as if caught in a whirling wind.

"YOU DARE TRY TO BOND ME?" she screamed at the old man. Power coursed in her arms and legs, the climb to the Eerie and all subsequent exertions forgotten. She felt that she could leap straight up the flue and land somewhere in Cheapsgate if she so desired.

His face went slack and turned pale as a fish's belly. Spittle dripped from his lower lip. He looked up at her from his crouch, hate etched into every line on his face.

A growing splotch of blood stained his robes where Cayne's last strike had finally penetrated his mercusine armor. He was worn down. His defenses now lost. Quinn continued to harry him.

"Do not kill him yet," Kila said. "He still possesses the bond to Nax. If he dies, she dies."

She turned to the demayne, who stroked Oly's head with black claws. The cat purred and reveled in the attention.

"We had a deal, Flaumishtak. One thousand dragon scales. Here they are." Kila kicked the pile of glistening scales, sending them scattering and tinkling across the floor. "Honor it."

"I merely need the name, girl. It shouldn't be so hard."

"Her name is NAX!"

Something beyond sound came with her shout, a reverberation that was not attributable to the echoey nature of the chamber. There were other notes pronouncing Nax's name with her. They were low, resonant, and beyond the range of Kila's voice. The floor trembled with her pronouncement and drifts of dust fell from the ceiling.

A sudden silence held the chamber, and a golden light

pulsed on her words as the sound left her lips. The glow found Nax, engulfed her. And then all was still.

Flaumishtak staggered backward. Oly mewled in annoyance.

Nax stepped across the stones. Kila was sent to her knees again as a warm rightness claimed her. The force of the returning bond stole her breath. Her heart paused as a flow of relief, love, and endless warmth flamed in her chest.

Nax had returned.

And suddenly the warm press of the slim gray's body was on her legs. Kila scooped Nax from the floor pressed the animal's soft whiskers to her cheek. Though the return of wholeness was a relief, it didn't mask the feelings Nax sent through the renewed bond. The cat's rage and ferocious hatred for the Hargothe joined Kila's.

Nax sent a command. *Kill him.*

Words and intention were simultaneous. Kila set Nax on her feet and faced the horrid old man.

It was time. Seeing the murderous intentions so clearly written on her face, the Hargothe lashed out with his mercusine probes.

Kila deflected them as easily as she could a child's slap. Combining scent and sound into her own unskilled mental bolt, she gripped him in a willshift. His body stiffened as he fought it, but her will held firm.

You are outmatched on the field of the mind, he said into her head. She stepped toward him, willshifting his arms apart. Her last knife strike had blotched the front of his robe with blood. She would finish it.

"Demayne," the Hargothe rasped. "You must satisfy the rest of *our* bargain."

"And so I must." The demayne laughed again, and Kila felt a wash of icy air sweep past her. The Hargothe convulsed, folding his arms across his chest despite Kila's attempt to keep them spread.

The Hargothe gasped, eyeless sockets gaping. "I see. Yes. I see it!" He raised a trembling fist over his head and squeezed his lids shut. A swirl of green appeared at his feet and quickly rose.

"No. No. I will not allow you to go!" Kila threw Cayne with all the power of her arm and her mercus. The blade left a blurry trail of violet as it flashed into the green. And then the Hargothe was gone.

Cayne clattered into the stone wall above Radiant Peline's head and fell to the floor. All that remained in the place where the Hargothe had stood was a slick of his blood. The room was filled with gasping breaths, from Kila, from Quinn, from the Radiant, and from Fallo.

Quinn ran to the boy's side and drew his head into her lap. "I'm sorry, Fallo. I had to help her."

Fallo rubbed the back of his head, but didn't make any effort to extricate himself from her grasp. His legs wept blood from two wounds.

Oly says you are stubborn, Nax sent. The gray leapt into Kila's arms.

Oly would know. He's as stubborn as he is faithless.

He sees differently. But now that I am here, he must go.

But I'm not done with Flaumishtak. She rounded on the

demayne. "Why did you send the Hargothe away? I was going to kill him."

"I did not send him away, Delicious One," he said. "I met the terms of our agreement. I taught him to dymense."

"Teach me. I must go after him. I'll give you a thousand more scales."

"Not for ten thousand dragon scales would I teach you. They no longer have value to you." He motioned with his claw and the scales arced to him, stacking in his palm with a stutter of sharp clicks. "Exactly one thousand. Let it not be said that Flaumishtak does not meet his bargains." Thousands more scales still lay upon the floor, spilling from the backpack.

He glanced at the Radiant. "Well?"

The Radiant remembered that she had summoned the beast. Before Kila could stop her, the woman flung her hands apart. "Begone."

The demayne vanished in mercus green.

27

TO BE SOLD AND TRADED

Flyer leapt over lively waves, leaning hard to port on a westerly tack. Ragin now lay on the bottom bunk, chin over the edge, bucket directly below. He had lost all of the small meal Henley had brought him courtesy of Captain Itello.

A small candle lantern swung from a beam, making the small cabin waver with a weak light that deepened the shadows. But there was no shadow darker than the one occupying the top bunk. From where Henley lay in his hammock, the large black mound of Dunne Yples seemed to suck in the light. Henley supposed the effect was a product of his own dark thoughts.

Getting the man to swallow Finta Sahng's bolus of mind-numbing medicine hadn't been as difficult as he'd expected. The man possessed virtually no will and seemed to accept whatever was pressed into his hand at mealtimes.

The ship thrummed with noise and tension. The wind

pressed the sails and made the rigging hum, and the great beams and planks that comprised the hull never ceased in their complaints. It was a familiar song to Henley, and it reminded him of better times.

Ragin retched again but didn't have anything left in his stomach. Henley pitied the older lad his weakness. Perhaps Henley's only remaining fortune was his immunity to the rising and falling of the ship. In fact, the swing and sway of his hammock was finally lulling him into drowsiness.

A tingle at the edge of awareness pried him from the edge of sleep. The smell of acrid smoke jerked him completely awake. Fire on a ship meant certain death. The candle was protected by glass, but a draft made it flicker and spit. Then the cabin went green, and the smell of burning hair made Henley cough.

Ragin looked up, face green with sickness and the flare of eerie light. Dunne Yples turned on his bunk and pulled back his hood. His mad eyes absorbed the green and his lips pulled back in a snarl.

The whole cabin filled with icy air and a looming presence. A giant figure maned with smoke and shrouded in thick robes hulked over Henley. "Ah, my gift," the beast said to him. "I see now why the Hargothe prized you so."

Henley struggled to jump from the hammock, but his fingers became entwined in the netting and his blanket came alive to squeeze around his legs.

"Save your strength for the voyage, lad," the demayne said. "You need not fear me."

Ragin fell from his bunk and popped up, holding his sick-up bucket over his head. "Begone!"

"You again?" the beast said, amused by Ragin's pitiful display of defiance. "Have you not learned to run when faced with superior strength?"

"You know this thing?" Henley said to Ragin.

"It came for Kila, twice. It does the Hargothe's bidding."

The demayne snorted and narrowed its flaming eyes. "I do not *serve* the Hargothe. It is true that we have struck a bargain. For instance, he has given this young man to me."

"I am not property to be sold and traded," Henley said. The beast's presence had awakened a familiar heightening of the senses. He knew it to be part of his mercus talent, but he didn't have the faintest idea how to use it for his own defense. "Leave us be."

"Or what?" the demayne said. It didn't seem effected by the motion of the ship. Though its height forced it to slouch beneath the low ceiling, it stayed upright as the ship tilted under its feet. "Will you threaten me?"

The frightful hell-spawn flourished a clawed hand, and a burst of red fire plumed into its palm. "I could end you all in any number of ways. I could rip your heads from your shoulders and consume your mercus and your souls. I could have ashed that one on several occasions," he said, pointing to Ragin. "But I do not kill without discrimination. There are consequences for all actions, and not just in this realm of humans."

Dunne Yples had managed to get seated upright, his legs

dangling from the edge of his bunk. His face had gone from animal rage to something akin to childlike wonder.

Henley stopped struggling against the hammock that squeezed him into immobility. "You haven't killed me, so what is your intention?"

"You have something I desire. I have your life in my hands. I am here to make a bargain."

Ragin hurled the bucket. It glanced from a spot in the air a foot from the demayne's face, deflected by a casual gesture of mercusine. The wooden bucket clunked onto the deck, splattering its contents across the planks. The stink of it was worse than the burning smell of the demayne.

"What do you want?" Henley asked, gritting his teeth to stifle a gag. "All I possess is in this room."

"That is not true, for your Beloved One is on the deck—creeping from shadow to shadow to avoid notice of these superstitious sailors."

"Huff is not a possession. And I would never trade him away. You must know that."

"I do. But I do not desire to remove him from you. Whether you believe me or not, I respect the desires of the Beloved Ones. We are beings of a similar kind. If one chooses you, who am I to argue against it? No. I do not wish to take a Beloved One."

Ragin was gasping. He had his hands on his knees and could barely stay on his feet as the ship pitched and rolled. "It's a trick. Whatever it says. Do *not* believe it."

Henley didn't see the point of the warning. The demayne

was clearly powerful enough to do what it wished. "Make your offer."

Huff's presence had remained solid and somewhat bored during the entire encounter. But now it became excited. *What is it?* Henley sent.

Oly is close.

Before Henley could ask what Huff meant, Wen's ornery cream-colored cat appeared in the demayne's arms. "I recently acquired this Beloved One. I cannot take him where I must go next, so I ask you watch over him for a time."

"Where is Kila?" Henley demanded. "What did you do to her?"

"I presume she is tending to the wounds of her friend, Fallo PiTorro. But she is otherwise well, if a bit exhausted. She has recovered her Beloved One . . . Nax." The beast gave himself a shake, as if recalling a disturbing event. "I anticipate your next question. Fallo is likely to live."

Huff was coming. The cabin door opened of its own accord to admit him, surely the demayne's doing. Oly hopped from the demayne's arms. The cats nosed each other, then Oly swatted Huff's ear and received a playful bite on the skull in return.

Flaumishtak tells the truth, Huff sent. *Oly says Kila named Nax and the demayne was forced to return her.*

What do you mean she named Nax? She did that long ago.

Not the same. Huff didn't elaborate. But the only feeling coming through the bond was contentment. He didn't seem the slightest bit alarmed by the presence of the demayne.

Oly is staying? Huff asked.

Henley didn't see what choice he had. "If I agree to watch over Oly, you'll let me live? You won't steal my soul or any of my life? You'll leave Ragin alone?"

"You dare to add provisions to the bargain? Your father was not as savvy—or nervy—as you, I think."

"It doesn't feel like much of a deal, to me. What choice do I have if I want to live?"

"A fair point. But it is nothing to me to accept your offer. I have no interest in killing and consuming Raginalt Keel. Or this Donse Master you keep be-stupored. I feel the force of destiny upon him. Much more interesting to watch the disaster of his life unfold than to prevent it, don't you think?"

Henley shrugged. The hammock had relaxed its grip on him during the conversation. "Where are you going that you can't take Oly?"

"That is none of your concern. Just see to it that he does not get thrown overboard. His way of being is jagged and he does not ingratiate himself easily."

Henley actually laughed. That was the most charitable description of Oly Henley had ever heard. The animal was as sharp-edged and welcome as a whipaxe. "I will do my best."

"If you fail, your death is assured." The demayne didn't wait for a rejoinder. In a flash of green he was gone.

Oly stood in the center of the cabin, hissing at Henley and Ragin, fur standing out.

What's wrong with him? Henley asked Huff, dropping to the floor. Huff rubbed along Henley's shin.

He didn't want to be left behind, and he thinks it's your fault he was.

Didn't the demayne tell him what was happening and why?

Oly won't say. But he thinks it's your fault. To emphasize this, Oly stomped up to Henley, clamped his fangs into his ankle, and then fled to hide under Ragin's bunk.

Instead of outrage, Huff passed a feeling so close to mirth it was almost human. Henley glared at his orange cat and climbed back into his hammock. Ragin had retrieved his bucket and was trying to wipe up the mess. Dunne Yples slumped back into the shadows of his upper bunk. A quiet mantra of "Dem-Kisk" and "thinnies in flames" wafted from him.

"How can the Hargothe give you to that thing?" Ragin said once he had fallen back onto his bed. His blond hair was matted to his head, the fever of sea sickness slicking his skull with sweat.

"I know nothing about demayncy. I presume he struck a deal with the Hargothe. Don't demayne need human permission to move about in our world? That's what the stories all say."

"You escaped with little cost. If I were you, I'd be terrified."

Henley knew this was true, but he couldn't bring himself to worry. The whole event had felt so dreamlike, he could scarcely believe it had happened at all. If Oly hadn't been there, he likely would have assumed it a dream.

But Ragin was right. In none of the stories did a demayne strike such a simple deal.

"I hope I never see that beast again," Ragin said.

"Most fearsome, isn't it?" Henley said, rubbing the shallow bite marks on his ankle.

"Yes. But that's not the main reason."

"Then what is?"

The answer was a long time coming and spoken so softly it required Henley's heightened senses to hear. "He makes me think of Kila."

28

THEIR BLADES SING

The greathouse of Radiant Peline was bustling with late-night activity. Servants were scurrying about, collecting trunks and packing all manner of things into them, most of it Quinn's seemingly endless wardrobe. But there was also food, most of it dried or smoked. A large portion of Quinn's bedroom furniture had been disassembled and bound up in leather straps. Some things were already loaded onto wagons bound for the docks.

Kila sat with Quinn in a maid's room she had once spent part of one night in. The Radiant had grudgingly agreed to have Fallo put there. Finta Sahng had been fetched from the Baths to tend his wounds, which she declared serious but clean.

The ancient woman had merely looked at Quinn's blade and nodded. "A Shadline will cut as cleanly as a razor. It is fortunate for Fallo. These cuts are deep, but did not severe major vessels. He will heal and have the faintest of scars."

Fallo was now half-asleep from the medicines Finta had given him. They had put him into a relaxed, jovial mood, too. "Well, Quinn-my-friend, I hate to be the kind of man who points out the obvious, but Radiant Peline will have you trussed like a turkey and carried to the ship if you do not go voluntarily."

The dark-haired young woman had changed into a different outfit of trousers and leather jacket. Both were black, but her ruffled shirt was crimson. A scarf of black wool hung over her shoulders. "My mother's plans for me have no bearing on what will happen to me. I make my own choices. I have taken sacred oaths to the Order and I will not abandon them because Mother is afraid. The Hargothe's disappearance is more reason to stay than it is to go. I will not abandon Kila to his next attack."

The Cloak's voice cut into the room. "Kila hasn't taken the oath. She isn't of our Order. You owe her nothing."

Kila spun and drew Cayne. He eyed her and walked purposefully past her to go to Fallo. "Are you well, brother?"

"My 'blade-sister' cut me, but other than that I feel quite well. I survived seeing both the Hargothe and a demayne today. One of them even"—He snapped his fingers at Kila —"what did you call it?"

"Willshift," Kila said. Nax sat on her lap, buzzing with contented warmth.

"Yes, I got willshifted," Fallo said. "The bastard controlled my body and made me grab Quinn." Fallo seemed delighted by this experience.

Quinn gave him a rueful look. Though she had been assaulted first, she had been the one to draw blood. Quinn had warned Kila that the Cloak—this strange man in all black—would be returning to hear her oaths.

Kila had no intention of making any vows to a stranger, especially one who was titled after a garment.

The man didn't seem particularly impressed with Fallo's story. His expressions ranged from solemn disinterest to hard suspicion. Humor—or even compassion—didn't factor into it. "The house is preparing for a departure. Is the Radiant fleeing?"

"No," Quinn said. "She is ordering me to embark for the Garden. She is paying some poor captain an excessively large sum to leave immediately."

"And you, Kila Sigh, are you going to the Garden as well?"

Quinn's mouth dropped open. "What? I'm *not* going."

He didn't even look at her. "Of course you are. But Miss Sigh should go, too, don't you think? She is a merculyn, is she not? Where else will she train and master her powers? We have brothers and sisters there who can continue training you both. And from what I can discern from events, both of you need much more training if you are to survive whatever lies ahead. But first, the oaths."

This was ridiculous. This man had no power to tell Kila what to do. "What's the power of an oath if I don't give it voluntarily?"

"That is a luxury, Sigh. The world faces many evils. Either you are on the side of Order, or you are indeed Dem-Kisk."

His words were so matter-of-fact, he might as well have been telling her about the weather.

She wasn't having any of it. "You don't sound that different from the Hargothe. Who made you the speaker of the gods' intentions? You sound like all the Donse Masters I've ever heard on a Tilsday lecture."

She stroked Nax's soft back. *What do you think about this man?*

He has a familiar way. Like Yiqa. Dangerous. This assessment did not come with any particular feeling of wariness.

The Cloak regarded Kila with his hard eyes. "I have spoken with others in the Order. They are fascinated by your blade. Yours, too, Fallo. Against my advice, they have requested you come to a meeting. They wish to see the blades and discover for themselves what might be learned of them. They possess different methods than I to learn a blade's name and power. You both might benefit. And if Radiant Peline could be prevailed upon to delay your departure, Quinn, you could come with your friends."

Quinn's jaw bulged with fury. Kila expected her to soon start spitting out shards of her own teeth. A sound came through her clamped lips that reminded Kila of one of Oly's irritated moans. "Does the Order have no better use for me? What can I learn at the Garden that you cannot teach me?"

"Nothing. But I will not be here to teach you. The Order has a mission for me. And Fallo. We will be away from Starside for a time."

"I don't suppose I have much choice," Fallo said, words

slurring. "But I'm not ready for a long walk at the moment. Maybe tomorrow."

Quinn's eyes glistened with frustration. Kila didn't much like her being sent away, either. She had found in Quinn a loyal friend, one who had risked her life to help. Maybe that was from her oaths, but whatever the reason, such loyalty was rare. The thing that hurt most was losing a young woman who Kila could talk to in ways she had never been able to before. Not even with Wen. She'd only had Finta for some things, but a one-hundred-year-old didn't have the same way of seeing the world. In Quinn, Kila had found a kindred spirit.

"You have Nax, Kila," Fallo said. "Remember what we talked about after Wen died. You said as soon as you got Nax back you were going to leave Starside and never come back. Now you don't even need a single copper plug for your fare. You can go with Quinn."

He wasn't wrong. But Kila didn't want to enter school at the Garden. There would be countless rules and Sensuals lecturing her and telling her to stay off the roofs.

Quinn looked to Kila with an expression of a drowning woman seeking a rescuer's hand. "Yes. Kila, come with me. At least we would have each other. And how long will it be? A year at the most. We can survive a year of the Garden. By then the Hargothe will have forgotten all about you. And I'm the heir to a Radiancy. You'll never want for anything."

Leaving Starside appealed to Kila more than anything. "Cloak, sir. How long will this meeting with the Shadline take?"

"An hour. No more."

"Fallo," she said. "Come to the Garden with us? Henley and Ragin will be there."

"He cannot," the Cloak said. "He must go with me, to train, and in some places to guide."

"I had a hunch you were going to say that," Fallo said. Then he brightened. "Maybe Kila will learn that vanishing trick the demayne taught the Hargothe. Then she can visit all of us along the way." His sideways smile, so full of snaggle-teeth, had a weird sort of charm once you got over the ugliness of it. It seemed Quinn already had. She went to him and took his hand.

Quinn whispered another apology to him about the stabbing. Kila looked away after Quinn bent to kiss his forehead, then changed at the last moment to press her lips to his.

"I think I can walk now, after all," Fallo said. "I'm feeling quite a bit rejuvenated."

"I'll go speak to Mother," Quinn said. "I will go to the Garden if Kila does."

"I will go," Kila said.

The commitment felt almost as forceful as her naming of Nax. Her skin chilled and the room seemed to shudder. No one else noticed. But it didn't bring with it the same feeling of rightness. If anything, it made her uneasy. That was nothing new. Her father had always insisted that she and Wen become friends with discomfort. Perhaps that was why she felt a weird sort of eagerness to meet these Shadline masters who bossed around a man like the Cloak.

The Shadline master took Kila, Fallo, and Quinn into Cheapsgate by carriage. The destination was a familiar tavern favored by sailors. Critt Sanglo's.

Kila was glad, if surprised. She hadn't yet told Critt that Wen had died. Fallo walked with grim determination, though his legs moved stiffly, knees bound by bandages.

They descended into Critt's place, and wove through the throngs of doxies and drunkards. The stink of trezz and smoke made the air thick and cloying to Kila. The crowd parted for the Cloak, and eyes shied away from him. Kila wondered if they knew he was Shadline or if they instinctively feared one who moved in such a predatory way.

He led them into a back room. There, a group of three people waited. All were masked by scarves or strange black hoods. One man was obviously Critt himself. He had been a friend of Kila's father and had kept an eye on Kila and Wen for the past few years.

He had seen Cayne on Wen's leg for years, and on Father's prior to his death. And yet, there he was. Kila had never seen a blade on him. Critt as a Shadline was as strange as anything Kila had encountered.

The women were opposites of each other. One was thin and tall with a youthful posture. Her cloak and trousers were fine and unstained. She might have been one of Quinn's peers from Gristenside. But when she opened her mouth, a highly accented Sorgani lilt came out. "She a small'un, Cloak Einlin. And the blade hasna ring nor name." Her dark eyes drifted to Fallo. "Misen-Tine?"

Fallo nodded. Kila hadn't the slightest idea what they were agreeing about. Unless the woman was requesting Fallo to sing the famous "Highs of Hiwonne," the long ballad about Misen-Tine.

The other woman was elderly, lumpy, and hunched. Her hood had fine lace over the eye-holes. Her dress was plain and road-worn. "I see nothing of the Shadline in the girl's blade. The boy's speaks to me. How about you?" she asked Critt.

He spread his huge hands apart. Unlike the women, he hadn't bothered with gloves. "I'm surprised as anyone to learn their blades sing. But if Cloak Einlin says they do, there can be no doubt."

"May I handle the blade you call Cayne?" the old woman asked Kila. She extended a doughy hand, sheathed in dingy, white cloth gloves.

Kila put a guarding hand on her blade. "I am not handing my blade to anyone, friend or stranger."

The woman cackled and nodded in approval. "It already has its claws into her. That is well. And what of yours, Fallo?"

He shrugged and handed his rusty blade to her. "I've never felt any eerie force keeping me from loaning it. But it does have a bit of sentimental value."

The woman sniffed it and tested its edge against the fabric of her glove. With a shrug, she handed it to Critt.

He barely looked at it. "Bludgeons are more my language."

He passed it to the Sorgani woman. No sooner did her fingers touch the hilt than she let out a pained hiss. Smoke curled from the fingertips of her black leather gloves and she dropped the blade onto the table.

"*Ugon-sli! Telt!*" The words meant nothing to Kila, but by the reactions of the Cloak and the other two Shadlines, she might as well have announced that Fallo had a tail and a forked tongue. They reeled away from him.

The old woman nodded, her hood puffing out as she let out a breath. "I smelled Misen-Tine on this the moment you walked in. But how is this possible? The curse should force you back there. And yet you brandish it as if is a butter knife from your father's table."

Critt shook his head, marveling. "The mythical Telt, sittin' there upon my table."

Fallo plucked up his sorry-looking blade. "It was a gift. In a way." His face seemed to close up, and Kila saw he would say nothing else.

"You are right, Cloak," the old woman said. "Fallo PiTorro will be a good apprentice for you. These others will do well to continue to the Garden. A teacher will seek them out there."

"Kila Sigh refuses to take the oaths," the Cloak said.

That shut them up. Only Critt nodded. And it was he who spoke next. "I knew her father and brother. An oath pulled from her lips with block an' tackle would 'ave no meanin'. I advise we train her anyway. In time, she'll come to see the good we do. And perhaps it'll give us time to study the origin of this mystery blade that hid its nature from me."

Both women nodded, if hesitantly. "Yes," the Sorgani said. "P'rhaps it be wiser to understand it afore we bring it into our Order. There have been other bad blades, and we bear a heavy burden for their sustenance."

Critt cleared his throat at the mention of these bad blades. The very term chilled Kila's skin.

The Cloak took this as a dismissal. He turned to go. Kila squinted at Critt Sanglo, wondering how he had come to be a Shadline. And wondering why the Order had left him to run this establishment. Surely a true Shadline would have more useful things to do.

"Enjoy yer time at the Garden, Kila," he said. "Keep yer eyes open an' yer blade close."

The two women echoed this, if with a bit less enthusiasm. Critt added, "Yer brother would be very proud of you. As would yer father be."

So Critt knew about Wen. There was nothing else to be said. With a nod, she turned and wound her way out of his establishment and into the winter chill of Cheapsgate. Nax met her on the rooftops.

"I have one other visit to make," she said to the Cloak.

The man raised a questioning eyebrow. Kila merely pointed—beyond the slums, past the wall, high over Gristen-side to the spires of the Citadel. "I've been summoned."

Fallo and Quinn stammered some questions, but Kila didn't answer. She didn't have any answers. They piled into the carriage to begin the long ride back to the Peline greathouse. Quinn said she would have the driver take Kila to the Citadel. Later, when they stopped at the greathouse to drop off Quinn, the Cloak, and Fallo, the Cloak cleared his throat. "Say your goodbyes, Fallo. You may never see Kila Sigh again."

It was an awkward moment. They studied each other, realizing the bonds of friendship had tightened upon their hearts in small degrees, but now had formed knots as sure and strong as their bonds to their cats.

Fallo gasped her forearm, she his. "All right, Kila?" he said. "It's a wide world and food isn't free." It was a common parting in Cheapsgate.

Kila gave his forearm a return squeeze. "As true as that?"

He grew solemn, eyes glimmering. "As true as that."

29

SHE IS OCCLUDED

Every gate was open to Kila, and not a single Fell Guard so much as looked at her as the carriage passed. At the courtyard before the Citadel, the carriage was met by a man in the robes of administrative office, wearing a red sash and pantaloons that cinched around his shins and billowed at the hips. "She awaits."

Remarkable. Usually a man like this would be shaking his fist at her and warning her away. If Wen could see her now . . .

She accompanied the man into the Citadel. Through the front entry, no less. The wide hallways and vast ballrooms and smaller sitting rooms each had a theme, usually dominated by a color. One blue-painted room had blue upholstered lounges and armchairs, the ceiling gilded and carved, the walls host to at least a hundred paintings of hunting scenes. The next room was deep maroons, with thick draperies and more paintings, these all of children at play.

Kila walked through a gallery with tall windows on one

side and mirrors on the other. Their footsteps echoed hollowly in the empty space, which she imagined was sometimes host to grand receptions or balls.

It was all empty now. Not even servants appeared along the way. Finally, the man took her to a staircase. "The climb," he announced, as if were a ceremonial part of her approach to the Enlightened. Perhaps it was.

Kila went alone. She had a long time to consider who it was she was about to meet. The stairs wound up and up, bypassing windows that gave views out over the Divide and then toward the mountains. She realized it was winding along the outside perimeter of the spire. There were few doorways to the interior. She began to wonder what occupied the central shaft of the spire. Surely it couldn't all be rooms. Was it perhaps a void that plummeted from the Enlightened's rooms to the basements? That was a chilling thought even to one who was not generally afraid of heights.

She still wore the sea-hound boots Marlow had provided. They made soft thumps and scuffs with every step. But she kept them on, not only because they were warm and the stairwell cold, but she didn't want to come into Her Enlightened's presence barefoot.

The top of the stairs ended in a widening hallway that approached a set of double doors. They were arched and made of deeply stained oak. The thick planks were ironbound, with heavy black hinges inset into the stone walls. Before them stood two Fell Guards, each in his eerie birdlike helm with the atlen plumes. Their scarlet cloaks poured down their shoulders and pooled behind their feet. Each held a spear and wore a sword on his hip.

They didn't acknowledge Kila as the doors swung inward at her approach. Waiting for her in a foyer on the other side was Marlow. He smiled and beckoned her in. "So. You lived."

Kila unlimbered her backpack and let Nax out. The cat pressed against Kila's shins and then stopped to lick a white foot. "I got her back. It was strange. Your brother—"

Marlow shushed her. "No sense in telling the story twice. Her Enlightened Majesty may want to hear it." He reached for her hand. Hesitantly, she raised it to allow him to grip her fingertips in the daintiest way. He led her down a short hall, still holding her hand.

The doors swung open by themselves and they stepped into the inner sanctum of the most powerful person in Starside.

"I present Miss Kila Sigh, Your Enlightened Majesty."

The woman was facing away, looking out a window. The glow of pre-dawn sun framed her raven-black hair. The braiding pulled the locks from her face, interweaving in a stunning arrangement as they traced down her back. Sheets of loose hair flowed free beneath. Her hair was a garment in its own right.

Kila was instantly aware of her own hacked-off boyish hair. She patted it self-consciously, wishing she'd thought to tie it back before coming into Her Enlightened's presence. "You told me to come," Kila said. "I'm here."

"I'm delighted to meet you. Finally." The woman turned to

face Kila. She was lovely, not merely from the magnificence of her gown or the perfection of her grooming. She had a shapely face, angular, perhaps a bit severe. Her high brows angled sharply down, regal, but not permanently angry. Her teeth were very white and even, her lips rosy as if she'd been biting them.

She was Kila's height, and appeared to be only a ten-year older. That wasn't possible, for she had been the monarch for many a ten-year.

She said, "Dunne Marlow told me of your swift mastery of mercusine masking. I am impressed. I can barely sense you even now. You must work diligently to perfect the skill. In particular, your sound negation is flimsy."

Kila was irritated enough to check her mask. The sound was dead silent to her. A perfect negation.

The woman must have sensed her confusion, for she said, "Attend."

Kila felt a wash of mercus flow over her: sound, light, touch, smell, and flavor. All dissipated except sound. The bell tone then slipped into negation, just as Marlow had showed her. And then Kila did hear it. A hiss, like the slightest rustle of wind through grass, or the bubbling foam left on the sand as a wave retreated. "You hear it now?"

"I do." Kila made an adjustment in her mask and the hiss went silent.

"Truly remarkable," the woman said. "Do that and not even I will be able to find you. Not quickly anyway." She strode toward Kila, and Kila was shocked to see bare feet appear from beneath the hem of her gown. Small, strong feet, but not soft. She walked like Yiqa, the Voluptuary's Alnassi friend.

Kila instantly liked the woman, though she kept her guard up. "Do I need to hide from you?"

This evoked a genuine smile and a melodic laugh. Kila noticed the woman had piercings in her ears. Sapphire and gold. The pendants dangled like blue stars against the black of her hair. "You hardly need to hide. Even unmasked, you were not always clearly seen. I sent messages. In dreams you are more present to me, but you are forgetful. So forgetful."

She did look somewhat familiar to Kila, but vaguely so. "I don't suppose you're joking about talking to me in a dream. That's hardly a comforting thought."

"The raven brings many messages on her wings. She does not explain them all. Not to me, not to you. But I need to tell you something, and I wanted to do it here, with you looking directly at me. Otherwise, I fear you will forget like you've forgotten so much else."

"I don't know what you're talking about. My memory is as good as the next person's. Better, I think." She was aware of Marlow withdrawing to the opposite side of the room. He watched them, but was giving them the privacy to have an intimate conversation. Also, the Enlightened was doing something to the sounds in the room. Her voice sounded boxy, as if they were in a much smaller space. The Enlightened took a seat on a richly worked armchair with her seal embroidered on the backrest. She crossed her legs and tilted her head in a curious manner. "Sit, please."

Kila sat.

Nax crept close to Her Enlightened and sniffed her bare toe. *Nax, stay back,* Kila sent.

The cat obeyed and returned to Kila's lap. The Enlightened didn't take any special note of the cat's presence. "Kila Sigh, tell me what you remember of your mother."

Kila shrugged. "I don't remember her. She died when I was very young. Father said she looked like me." A sharp pain sliced through her head.

She needed sleep. And probably food. Maybe she would visit the mistress of kitchens on her way out. Fallo had mentioned a name. Kinnon Swile. That was it. See? she thought. Her memory was just fine.

"Kila," the Enlightened snapped. "Your mother. Surely you remember something. What color was her hair? Fair like yours?"

Why was this woman asking about her mother? Surely her father was a more interesting person. He had been a locksmith for many years, and then he'd left Starside to live in the wilds of the Honor Mountains for a while. He had left Wen apprenticed to a locksmith. Besides, Father had discovered or acquired Cayne somehow. That made him a Shadline, sort of. She wondered if he'd known—

"Kila! Your mother. Remember her." The Enlightened's voice was so loud Kila thought the earth would shatter. She covered her ears and cried out as searing pain coursed through her head. It was almost as bad as when the Hargothe performed his vile penetrations into her mind. "Tell me of your mother."

"I never saw her," Kila cried. "I don't remember anything."

But that wasn't true. She remembered an image of a woman with black hair. A violet glow surrounded her. The jolt of pain that attended the memory sent Kila spilling to the rug, Nax tumbling out of her lap.

On all fours, Kila retched. A hang of drool dangled from her lips. She sucked in air. "Apologies, Your Enlightened Majesty. I feel ill all of a sudden."

The woman knelt next to Kila and gripped her elbow with one hand and pulled Kila's hair back with the other. "Be sick if you must. It is merely a rug." As if the permission were a cue, Kila spilled the little she still had in her stomach. She was very glad she hadn't eaten prior to coming here. It was mortifying to be weak in front of her sovereign. Wen would have laughed until he wet himself. She couldn't imagine the guff she'd take from Fallo and Henley if they ever found out.

Marlow had come to assist. He knelt on Kila's other side. "I didn't hear what was said. Should I call for a girl to clean this up? Perhaps a soothing draught of tea?"

"She is not ill," her Enlightened said. "She is occluded. Her mind has been touched to keep certain thoughts and memories away from her awareness."

"What do you mean?" Kila said. She was feeling much better. In fact, she was starving. "I have an excellent memory."

Marlow and the Enlightened shared a meaningful look, a bit too conspiratorial for Kila's taste. "What was it you wanted to tell me?"

Nax? Do you trust this woman?

The cat sent the equivalent of a shrug through the bond.

She sniffed at Kila's sick-up then walked to sit near the fire and commenced grooming herself.

The Enlightened helped Kila to her feet. "I asked you some specific questions just now. Do you recall what any of them were?"

"You asked about my family. My father was a locksmith, and so on."

Her Enlightened Majesty smiled and patted Kila's shoulder. "I have something for you. It may come in handy during your time at the Garden." She went to a small table under the window she'd been at when Kila had come in.

"I got this from my father when I was about your age." She removed a small item from a drawer and brought it to Kila. A hand mirror. It was quite dainty, the oval of glass no bigger than a chicken egg. Kila glanced at her reflection and was shocked to see how smudged her cheeks were. She turned the mirror over and appreciated the fine craftsmanship. Pewter, with a floral pattern carved into it. The handle was bone of some sort. It would fetch a gold skillet at market. But if she could convince anyone it had belonged to Her Enlightened, she would fetch many hundreds of skillets.

"Sorry about the grime," Kila said. "I'm just a lowly—"

"Do not say 'Cheapsgate waif,' Kila." The words were stern but her expression was earnest. "You are no more a waif than I am a headsman. The mirror will serve to show you yourself. But it can show you other things if you are patient. It can be cagey and does not like its secrets revealed by others, so I can tell you no more. Look into it often, and its power will soon be revealed. Tell others, and it may refuse to help you when you most need it. In that, it is like your blade."

Kila tucked the mirror into an inside pocket, next to the canvas roll containing her father's lock-picking tools. "Thank you, Enlightened."

Marlow grunted and Kila realized she had used a very informal title for the woman. The monarch didn't appear offended by it.

"You have several thousand dragon scales in your pack," Her Enlightened said. "It may serve you better to exchange them for gold."

Kila shrugged. "There's not much of a market for them. I would spend so much time trying to convince people they were real. I'd be better off doing other, uh, work."

"I will buy them. One gold Raven each. Obviously, that is too much coin to carry." She went to a writing desk and drew out a slip of paper and wrote a few lines. She handed it to Kila. A bank draft for three thousand four hundred and fifteen gold Ravens.

Kila laughed. "No banker will honor this. If I present it to them they'll think it's a forgery."

The woman merely raised an eyebrow and said, "No they won't."

Marlow nodded, his mouth twisted with unusual seriousness, a confirmation that Kila would have no trouble redeeming her note for coin. The amount was worth more than she and Wen had dreamed of stealing. They had thought to amass only fifty skillets to set up as legitimate recovery agents. With this amount, Kila could retire and buy a house in upper Terriside and have a maid do her cooking and washing up.

But upon closer study, Kila noticed the draft clearly stated it was for redemption solely at the Bank of Fries and Posson at the Garden. Kila flapped the paper. "How did you know I was going to the Garden?"

The woman gaped for a moment. "I didn't. This note was to induce you to go. And here I could have saved the realm so much coin."

Kila quickly folded the note, and it joined the mirror in her pocket. "Thank you, Your Enlightened Majesty. Thank you most kindly."

The monarch gave Kila a last considering stare. "You are a blur upon the future, Kila. You may be here for good or ill. I cannot say. I assist you in hopes that the force of destiny can be nudged in the service of good. But you must make the choices that count. May the Triumvirate guide you."

Kila made a terrible attempt at a curtsy, which forced a moan from Marlow. He guided her to the steps. Once out of Her Enlightened's presence he patted the sides of her arms and stared her full in the face. "I am not a good man. Nor do I think I'm wholly bad. Just a man. I do not know how long I will retain my post here at the Citadel. But if you need to get word to me or Her Majesty, do not forget the flashtowers. They are for just that sort of thing."

The flashtowers were far out to sea, spires towering over a string of sea bastions designed to relay flash signals the thousands of miles separating the Colony from the Citadel. How far to sea did Marlow think she was going?

Nax hopped into the backpack and Kila hefted it onto her shoulders. "Thank you for not being on your brother's side, Marlow. Compared to him you're a prince."

"That's not saying much."

"No. It isn't. You might want to keep an eye out for him. He dymensed away from our confrontation."

Marlow swore. "Take care, Kila Sigh."

She started the long climb down the spire.

30

A NEW SEASON

Marlow returned to Her Enlightened's presence. She sat near the fire, gaze lost in the flames. Without looking at him, she said, "Kila's mind has been clouded. Her own past is hidden from her."

"Do you know what is hidden?"

"I do not."

"But you suspect something in particular. Perhaps a prophecy you have not shared?"

She pulled her eyes away from the firelight and looked him, direct and open. "I do not know you that well, Dunne Marlow. I will confide nothing more to you."

"I understand."

Time would build trust. And the more useful he became to her, the more secrets she would reveal. He had the posting he had always sought, the one best suited to his skills. All that remained was to do the job. Maybe one day he would pay off his debt to Flaumishtak. If not . . .

Best not to think of such things. He bade her goodnight and began the long descent to his quarters.

IN THE HIGH Eerie above Starside, a dragon stirred in its sleep. It raised a wing and sniffed the air. A new season was beginning, one not seen in a thousand years. The beast adjusted its weight and returned to its slumber.

A raven winged by far below, sending chills through a people who had suffered repeated chills throughout the night. The goodwives of the city all agreed that evil was afoot in Starside.

Far out to sea, a ship leaned hard into a gale as it sailed southward. A madman sat up in his bunk and screamed before his companions quieted him with a dose of mind-numbing medicine.

At mouth of the Moriterren Pass, a boy with bandages on his knees followed a man who was more shadow than light. He spared one glance back at the city before plunging into the subterranean darkness.

In a cave far from Starside, an eyeless merculyn shivered, body wracked with fever, while a storm raged outside. His mind drifted upon the mercusine, calling for a distant spark to come aid him.

Upon the Street of the Diadem, a young woman who might be Dem-Kisk rode a carriage down the slopes of Gristenside. She held a small mirror in her hand. It was too dark in the unlit carriage to see her reflection. A cat curled into her lap, warm and calm. The young woman let the sway of the carriage lull her.

Somewhere above her, winging through the crisp winter night, the raven soared. It circled toward the Citadel, a shadow upon the shadow of night. The black-haired woman standing at a high window listened to its cries, a voice beyond hearing.

Fly, Kila Sigh. Fly.

The End of *The Raven Throne*
Book Four in Starside Saga